DRY AS RAIN

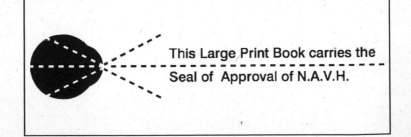

This Large Print Book carries the
Seal of Approval of N.A.V.H.

DRY AS RAIN

GINA HOLMES

THORNDIKE PRESS
A part of Gale, Cengage Learning

Detroit • New York • San Francisco • New Haven, Conn • Waterville, Maine • London

GALE
CENGAGE Learning

LIBRARY OF CONGRESS CATALOGING-IN-PUBLICATION DATA

Holmes, Gina.
  Dry as rain / by Gina Holmes.
    pages ; cm. — (Thorndike Press large print Christian
  fiction)
    ISBN 978-1-4104-4480-6 (hardcover) — ISBN 1-4104-4480-5 (hardcover)
  1. Marriage—Fiction. 2. Husband and wife—Fiction. 3.
  Amnesiacs—Fiction. 4. Large type books. I. Title.
  PS3608.O494354D79 2012
  813'.6—dc23   2011047829

Published in 2012 by arrangement with Tyndale House Publishers, Inc.

Printed in Mexico
1 2 3 4 5 6 7 16 15 14 13 12

For Adam, my oasis.

He has removed our sins as far from us
as the east is from the west.

PSALM 103:12

ACKNOWLEDGMENTS

As always, I am so very grateful to my children — from oldest to youngest: Catherine, Jessie, Jacob, Becky, and Levi — for their undying support, encouragement, and understanding when I'm stuck to the computer or having a bad day.

I thank Dr. Frank Shelp for advising me on some psychiatric issues early in the process, as well as Charles Martin, who shared a little of his overflowing genius. The good folks at ACFW (American Christian Fiction Writers) were so kind to answer my many questions. I am grateful for their support not only of me, but of all of us who write with the Kingdom of Heaven on our hearts.

A very special thanks to Karen Watson, Chip MacGregor, and my amazing editor, Kathryn Olson, who stuck with me through multiple rewrites. Thanks for not letting me take the path of least resistance and for holding my hand through the birth of a particularly stubborn baby. You all went above and beyond on this one. You're the best. And of course, Ane Mulligan, who read every word no matter how busy. Ane, I'm always in your debt!

I can't thank the marketing team at Tyndale House enough — especially Babette Rea — for their support. I know how hard you all work and how much you pour into what you do. Thanks to Ron Beers, whose kind words will stay with me whenever I doubt myself as a writer, and sweet, capable Stephanie Broene, who always makes me feel like the only author she has to attend to. The hardworking sales reps and the rest of the Tyndale team have been incredibly flexible, supportive, and all-around fantastic. Meeting you really opened my eyes to how much heart you pour into your work and just what a ministry it is to you. I couldn't ask for a more wonderful group to represent my work.

As always, thank you to the Novel Journey crew, who aren't just blogging teammates but friends and talented writers as well. In no particular order: Ane Mulligan, Jessica Dotta, Kelly Klepfer, Mike Duran, Noel DeVries, Yvonne Anderson, Michael Ehret, Marcia Laycock, Anita Mellot, Ronie Kendig, Athol Dickson, Mary DeMuth, and Chip MacGregor. I pray you all are being blessed as much as you're blessing others.

I couldn't successfully wear all the hats I do if I didn't have such a supportive husband, and I have the best of the best. Adam, you are my hero, the best friend I've ever had, and the absolute love of my life. Baby, thank you for being my biggest fan, listening to every idea, plot summary, etc., and reading aloud to me every last word that makes up one of my stories no matter how tired you are. Someday soon it will be your turn with all of those amazing songs you write, and I'll get to return the favor.

Above all, thank You to my Father in heaven. Please take my words and make them more.

ONE

When I first became a Christian, I read what Adam and Eve had done in the Garden of Eden and it really ticked me off. Until that fateful moment, humanity had it made. If Eve hadn't allowed emotion to overwhelm logic, and Adam hadn't been so whipped, everyone would be living in Paradise right now.

If God Himself directly tells you not to do something, do you really think you'll get away with doing it anyway? Did they honestly think they could hide from the Creator of the universe? I mean, come on.

I don't know why the Garden of Eden should pop into my mind again on that January evening except that my toes were freezing inside my dress shoes as I trudged along the slushy sidewalk, and if sin had never entered the world, then probably neither would have bitter cold. If Adam had been there with me, I'd have shown him what I thought about his shortcomings with a snowball to the head.

Maybe blind dates were also the product of sin. It made a certain amount of sense. The trepidation I felt about my upcoming one certainly felt like punishment. Maybe I was the one who needed a good snowball pelting. What was I thinking agreeing to spend an evening with a woman I'd never so much as exchanged a smile with? I'd always said blind dates smacked of desperation, but here I was on my way to meet my coworker's sister.

Bobby showed me a photograph of her earlier in the week. Long hair, long legs . . . long shot. If the picture wasn't old or doctored, she was an easy ten. The way I figured it, I was an eight — nine at best. Now, as I hurried under the light of the streetlamp on my way to Sophia's to meet her, I'd have given anything to turn back the clock and undo the mismatched arrangement.

Digging my hands deep into the pockets of my wool coat, I hurried from the parking lot toward the restaurant. The brittle night air burned my lungs as plumes of white rose from my chattering teeth. More to stall than to warm myself, I cupped my hands over my mouth, puffed onto my palms, and glanced at the canopy arched over the restaurant entrance. It looked like a big, red eyebrow raised in my direction. On it was stenciled the restaurant's name in gold calligraphy. Ivy, browned from winter, crawled up bricks on both sides of the entryway.

I'd been warned that the place was every bit as pricey as it looked. The fact that my date had chosen it should have been my first clue of what kind of woman she was — or at least what kind of man she was looking for. With a sigh, I grabbed the cold brass door handle and pulled.

When I stepped inside, the first thing I noticed was the immediate warmth; the second, the darkness. Other than strings of white lights winding around strategically placed artificial trees, the only illumination came from globe candles centered on each table.

The jewel-toned lighting seemed almost magical in the way it made everyone and everything look rich and attractive. I could only hope it had the same effect on me. The instant I laid eyes on Bobby's sister standing by the podium, I knew it was going to be a long night. She was just as hot as her picture, but one glance down her perfectly sculpted nose at me set my high-maintenance chick detector squalling like a siren.

Everything from her diamond earrings to the designer purse she carried was too fat for my wallet. I had always been the Mary Ann type, but this one was definitely a Ginger. I could tell by the twisted pucker of her heart-shaped mouth that I wasn't exactly her dream date either. I wondered if her brother bothered to inform her I was half-Japanese.

When the hostess told us there was a wait, I moved Bobby's sister over to the bar. I figured this girl was going to be a lobster and champagne type, so I ordered the cheapest draft they had so maybe she'd get the idea early that I wasn't Mr. Howell. Not taking my hint, she ordered a top-shelf martini.

I glanced at the wall of mirrors hanging behind the penguin-dressed bartender. That's when I first noticed the baby grand behind me . . . and the redhead making it sing. I listened to her play against the backdrop of laughter, clanking wineglasses, and couples stealing kisses over ravioli.

Her hair was the color of spun sunshine, her skin as creamy and flawless as a porcelain doll, and her beautiful fingers flew over those ivory keys with such grace I couldn't

16

help but be infatuated.

I've never been one to believe in love at first sight, but I just knew in the smoky reflection of that bar mirror that we were going to have one heck of a romance. Well, maybe I just hoped we would. She played "Fly Me to the Moon" as a waiter passed by with an oval tray perched atop his fingertips. The air filled with steam and the scent of beef and marsala cooking wine.

Something told me if I didn't make a move then, I might never get another chance. Having my date and her brother mad at me was something I could live with. Not finding out if the piano player was my soul mate was not. I turned to Bobby's sister to apologize for what I was about to do, but she'd already started flirting with the man on the other side of her.

I made my way from one end of the bar to the other and leaned between a middle-aged couple toasting something or other. After a few rounds of lighthearted negotiations, I'd purchased the rosebud the man had been wearing on his lapel.

When I walked over to my date holding the flower, I'm sure she thought it was hers. Instead of smiling, she looked embarrassed. I told her I had met the woman I was going to marry. She was so relieved to find out it wasn't her that she laughed, threw a look over her shoulder at Kyra, and grabbed her purse.

Feeling suddenly emboldened, rose in hand, I turned around on my stool and made no secret of studying her. Sophia's was warm with so many bodies confined to such a small area, but with my gaze fixed on the pianist, I felt like I was baking in a thermonuclear reactor. When she stood to take a break, some mafia type stuck a fifty in her jar and told her when she got back, he'd appreciate it if she'd play anything but Frank Sinatra.

She walked to the far end of the bar where the waiters picked up their patrons' drinks and the bartender gave her a bottle of water. I strolled right up to her and handed her that rose.

"Thanks," she said, holding the stem, which had been clipped short. "Where's the rest of it?"

I felt my throat close in until she laughed. It was the most beautiful laugh I'd ever heard. We had dinner the next night — and every night leading up to our wedding reception.

If you had told me that twenty years later she'd be divorcing me, I wouldn't believe it.

I loved her so much. I still do. But one person in love does not a marriage make.

Two

I woke up in bed with a woman who was not my wife. The candlelight that had cast the room in shades of gold earlier had long since died, taking with it the flickering illusion that all was rosy and right. Beside the bed, a merlot bottle sat empty next to two glasses stained with crimson.

How beautiful and exciting my coworker seemed just hours ago. Light from the adjacent bathroom fell on her face, still full from youth. I wondered what exactly I'd found so remarkable about this ordinary girl, barely a woman.

She wasn't half the beauty Kyra had been in her twenties, or even now. Her curves could not compete with my wife's willowy grace. She didn't have Kyra's intelligence, talent, or my promise on her finger. But what she did have had intoxicated me completely. She'd looked at me with wide, innocent eyes as though I was some sort of hero. As though I wasn't the disappointment I'd become to Kyra. As though I was the man I used to be.

Danielle's eyelids twitched from dreams, her fine lashes fluttering against her skin. The heat of her breath puffed against my neck. Careful not to disturb her, I rubbed a lock of her flaxen hair between my thumb and finger. It had seemed so much more wild and beautiful as we'd made love.

Love — I almost choked on the word.

When I closed my eyes, it was no longer Danielle's blonde hair I touched, but Kyra's red. I remembered a time not so long ago that I lay with her in this very position. The light of dawn traced the outline of her face and her long, lean body like a golden aura. How I'd wanted to ravish her at that moment with a desire that was so much more than mere lust. So much more than what I'd shared with this girl.

When I opened my eyes, it was Danielle once again lying next to me. This was what I had fantasized about for weeks, but now that my belly was full of it, I barely remembered what the hunger had felt like. She hadn't changed, but somehow I felt no residue of my earlier lust.

As I watched her sleep, I knew it wasn't the shape of her young body, the curve of her hips or legs I was really looking at, but the death of my marriage. The finality of my actions struck me with unexpected force. Kyra and I were never supposed to come to this.

I shouldn't have done what I'd done — two wrongs would never make a right — but after being accused of it for so long, at least now the punishment would fit the crime.

And anyway, wasn't it Kyra, not me, who had insisted on the separation? Those almost always lead to divorce, I'd rightly argued, but she wouldn't be reasoned with. She'd seen a suggestive e-mail that had her convinced I'd been having an affair. I wanted to work things out. Begged her to attend counseling with me, but she'd had one foot so far out the door, it was a shorter walk out than in.

A small smile pulled at the corners of Danielle's lips. She stirred in her sleep and laid her arm across my stomach. I waited for her to settle before gently removing it.

Careful not to wake her, I pushed myself up, cringing as the bed creaked. She sighed, curled into the fetal position, and tugged the blanket up to her neck. Before my foot hit the floor, my cell beeped. I had to lean over her to get it. My arm brushed her chest and she awoke.

I faked a smile. "Good morning, beautiful."

Her eyes lit up as she covered her mouth. "Hey, there."

I put the phone to my ear. "Eric Yoshida."

"Hi, Eric. It's Al."

I shook my head at Danielle to indicate my regret in answering. "You got a new number, I see."

"Yeah, it's a TracFone. You know your mother and bills."

I cleared my throat. I didn't have it in me to worry about my stepfather's constant drizzle while I was dealing with my own tsunami. "What can I do you for?"

"Are you sitting?"

Looking down at myself perched on the edge of the bed, I felt the dread of the coming news. "Is it Mom? Is she — ?"

"Your mom's fine. Everyone's fine."

I exhaled as Danielle watched me intently. Without her makeup, she seemed even younger. At forty-five, I probably looked like an old man to her in the stark light of day with my sparse, gray body hair and the not-so-subtle pull of gravity. With my free hand, I picked my pants off the floor. I was relieved that she had the decency to look away as I slid them on.

"It's Kyra, son. She's been in an accident."

I'd barely gotten my foot in the second leg hole when I had to sit again. "What kind of accident? Is she okay? Where is she?"

"Whoa, slow down. They told your mother that physically, she's fine. Anyway, I had the car towed to that body shop with the big eagle on the side. You know, the one down the street from Waffle House."

"Why didn't they call me or Marnie? Why did they call you?"

"They said her phone just goes to voice mail and Kyra gave them the number you used to have back in Braddy's Wharf."

I didn't bother asking why she would do that because the answer was obvious enough — she didn't want me to know. I closed my eyes and pinched the bridge of my nose. "Is she home?"

"Not exactly. They admitted her to Batten Falls Psychiatric Hospital for observation."

I sat there stunned to silence as I listened to the bizarre news of my wife's whereabouts, all the while feeling the weight of Danielle's gaze. When I hung up, I found her sitting with the blanket wrapped around her like a beach towel.

"What is it?" She looked confused. "Who's hurt?"

I licked my lips, not knowing what to say.

"It's her, isn't it? It's Kyra." She frowned as her eyes searched mine.

"It's okay," I said, standing. "She was in a minor accident."

When Danielle stroked my arm, her touch possessed all the comfort of burlap. "I'm sorry."

I pulled away. "No biggie. She'll be fine." But even as I said the words, I doubted them. She was in a psychiatric hospital. How okay could a person be to find themselves there?

She focused on my knees. "Thank goodness. Are you going to see her?"

"What else can I do? She's still my wife."

"No. I know. I'm just asking."

I said nothing for a moment, then set about picking up the rest of my clothes from the rug. Scratching at my freshly grown neck stubble, I asked, "Would you mind if I borrow a razor and some toothpaste?"

Without so much as looking at me, she shrugged. I ducked into her bathroom and opened the medicine cabinet. A pack of disposable pink razors sat next to a battered box of Band-Aids, a bottle of watermelon body spray, and some peroxide, which, according to its expiration date, should have been thrown away two years ago. I grabbed a razor and the apple-scented shave gel resting on the edge of the tub. I'd smell like an orchard, but at least I would look presentable.

After squeezing a dab of toothpaste onto my finger and doing the best job I could for my teeth, I looked at my reflection in the mirror. Veins of red fractured the whites of my eyes. When I frowned at my weary reflection, fine lines etched themselves around the corners of my mouth. Strands of silver had infiltrated my thick black hair so much that it was now almost a fifty-fifty blend.

Where was the dashing young man of my youth? The one my wife couldn't keep her hands off of? I sighed, turned the light off, and stepped back into the bedroom.

Danielle was looking at me once again with wide, admiring eyes. She now wore a white T-shirt and men's boxer shorts — trophies of a previous relationship? The thought both nauseated and relieved me. I didn't like thinking of myself in a long line of lovers, but then again, if I was, maybe she was less likely to have mistaken our night together for more than it was.

The way she looked at me, though, told me our tryst had meant something to her. *Great,* I thought, patting my pockets for my cell phone. Just what I needed, to add another boulder of guilt to my quarry.

I glanced around until I spotted my car keys resting atop her digital alarm clock. "I've got to go. I'm sorry."

Though she smiled stoically, her eyes betrayed her.

"I wish you could stay," she whispered.

I kissed the top of her head. "I'm sorry," I repeated, feeling sorry indeed.

THREE

I felt like an actor in a bad B movie as I made my way to the front desk of Batten Falls Psychiatric Hospital and signed in. I just wished somebody would yell, "Cut!" so I could take Kyra home. The receptionist eyed my wrinkled suit with disapproval and pointed to the waiting area.

The pleather couch looked like a relic from the fifties, but it was comfortable enough. I leaned forward with my elbows on my knees and tapped my foot. A line of gilded-framed portraits stared at me from the wall to my left. Male and female, young and old, each board member shared the same baleful expression as if they knew what I had done.

Farther down the dimly lit corridor, sad plants drooped over macramé-hung pots. The dreariness of the place had permeated my soul the moment I'd walked through the door. Maybe it was the eerie silence, so stark

I could hear my own breathing, or the vague nursing home smell lingering in the air. My gaze moved across the tiled floor, polished to a mirror shine. At least it was clean. That was something.

Running my tongue over inadequately brushed teeth, I pulled a stick of gum from my suit jacket pocket, unwrapped it, and shoved it in my mouth. As I chewed, cinnamon burned my tongue, but the taste soon died. Nothing lasted long these days. Not Kyra's love for me, not Benji's childhood, not my faithfulness as a husband, not anything . . . but then again, neither would this nightmare.

Kyra would be home soon. Then what? As if I didn't already have enough to feel guilty about, she'd find a way to blame me for this as well. If it rained when the weatherman called for sunshine, she'd find a way to pin it on me.

Still, being contentious was a long way from being insane. What on earth could have made them think she belonged here? I pressed the chewed gum from my lips back into its wrapper, balled it up, and tucked it in my pocket. I knew our separation and Benji's enlistment affected her more than she'd let on . . . but a breakdown?

This was a woman who was as grounded

as they came. Her no-nonsense approach to life was one of the things I'd loved best about her. What must she be going through at this very moment? Probably wondering if she died and woke up in hell. I gritted my teeth, knowing that last night I'd given up any rights as her protector.

Sheets of sunlight streamed in through the generous windows at my back, but they did nothing to warm me. Across from the waiting area, the receptionist with unnaturally black hair sat behind glass, answering phones and glancing every few seconds at a security monitor. When my eyes met hers, she cleared her throat and glared at my tapping foot. Feeling no desire to appease her, I closed my eyes and continued the rhythm.

After a few minutes, someone said my name and I looked up. A fiftysomething-year-old man gave a quick bow of head and held out his hand. I had grown used to the stereotypical greeting, though it still annoyed me. Ignoring the bow, I stood to shake his hand and was disappointed to find he beat me in stature by a good two to three inches. The calloused hand I shook was that of a laborer, not the professional it was attached to. His grip was firm. I made sure mine was firmer.

"I'm Dr. Hershing."

"Eric Yoshida." As I let go, I noticed his left hand did not sport a wedding band.

"Let's talk privately, Eric."

The unearned familiarity of addressing me by my first name made me feel an instant dislike for him. It also didn't help that he was fit, besides being a doctor. Women were suckers for success, and Kyra was no exception. Although he'd have a hard time impressing her even if he'd been the surgeon general. The thing with Kyra was that she was never satisfied.

I followed him down a long, white corridor. We walked by a line of small offices. A face in each one glanced up as we passed. At the end of the hallway, a door stood open and the doctor motioned for me to enter.

A polished wood conference table took up most of the rectangular room. In the center of it lay a scattered pile of miniature tissue boxes, a few legal pads, and some plastic pens. The room smelled strongly of alcohol. A glance at a small desk pushed against the farthest wall explained why. An open bottle of rubbing alcohol sat beside a mannequin cut off at the waist. The space must have recently doubled as a training room for CPR.

Tucked under the conference table were tall, fabric-covered chairs. I took the one at the head of the table. The doctor raised his eyebrows but said nothing. After taking the seat across from me, he slid a pad and pen over to himself. He flipped the top page and tilted it toward himself, away from my line of vision.

I leaned my clasped hands on the table. "Let's cut to the chase, shall we?"

He scribbled something.

I felt my face flush. "What are you writing already?"

Hershing smiled. "I just remembered my mother asked me to bring home coffee filters."

I squinted at him. One thing I couldn't stand was being patronized.

He studied me a moment. "You don't believe me." He turned the pad around to reveal the two words he claimed to have written. "Sorry. If I don't write things down, I forget them. She'll have my hide if she doesn't get her java in the morning."

I felt like I'd been deliberately played for a fool, but of course I would just look paranoid if I voiced my suspicion. Learning that Hershing still lived with his mommy at least gave me a feeling of satisfaction. So much for being a lady-killer. "How do I go about collecting my wife?"

He set his hands on top of the overturned

pad. "Collecting?"

"She doesn't belong here."

"I'm sure you also want what's best for Kyra."

The sound of her name on this man's lips sent pricks of jealousy through me. Was it my imagination or had his voice lowered an octave when he'd said it? "Of course I want what's best for her and that doesn't include her staying here. She's not crazy."

He cleared his throat. "I'm sure your stepfather has told you by now Kyra isn't herself at the moment. She's here because the paramedics thought she might be suicidal."

Suicidal? Kyra? I shook my head. "He didn't mention that, but I have a hard time believing that's true. She's the most level-headed person I know."

The doctor scribbled something else on his pad, then turned it over on the table. "One thing I've learned in my many years here is that everyone has a breaking point, Eric."

I could agree with that. After all, I'd certainly found mine. "What made them think she was suicidal?"

"She said more than once that she wanted to die."

I felt my Adam's apple rise and fall as I

swallowed. She couldn't have known about last night, could she? No, I reassured myself. No one but Danielle and I had known. I hadn't even known it was going to happen myself until yesterday. Maybe it was her own guilt that finally caught up to her. "Everyone says stuff like that from time to time."

Wrinkles formed in Hershing's brow. "Maybe so, but not right after they've driven their car into a signpost."

Drawing in a breath, I tried to really digest for the first time that my wife could have been seriously injured or even died. What would our last words to each other have been? Something horrible, I was sure. "My stepfather said she wasn't hurt. Is that true?"

"I wouldn't go that far. She's hurting, just not physically."

A familiar pain passed through me but I refused to entertain it. *She wants a divorce,* I reminded myself. *She doesn't care about you. Why should you care for her?* But of course, I did. "What do I need to do to get her out of here?"

"This is one of those things that aren't within your control. It's really up to Kyra."

I glanced out the window at the trail of fog making its way across the distant mountain range, right into my head. "Are you trying to say she doesn't want to come home?"

The doctor crossed his arms. "Where *is* home, Eric?"

And so the psychobabble begins, I thought. "Rolling Springs."

His eyebrows shot up. "Nice area. Pricey. Do you mind me asking what you do for a living?"

"I sell luxury cars. Well, I manage a team that sells them."

"I didn't realize there was that much money in car sales. Long hours?"

My muscles tensed. Obviously Kyra had been griping to the good doctor about my schedule. Before I'd gotten the promotion, she complained about scraping by. Like I said, never satisfied. "Ten- to twelve-hour days, six days a week."

"That sounds like a tough schedule."

"I've tried to give Kyra the best."

"I see. She likes the finer things, then?"

What was this guy getting at? Probably some sort of mind game to prove we were both nuts. "Don't we all?"

"I'd say that's true. Of course, everyone's definition of what those things are can be quite different. Would you say your wife is high maintenance?"

The question sent blood rushing to my head. What business was it of his? Next he'd be asking about our sex life. Nosy son—

"Mr. Yoshida, I'm not trying to pry. I'm trying to help. I can see by your body language I've probably angered you. That's not my intention."

I made an effort to relax my clenched hands and calm myself. I didn't like the idea of anyone, especially this man, having that sort of power over me. "What exactly is your intention?"

"You want Kyra to come home. Kyra wants to come home and I want that too. The problem is that we have an otherwise-sane woman insisting you're dead."

All the anger drained from me. "Dead?"

"That's what she's saying."

I felt suddenly disoriented as I attempted to wrap my mind around what he had said. "Who would tell her that?"

He straightened his tie as if we were discussing nothing more concerning than an impending rainstorm. "She thinks you've been dead for something like a week."

Dead? I sat stunned trying to make sense of it. This was crazy. She was screaming at me about cutting off her credit card two nights ago and now she thought I was dead? "Did you tell her I wasn't?"

"Yes, against better judgment. I thought she was what we call a malingerer — someone who pretends to be mentally ill, but —"

"Kyra would never do that."

The doctor pressed his lips together as though considering it. "How long have you been married?"

"Twenty years."

"*Good* years?"

Under the table, I traced the smooth gold of my wedding band, searching my mind for the right answer. I wanted to tell the truth, to help the doctor help my wife if she really did need it, but the humiliation of spilling my guts to this stranger would be too much. "Yes, good years."

He nodded. "Tell me about the phone call from Benjamin."

"Benji called?"

His lips drew up in a smile revealing perfect teeth. "Or *I* could tell *you*. Apparently your son called from the naval base. He's arrived safely."

My son was safe. A mixture of relief and pride filled me as I leaned my head back. *Thank God.*

"I think the call was very traumatic for your wife."

Everything made sense now. I could just picture Kyra cradling the phone to her ear as she cried. Taking a drive, like she often did to clear her head. Her vision blurred from tears. She hits a sign. The paramedics come and she's upset. They blow it out of proportion and voilà . . . here we all were. I just needed to set the record straight and everything could go back to normal. Whatever normal was these days.

Wishing I had a drink of water, I cleared my throat. "She pretended for Benji's sake that she was excited about him joining the Navy, but I knew better. She cried herself to sleep worrying about the what-ifs. I figured it would pass once he left home." *Prayed* was more like it.

Hershing nodded. "She and Ben are close?"

"Benji's always been a mama's boy." Seeing Hershing's concerned look, I quickly added, "I don't mean that in a derogatory way."

"Of course not." He clicked his pen against the pad, making the point protrude, then disappear, again and again.

"He's just always been tight with his mom. You've never seen a boy love his mama the way that kid loves Kyra."

"That's nice." Dr. Hershing's face lit up as if this was the first good thing he'd heard yet.

Was it? I hadn't always thought so. I had never admitted to anyone but I'd always been jealous of their relationship. Benji obeyed me out of fear of punishment, but Kyra he obeyed out of love.

"So my wife thinks I'm dead. Do you see this kind of thing a lot?"

He shook his head. "Never." Looking to the side, he tapped his chin with the butt end of his pen. "Well, let me take that back. I deal with dementia, where patients confuse reality or are confused about who they are and that sort of thing, but never a woman in her early forties with no psychiatric history." He paused. "She doesn't, does she?"

I shifted in my seat. "Of course not." Kyra's adopted sister, Marnie, came to mind. She was diagnosed with obsessive-compulsive disorder, but since there was no biological relation between them, and everyone else in the family was more or less normal, I decided it served no purpose to mention her.

Hershing continued, "The idea that someone suddenly thought their living spouse was deceased but seemed otherwise oriented to reality . . . well, I admit, it had me quite intrigued on a professional level. I thought it an unusual form of disassociation."

I felt myself tense. "My wife's not a science fair project, Doctor —"

"Easy, Eric, your knuckles are white

39

again." He motioned with a tilt of his head toward my clenched hands.

I put them back on my lap, out of sight.

"When the ambulance brought your wife in last night, that's what I thought. This morning, however, a small bruise has formed in the center of her forehead." He smiled as though sharing a private joke. One I didn't get. "Mr. Yoshida, I now believe your wife has a simple concussion."

Alarm filled me. "Then she needs medical care."

He interlocked his hands and set them on top of his head. "Besides being a psychiatric hospital, Eric, we also are able to offer non-intensive medical care. She's already been sent out for a CAT scan to make sure there's no serious damage — an internal bleed or anything of that nature. The facility performing it will call me with the results this afternoon. I suspect the scan will come back negative. Negative being good, of course."

Why did the educated assume everyone else was a moron? I felt my nostrils flare. "I know what negative means."

Dr. Hershing either didn't notice my irritation or didn't care. "Concussions often have the side effect of memory loss."

Finally he was making sense. "How long

will it last?"

"Not long, I suspect, although permanent damage isn't unheard of."

So Kyra might spend the rest of her life thinking I was dead? "Can't I just go to her and show her I'm alive?"

He unlocked his hands and wagged his finger at me. "I wouldn't. When I told her you were down here, she didn't believe me. She called me a liar, then started hyperventilating. So I'm fairly certain that's not the best avenue to take right now."

"So we just let her walk around the rest of her life thinking I'm dead?"

"Of course not. She's here for a forty-eight-hour observation anyway —"

I set my palms flat on the table. "Forty-eight hours? No way. I'm taking her home today."

"Mr. Yoshida, hitting the table and yelling at me isn't going to get your wife out of here any sooner."

I looked down at my stinging hands, then back at him. I hadn't yelled, had I? "This is nuts. My wife has a concussion, so she gets locked up in a psych ward?"

"I *suspect* she has a concussion, Eric. I'm not positive. If that's all it is, she'll most likely regain her memory in the next few days and I'll be releasing her."

"She's here for two days no matter what?"

"At least."

I leaned back in the chair and ran a hand through my hair. Maybe I needed to call a lawyer or Kyra's doctor. Of course, the forty-eight hours was practically half up anyway, and her being in here would at least give me time to smooth things over with Danielle. "She's safe?"

He scribbled something else in his pad. Probably *sucker.* After he finished, he looked up. "Perfectly."

"What if it isn't a concussion? What if she — ?" I stopped myself. Of course there was a medical reason for her memory loss. This was Kyra I was talking about, not some lunatic.

Dr. Hershing stood. "I don't like to deal with ifs, Eric. There's no sense in trying to cross a bridge that hasn't been built yet."

Four

Inside Thompson's Imports, the smell of brewing coffee began to eclipse the scent of new rubber tires. I glanced inside my empty mug and wondered if it was too late to get just one more refill. My watch told me I'd better not.

Danielle strolled by my office for the third time in an hour. Again, I pretended not to see her. Her expression grew darker each time I didn't greet her with my usual playfulness. I was going to have to deal with her soon, but hopefully not today. My head was still reeling from learning my wife had been institutionalized.

Before I could even attempt an explanation to Danielle, I would need a good night's sleep and some time to make sense of things myself, so I could make sense of them to her.

A car alarm blared. I grunted and picked up the phone. Through my wall of windows,

I watched Stan Jacobs answer my call. "Hey Jacobs," I said into the receiver, "go show Jim for the hundredth time the difference between the trunk release and the alarm button."

Stan held his thumb up high enough for me to see and we both hung up. Before he could push away from the front desk, the alarm stopped.

I pulled another contract from the pile in front of me and began to review it.

"Hey man, what'd you do to Danielle?"

I looked up to find my best friend, Larry Wallace, standing in my office doorway. The overhead light reflected off the lenses of his black-rimmed glasses, making him look possessed. I squinted at him. "Say who?"

He frowned. "I asked her to work the back end of my deal and she sulks through the entire presentation. Needless to say, we didn't sell them any extras."

Tilting to the side, I slid my hand in my back pocket and pulled out my wallet. "What's the spiff on Scotchgard? Fifty bucks?" I counted two twenties and a ten and held out the money.

Larry kept his eyes glued to mine. "That's not the point and you know it."

Hoping he would get the hint, I put the cash away and went back to reading. "You know how women are."

He crossed his arms over his protruding gut and frowned. "So how are they, Eric. Or more specifically, how is *she?*"

Knowing the gig was up, my heart stopped. Still, I did my best to look like I had no idea what he was talking about. "What are you getting at?"

"I think you know."

I picked up my mug and took a sip, remembering too late that it was empty. A drop of cold, sickeningly sweet coffee hit my tongue. I grimaced and set the cup back down. "Know what?"

"Ever since Kyra kicked you to the curb, you and little Miss Sales Associate have been fawning all over each other."

Beneath the desk, I rubbed my damp palms down my dress pants. "Danielle? Give me a break."

"You give mc a break." Larry scratched his goatee. "You know you can lose your job over this? Try to remember that you're her boss, Einstein."

Sitting up straight, I gave him what I intended to be a threatening look. "I'm yours, too."

"Not for long if you don't —"

Juan Santana appeared in the doorway, cutting off Larry's lecture. One rogue curl broke away from the rest and lay plastered against his perspiring forehead.

Glad for the diversion, I swiveled my chair to face him. "What do you need, Santana?"

Neither finishing his thought nor turning around, Larry just kept glaring at me. If he was trying to unnerve me, it was working.

Behind Juan, a businessman was busy kicking proverbial tires on the showroom LX.

"Dude's upside-down on his trade," Juan said. "There's no way we're going to be able to eat that difference."

I tried to ignore Larry's eyes on me. "Putting up any cash?"

Circling his thumb and finger to make a big, fat, zero, Juan shook his head.

Larry finally turned around. "What car do you have him on?"

"LX," was Juan's reply.

I glanced through the window at the man. He looked like he had money, but then so did every sales guy on the lot in their crisp, tailored suits. I'd learned a long time ago all that glittered wasn't gold. "Move him down to an LT."

Juan hesitated. No doubt he wanted the bigger commission, but sometimes aiming lower meant not losing the sale altogether. "He really likes the leather seats."

Larry shrugged. "Tell him he can't be drinking Dom Perignon on a Budweiser budget."

I dismissed Juan with a wave of hand. "You heard him. The LT, Santana. Tell him cloth's warmer."

Looking dejected, he nodded.

When Juan was out of earshot, Larry turned back around. "Where were you last night?"

I had planned my answer for the inevitability of this question. Why my friend hadn't asked earlier in the day was the only surprise. "I was feeling sorry for myself, so I went to Millstone's, had one too many, and woke up in the backseat of my car in their parking lot."

His eyes narrowed. "Millstone's, how appropriate. Was she with you?"

I laughed, hoping it didn't sound as phony as it felt. "C'mon Larry, is she old enough to even drink?"

He sucked his teeth. "You tell me."

I tried to answer him, but he barreled ahead. "She's a pretty girl, man, but she ain't your wife."

"I just told you I wasn't with her last night."

"I'd like to believe you, but . . ."

"But what?"

"But I don't." He took his glasses off and pointed them at me. "You're talking to someone who's been cheated on. The damage you're getting ready to do can't be undone."

I wanted to tell him that he was a day late and a dollar short with his warning, and that this was nothing like what he had gone through with his ex anyway. Tina had cheated on a faithful, hardworking man who adored her. I only strayed after Kyra accused me of it then kicked me out of my own house. "You know, as long as we've been friends, I would think you'd have a little more faith in me. That you'd know me better than that."

"I do know you, and that's why we're having this conversation. You've been eyeing Dani like a cat in a canary cage and she's been sprinkling herself with hot sauce."

Just then, my cell phone beeped three times, indicating I had a text message. Even before I looked, I knew it was from Danielle.

Hey U. Can we talk?

I had all the talking I could stand for one day. After deleting the message, I set the phone on my desk. "Man, give me a break. You're my friend, not my mother. Next you're going to tell me as long as I live

48

under your roof, I have to do as you say."

"You don't have to do anything. But I ain't going to aid and abet a cheater. You're separated, not divorced. Big difference."

Juan stuck his head back in the doorway. "I need your dealer tag."

I huffed. "Where's yours?"

"I got a guy out on demo."

I yanked the desk drawer open and grabbed the metal plate. "You just gonna let everyone drive our cars around, or you planning on closing one of these deals?"

Juan looked like he might cry. Of course his basset hound eyes looked like that even when he was laughing. "I'm working on it."

Paper clips clung to the magnet bar on the back of the plate. I swiped them off and handed it over. Smiling a thanks, he hurried out with it.

"What are you doing tonight?" Larry asked.

I shuffled papers around my desk. "Working, what else?"

"I mean after."

"Hopefully, sleeping on your couch."

Tucking in his lips, he nodded at me. "Good. Do the right thing, brother. Not just for Kyra or Danielle, but for yourself."

"When are you off again?" I asked picking up a pen and trying my best to look disin-

49

terested.

"Tomorrow and you know it."

"Good." I pulled an invoice off the top of my inbox, scanned, and signed it.

"But just because I'm not here to keep an eye on you doesn't mean you're not being watched."

Static broke in from the overhead speaker. "Larry Wallace, please report to the service center."

I looked up at the ceiling speaker, then him. "That'd be you, Larry. Go take care of your business and let me take care of mine."

FIVE

My father, looking as though he'd lived to grow old, stood beside my mother and stepfather, Alfred, in the house I grew up in. In this strange dream, the three of them were a couple, which didn't seem at all unusual to dream-me. When I held out my glass to have it filled, it was toward my dad, not Alfred. Looking dejected, Alfred shook his head and shuffled sadly away.

I felt awful and knew I should go after him, but I didn't. I just stood there filled with regret. I turned to my father for advice, but just like in real life, he was gone.

I started to call for him, but instead of words, my mouth rang like a cell phone.

Realizing the noise was real but the dream was not, I opened my eyes. In my semi-comatose state, I thought it was my phone alarm telling me it was time to get up for work. I reached over and hit the snooze button and drifted back off.

What sounded like a tiny and distant Benji said, "Dad? You there? Hello?"

I bolted to a sitting position and grabbed the phone off the floor. I guess I hadn't hit the snooze button after all. "Benji?"

"Hey, Dad, we must have a bad connection. Can you hear me?"

"Yeah," I said, feeling dazed. "What's going on? Are you okay?"

There was a pause, followed by, "Well, that's why I'm calling."

Adrenaline slapped the sleep off me. "What's wrong?"

"They're making me call."

"What is it?" My mind reeled with possibilities, each worse than the last.

"It's stupid really."

"Will you tell me already?"

"I'm in the infirmary."

Even though he was still in boot camp, I pictured my son lying on a MASH-style cot, with a bandage around his head and stumps where his legs used to be.

"I was bitten by some fire ants and had an allergic reaction."

I hadn't realized I wasn't breathing until I finally allowed myself to suck in air. "Thank God," I said. "You okay now?"

"Yeah, I'm sort of weird looking, swollen and stuff, but I'm fine. They gave me a shot that's helping."

"Sounds bad."

"Nah, it was just an allergy. The only thing is —" he hesitated — "one of the medics says they can give me a medical discharge for this."

"For an allergy?"

"He's kind of a smart-aleck type, so I don't know if he was just messing with me or what. Hang on; my sergeant just walked in." After a pause, Benji said, "He wants to talk with me. I gotta go."

Knowing the conversation was already coming to an end made me start missing him before we'd even said good-bye.

My words were fast and clipped as I tried to shoehorn in the million-dollar question. "Is it everything you thought it'd be? The Navy, I mean?"

"I was born for this. Hey, I really gotta go. Don't tell Mom, okay? I don't want her freaking over nothing."

"You got it," I said, trying not to sound as worried as I felt. "I love you, Son."

"You too," he mumbled before hanging up. In so many ways he was still a teenager, even if he was a man.

Setting the phone on the table, I lay back on my pillow. With my arms bent behind my head, I stared at the window watching dusk turn to dawn, wondering if Benji really could be kicked out over an allergic reaction. I didn't think so and I couldn't allow my mind to dwell too much on that possibility. It would devastate him. Being a sailor was the only thing my son had ever wanted for himself.

Trying to push the worry from my mind, I closed my eyes and attempted to fall back asleep so that I could get another few minutes before having to get showered for work.

Birds chirped outside my window. I'd started to grow used to their sounds, which were different from the ones at my house. The kind in my yard just chirped and sang like normal birds. Here they sounded like they were spewing accusations and naming names. I listened to one screech, "Stell-a! Stell-a!" over and over.

Trying to get comfortable and keep the sunlight streaming in through the untreated window out of my eyes, I flipped to my stomach and pulled the thin cover over my head. No sooner did the Stella bird shut up than another cried what sounded an awful lot like "Cheater. Cheater. Cheater."

After a while, irritation won out over fatigue. I huffed, climbed out of bed, and banged on the glass. The judgmental bird finally shut up.

I hurried back to the couch, hoping to fall asleep before the birds could start their racket again. As soon as I closed my eyes, my phone beeped. Thinking maybe Benji had sent a follow-up text message, I snatched it up, but it was from Danielle.

I can't stop thinking about you. xo

Right on cue, the bird restarted his obnoxious chirping, "Cheater. Cheater. Cheater."

I jumped up and threw open the window. "Shut up!"

A bang sounded from the wall connecting the living room to Larry's bedroom, and I knew he'd either elbowed or kicked it to tell me to do the same.

Feeling sick to my stomach — over Kyra, Benji, and now Danielle — I threw on a pair of jeans and a T-shirt and decided that maybe taking a walk might help clear my head or at least get me away from that stupid bird.

Six

I should have been hungry. Except for a few stale donut holes, I hadn't eaten since lunch the day before, but still I had no appetite. Particularly not after coming through Larry's front door, fresh from my walk, to find him sprawled on the couch in a T-shirt and boxers with a half-eaten breakfast sandwich parked on his protruding gut. His hairy legs rested on the cluttered coffee table between a stack of *Runner's Life* magazines and a mangled box of tissues.

I closed the front door, shutting out the morning light, and hung my keys beside a well-worn Miami Dolphins cap on the wall rack.

With one giant bite, he shoved the rest of his sandwich into his mouth and set his feet on the floor. He managed to speak around a mouthful of egg, cheese, and — by the looks of it — bacon. "Please tell me I didn't get our days off backwards. Today is Tuesday, not Saturday, right?"

"It's Tuesday," I said, taking off my Nikes. I lined them up side by side next to a small mound of sneakers and shoes, most of which still had dirty socks tucked inside them.

Larry's arm lay draped over the back of the couch as he looked over his shoulder at me. "So, why are you home?"

"I called in sick."

"Seriously. Did Thompson's burn down or something?"

"You think I can't get sick?" I knew I sounded defensive and I guess I was.

"Chill, dude. I'm just saying you'd go to work if you had a chainsaw lodged in your skull, that's all." He turned back to look at the TV weatherman apologizing for the promise of rain that hadn't materialized.

"Sorry, man, I'm just —"

"Forget it." He scratched at the fur on his forearm. "What happened between last night and this morning anyway? You look rougher than a drunk on payday."

"That's better than I feel." I rubbed my gritty eyes and gave him the lowdown on Benji.

He grabbed the remote off the table and pointed it at the TV, silencing it. "Listen, why don't I get out of here so you can have

57

some quiet?"

"No way. I'm not kicking you out of your own house."

Waving a paw in dismissal, he said, "I've got errands to run anyway."

Of course he was just saying that to be nice. As tempted as I was to pretend to be clueless to my friend's need for downtime, my conscience wouldn't let me. "What errands?"

His gaze roved around the room, finally settling on a balled-up napkin sitting on the windowsill. "Uh . . . toilet paper."

"Toilet paper — that's the best you can do?"

He shrugged.

"How about a compromise? You stay, but maybe keep the noise down to a dull roar?"

"Deal." He pulled at the gray patch in his goatee. "Listen, why don't you go crash in my room? My bed is a heck of a lot more comfortable than that block of cement I've got you sleeping on. Besides, it's like a cave in there."

I opened my mouth to protest, but then surrendered. A dark room and soft bed sounded pretty good. "You sure you don't mind?"

"If you don't mind a little mess, it's all yours."

Helping myself to Larry's bedroom, I shut the door. The smell of kitty litter was immediate and pervasive. It emanated from an open bag leaning against the wall by the closet. In the divorce, Tina had traded her claim to their small house in exchange for custody of their three cats and the Lincoln. Larry said he missed having pets but decided, with his long work hours, it wouldn't be right to replace them. I guess maybe the smell still reminded him of them. To me, it just plain stunk, but I figured after a few minutes, my nose would stop registering it. At least I hoped so.

Larry's bed was nothing but a couple of mattresses piled atop a metal frame, but under the circumstances, it looked fit for a king. Stepping around an empty bowl lying on the carpet beside an unused paintbrush and a bent spoon, I pulled off my T-shirt, then crawled into bed.

The sheets were a soft flannel and looked clean enough. So was the brown comforter, although a bit threadbare. Finding no pillow, I leaned over the edge of the bed and peered down. Sure enough, I spotted one lodged between the mattress and wall. After yanking it free, I folded it in half to double it and slid it under my head. I pulled the cover up around my waist and lay there on my side staring at the empty computer desk. It was the only clean area in the room.

When I closed my eyes, I tried to imagine what Kyra might be doing right then. Would they have her in a group therapy session where she'd ramble on about what a horrible husband she'd been saddled with?

I thought of Benji and the chance, however slim, that he might be medically discharged from the Navy. My cell phone beeped and I knew without pulling it out of my pocket that it would be another message from Danielle, asking why I hadn't answered her last one and maybe asking if I was really sick or just trying to avoid her. The answer, of course, was a little of both. Restless, I turned from my back to right side, then left, then back again, and finally sat up. A soft tap came from the closed door.

"Yeah?" I called.

"I'm running down to Quick Way," Larry said through the closed door. "You want anything?"

"Just a noose if they've got one."

There was silence, followed by the sound of the knob turning. The door opened and he stuck his head in. A white splotch of what appeared to be toothpaste clung to the corner of his mouth. "You're not laying there naked, are you?"

I made a face. "What? No."

"Good. I don't want to have to burn my sheets. Get ready. You're going with me."

"I'm trying to take a nap, remember?"

"Sorry, you lost the privilege of being alone when you mentioned hanging yourself."

"I was joking."

"Get your shoes on."

I yanked the pillow from behind me and chucked it at the door. He ducked just in time. It thumped against the doorjamb and hit the floor. "Get out and let me sleep."

He eyed the room like a cop. "Not a chance. You're coming with me if I have to drag you."

I wanted to either bawl or brawl but didn't have the fortitude for either. "Come on, man, give me a break."

His expression hardened. "I'm counting to three, then coming over there and yanking your skinny butt out of bed."

I gave him a dull stare.

He held up a finger. "One."

I didn't react.

"Two."

I could tell by his face, he wasn't playing. Since he was built like a grizzly, I didn't stand a chance. "Thr—"

With a groan, I yanked the blanket off and

swung my feet over the side of the mattress. "Would it matter if I swore on my father's grave that I was only kidding about the noose?"

"It might if you actually liked the man. Get your shoes on."

My father was more obsessed with baseball than any American. Most of the memories I had of him centered around the game. He couldn't play to save his life, but that didn't stop him from expecting great things from me.

The last memory I had of him was the day he taught me to hold a bat. I was five and kept spacing my hands too far apart.

"Not like that," he'd said. Or at least that's how I remember it.

My mother kept my hair sheared in a tight buzzcut back then and the summer sun baked my scalp. I wanted to go inside to escape the heat but was too afraid of my father to ask. I had, after all, seen his temper directed at my mother and didn't want it aimed at me. And so I tried again.

He took the bat from my hands. "Why can't you get this? It's so easy."

I felt my breathing come fast and my eyes try to fill with tears, but I knew better than to cry. Dad said tears belonged only to women and the weak. I was neither, so I swallowed them down and watched his flash of anger disappear.

"Let's forget about baseball a minute and play a different game," he said.

Relieved, I smiled.

"Make two fists like I'm doing."

I did.

"Good. Now keep them there."

He took his own fist and gently tapped mine with it. "One potato." Then he tapped my other fist. "Two potato."

I watched him, confused. This was a baby game. When he got to "seven potato more," he kept his fist on mine. I tried to move my hand away, but my father grabbed my wrist keeping it in place. "Now, look at our hands."

I studied his big fist resting on top of my own small one.

"That's the way you hold the bat."

And that is the way I still, to this day, hold a bat. After getting an ultimatum from Larry that I could either take a trip to the ER or the batting cage, I reluctantly chose the latter. It was there that I gripped the aluminum shaft and raised my elbow behind me.

"You ready?" Larry held the knob on the red metal box that controlled the pitching machine.

I slid the heel of my right sneaker around in the dirt and lifted my elbow. "Ready," I said.

He turned the knob on the box. The tire operating the pitching machine turned, followed by a loud *shoop* indicating a baseball was flying at me. I kept my eye on the white orbit until it flew within range, then swung hard. I heard the ping, felt the force of impact as the vibration moved down the bat to my hands, and finally heard the sound of the ball jangling the metal fence.

Larry watched it roll to the corner of the cage. "Good one."

Resuming the position, I waited for the next one. I hit baseball after baseball, until my muscles ached and I stood drenched in sweat. I glanced at the barrel of balls the pitching machine fed from. It was still three-fourths of the way full. I'd planned to empty it but was already on the verge of complete exhaustion.

"Enough," I said through heavy breaths. A ball shot at me so fast, I didn't have time to do more than raise my leg just in time to protect the jewels. It nailed me in the side of my right thigh. I howled and grabbed my leg.

Larry grimaced at me. "Turned it the wrong way. Sorry about that." He yanked the knob in the other direction then turned his attention back to me. "You all right?"

Even though my leg throbbed with pain, I waved it off as if it were nothing. Trying not to grimace, I limped over to where Larry stood and looked down at the knob he'd just adjusted. It was clearly labeled with big black letters. How could he have confused *curve* with *off?*

"You almost made it so I couldn't have more children."

He laid a hand on my back and smirked. "The last thing the world needs is another one of you anyway."

Picking the bat off the ground, I said, "Your comedic aptitude is second only to your abilities as a pitch machine operator." I held the bat out to him. "Here, your turn."

He took it from me and leaned it over his shoulder like a hobo with his bindle. "Nah, I'm not in the mood. This was just for you."

Good old Larry. I gave him a tired smile, then followed him out of the batting cage. The sun still played hide-and-seek behind a stream of clouds. We sat side by side next to our water bottles that had been waiting for us on the wood bench outside the fence. He handed me mine and watched as I took a long, cool swig.

"Still cold?" he asked.

"The water, or me?"

"Both."

"The water's lukewarm and I guess I'm about the same."

"Still want that noose?"

"I told you I was joking." I lifted up my T-shirt and wiped the sweat from my face with it. "Maybe I kind of did, but I feel better. Thanks."

"Good," he said.

We sat silent a few minutes listening to the pings of aluminum bats whacking balls in surrounding cages, along with the occasional grunt and expletive.

"So, were you picturing her face on it?" Larry asked.

I turned to face him. "Whose face on what?"

"Kyra's on the ball when you were hitting it," he said. "When I found out about Tina and her dirtbag lover, I used to come here and smash the heck out of those balls picturing their faces on them."

I couldn't believe my friend was actually admitting to an un-Christian thought. "Why would I do that? She hasn't done anything like that."

He took a gulp of his water. "She must have done something."

I thought of Kyra's mood swings and her

ongoing accusations and rejection, but I couldn't conjure an ounce of anger. "No, I wasn't picturing her face."

He gave me a sidelong glance. "Come on, man, you can be honest. I'm not going to judge you."

My phone rang from my pocket. "I wasn't picturing her face," I repeated. "I was picturing mine."

As Larry considered my answer, I pulled the phone out, glanced at the number and put it to my ear. On the other end, Dr. Hershing told me I could pick up my wife tomorrow morning.

"What if I'm not ready?" I asked with Larry's eyes glued to me.

"My asking if you wanted was really just a formality, Eric. If you prefer, I can try again to contact her sister."

When I said that wouldn't be necessary, he filled me in on her progress and lack of.

When I hung up, Larry gave me a funny look. "Who died?"

SEVEN

She was the bridge between heaven and earth. That's how I'd felt about Kyra, but something happened to turn our marital utopia into a living hell. I knew how it had started — with her growing disappointment in me and our lives. But until I woke up in Danielle's bed, I hadn't known how it would end. Until that moment, reconciliation was at least a possibility.

It was the irreversibility of my actions I thought of as I unlocked the door to what used to be my dream home. I wasn't exactly sure why I'd come by here. Maybe I just wanted to see my house one more time before she banned me for good.

It hadn't seemed fair that I'd been the one who had to move out when we separated. Wasn't it my money that had built the thing to begin with? Besides, it was Kyra, not I, who had wanted the split. She should have been the one to go.

As I unlocked the door, the house key had never felt so cold and foreign in my hand. Memories of toting my wife over the threshold of our honeymoon suite flashed through my mind.

"You don't have to carry me," she said through laughter. "You're going to give yourself a hernia."

"If I'm going to strain something this week," I dipped her down to slide the room key into its slot, "it's not going to be there."

Her ivory skin turned pink. Although I'd tried everything to get her to make love to me during our short courtship, she hadn't given in. Glancing down at the platinum symbol of forever wrapped around her finger, I was thankful she lived the faith she professed. So few — myself included — really did.

I almost dropped her as I turned the doorknob. This made her laugh even harder. I used my hip to push the door open. Holding tight around my shoulders, her giggles rang in my ears.

"Did you just snort?" I asked her. It was the first time I'd ever heard her do what I would, over time, grow quite used to.

Bobbing along in my arms, she stopped laughing and her expression turned severe. "There are a few things you need to know about your wife, Mr. Yoshida."

I gave a hurried glance around our hotel room. One king-size bed with four fluffy pillows and thick white comforter, a desk, one chair, two floor lamps, one TV with remote, and a balcony overlooking a halfway-decent view of the Atlantic — patio furniture included. Perfect.

I set her down on the bed. Although she didn't weigh much, my arms still ached with the reprieve. "What's that, Mrs. Yoshida?"

She batted her lashes at me, melting my heart for the hundredth time that day. "I don't snort, fart, or use the bathroom, except to brush my teeth and powder my nose. Understood?"

I raised my eyebrows, faking surprise. "Wow. Ever?"

She turned her head to indicate the conversation was over.

"Understood." I kissed her forehead, pausing to take in her vanilla-almond scent.

With a sudden fire in her eyes, she grabbed my face and kissed me with more passion than she'd ever shown me. Than maybe anybody had ever shown anyone. I couldn't stand not having her a moment longer. I spun her around and wasted no time unfastening the hooks on her wedding gown.

She jerked around and grabbed my hands.

"Not so fast. I want this to be perfect." She glanced around the room. "I need my suitcase."

I started to object, but her pleading eyes were no match for my protests. "Please, Samurai, the candles are in there."

I loved that we already had pet names for one another. It made it all feel so right. I pulled her to me. "We don't need the candles. You, my little chili pepper, are hot enough to warm us both."

She pulled away. Even then, Kyra could be so stubborn. Until the scene was perfectly set, love would have to wait.

Shutting the front door behind me, I grinned at the bittersweet memory. Oh, but that wait had been so worth it. I could almost taste her cherry lip gloss, feel her breath on my neck and imagine her silky hair between my fingertips. I hadn't known when I'd given her the nickname that she'd live up to it.

An undercurrent of longing pulled at me with such unexpected force I felt as though my guts were being yanked right out. Ushering the memory from my mind and my feet forward, I made my way to the dining room.

Ghosts of holidays past lingered around the table as well as the countless meals Kyra and I shared there over the years. If I had known the last time we sat there together would be the last time, what would I have done differently?

On the oval mahogany table rested a picture of me hugging a younger Benji. It was winter and we both wore toboggan caps and the thick, itchy sweaters Kyra's mother had made for us the Christmas before she died. In the photograph, a snowman, who had lost one of its pebble eyes, leaned beside us. Benji had an arm wrapped around its misshapen shoulder, wearing a smile more blinding than the snow.

It was the first and only snowman we'd ever made together. Kyra had taken over that job in winters that followed. Although I was glad my salary could afford her staying home, I still found myself jealous about all I had to miss that she was able to enjoy. Especially the snowmen.

I traced Benji's sweet photographed face, regret eating at my insides like battery acid. The picture was displayed inside a simple black frame and rested in front of Kyra's spot at the table. Her chair was still pulled out and a glass of water, half-empty, stood beside it. This was where she had been sitting when Benji had called from Great Lakes; I was sure of it. Maybe she'd been looking at the picture, thinking about how, despite her protests, I had bought our son a bucket of army men for his seventh birthday.

I left the dining room and headed for our bedroom.

As I walked down the hall, my fingertips dragged along the shelves holding our family photos. I paused in front of our wedding portrait. In her flowing white gown, Kyra stood before me, her arms draped over my tuxedo-clad shoulders. Bride and groom stared into each other's eyes as all the hope in the world passed between us in the form of a smile.

My hands trembled as I fought the urge to slam my fist into it — shattering the lie of that promise of a happily ever after. Why did she still display it while kicking me out of her life? She was never one to worry about keeping up appearances. It made no sense, but then neither did she most of the time. That was the one thing that hadn't changed over the years — I knew when I'd said "I do" that when it came to understanding her, I didn't, and never would.

Standing before our closed bedroom door, I leaned my forehead against the painted wood. How was I going to face her today? She'd take one look at me and know what I'd done. Maybe I should just sit her down and tell her the whole truth. Maybe if she understood why I'd done it . . .

Yeah, right after she puts a lawyer on retainer.

I opened the bedroom door and the smell of flowers hit me. A powdering of deodorizer blanketed the beige carpet. The vacuum cleaner stood plugged in and ready to suck it up. I walked to my closet and opened the door. Half my suits and shirts still hung there, but not for long. She'd be throwing my stuff out the windows soon enough. I closed the door and turned around.

Our poster bed stood neatly made and looked the same as always except that all four of the pillows were now piled on her side with a novel resting beside them. I turned it over and glanced at the cover. A man held an adoring woman in his well-dressed arms. Since when did she take to reading romances? She was already disappointed enough in our relationship, the last thing she needed was an idealistic hero to compare me with.

"You think you'd know what to do with her?" I asked the one-dimensional man, before setting the book back down as I'd found it.

I left the bedroom and walked into the living room. Everything was tidy as usual. Kyra had been such a pack rat when I'd first met her, but over the years my anal need for order and cleanliness had rubbed off on her. Now, like me, she preferred everything in its place.

A fish bowl sat on an end table beside a lamp. A small blue beta floated between two leaves of a fake plant nestled into blue gravel. I'd forgotten all about our fish, Steve. I tapped on the glass, wondering if he was dead, but he took off like a shark was hot on his tail.

Good old, hearty beta fish, I thought. The perfect pets. They didn't need to be walked or petted and could even go days without food. Too bad I didn't marry one.

I sprinkled a few flakes on top of the water, then checked my watch. This time tomorrow my wife would be home. I re-capped the fish food, took one more look around our home, and shut the door behind me.

EIGHT

You only want what you don't have until you get it.

Who was it who had said that to me recently? I rubbed the back of my neck, trying to remember. Right now, I wanted only to see Kyra walk through the door so I could take her home. Of course, solving the dilemma of getting her out of Batten Falls was only going to force me to face bigger problems.

I felt like a weary old man as I sat in the now-familiar conference room waiting for Dr. Hershing to join me. I looked at the wall clock. Already twenty minutes had passed. What was taking him so long? If the man would come on already, I could still make it to the lot by noon and get a halfway-decent nine-hour shift in.

Air-conditioning poured in from the vent right above me, causing a single cobweb strand to flutter in its breeze. Feeling the chill, I slipped my suit jacket off my chair and put it back on. When I looked up, Hershing stood before me.

In one hand he held a notepad. The other was extended toward me. "Good morning, Eric."

I shook his hand, looking at the door. "Good morning. Where's my wife?"

He slid his fingers from my grip. "Kyra will be down shortly, but I wanted to discuss a few things with you first."

I gave my watch what I hoped was an obvious glance. "I'm kind of in a hurry."

He pulled out a chair and sat. "What could be more important than your wife, Mr. Yoshida?"

Deciding whether or not to respond to the jab, I licked my lips, tasting the cola I'd drunk on the way over.

He flashed an almost-genuine smile as he set his interlocked hands atop the pad he'd carried in. "I have a few questions for you before I release Kyra to your care."

Oh good, more questions. "Have at it."

"Is it true you and your wife are separated?"

I felt my face catch fire. "Who told you that?"

"Your stepfather, Alfred."

"You spoke with him again?"

"No, just when Kyra was admitted."

So Hershing had already known the state of our marriage when he asked me the other day if our twenty years together had been good? That figured. "Stop playing games. You already know the answer, so why bother asking? Why don't you tell *me* about my marriage since you know so much?"

He looked down at his hands as though in prayer, but instead of praying, he read something on the legal pad. "You're very defensive, Mr. Yoshida, but you don't need to be with me. I was married once. I understand how difficult things can be at times."

I studied him. So he was divorced and planning on giving *me* advice? The blind sure did love to lead the blind.

"My wife passed away last year. While it was a good marriage all in all, we separated twice for short periods in our twenty-four years together. Rough patches happen to the best of us. You don't need to be embarrassed. I know as well as anyone how painful love can be. Most people find it helps if they talk about it."

The hands of misery squeezed tight around my throat. No matter what hocus-pocus Hershing pulled, though, he was not going to manipulate me into crying. No way.

I opened my mouth to say that I wasn't

embarrassed, that it was no big deal, things weren't that bad between us really, but the lump rising in my throat told me my voice might crack if I did. Instead, I crossed my arms and stared down the light switch.

He laced his fingers and tapped his thumbs together. "Here's what I've been told, Eric. Stop me if I get something wrong. You work a lot. Kyra is alone a lot. She was very upset by your son's departure." He paused, looking at me as though expecting confirmation.

I just blinked back. This was my personal business. Between me and Kyra and maybe our son, but no one else. Certainly not this stranger.

After a few seconds, the doctor sighed. "The good news is she no longer thinks you're dead."

I straightened my collar. "So you told me on the phone yesterday. Are we finished here?"

"Not quite. There's still a problem."

I looked at my watch again. Why wouldn't he just come out with it already? "I'm listening."

"I don't think Kyra remembers that you two are separated."

At last, I let my eyes meet his. "Why do you think that?"

His hands stilled. "Once she realized you were alive, she was so relieved, she couldn't stop crying. She spoke about you like a woman in love. She gushed about what a hard worker you are. How perfect you two are together, and your upcoming vacation." He studied me a moment. "Frankly she went on and on so much so I had to cut her off so I could make time for my other patients."

I was stunned to silence. I had no idea what to make of any of it. Kyra hadn't acted that way toward me in years, and the last time we'd discussed the possibility of a vacation was well before she'd found my and Danielle's e-mail exchange. "Wow," I finally said.

"Wow is right."

I couldn't stop my head from spinning. What did this mean for her? For us? "Did you tell her the truth?"

The beeper clinging to Hershing's waist wailed. He unclipped it, read the number, then hit a button and slipped it back on. "I didn't think that best. She's fragile right now. You just came back from the dead for her. I think it would do more harm than good to take you away again."

My leg bounced up and down as I considered the situation. "What am I supposed to do in the meantime? I can't tell her and I can't not tell her. This is terrible."

He nodded empathetically. "It's a difficult situation. There's no clear-cut right or wrong, but if I were you, I'd let her figure it out in her own time rather than overwhelming her too soon."

This was just great. Was I supposed to pretend I wasn't staying with Larry? Just crawl into bed with her like nothing was wrong? Then what would happen when her memory returned? I could just hear her screaming for me to get out of her bed before she called the police or threatened to kill me. No, I would definitely have to tell her.

On the other hand . . . I'd never wanted this separation in the first place. What if this was my do-over? a chance to get it right the second time around?

"I can see your wheels turning, Eric."

I stilled my leg as an idea came to me. "Maybe she should stay here a little while longer. Just until the rest of her memory comes back. I think that would be —"

He put a hand up, motioning for me to stop. "There's no real reason to keep her here. We know why she has memory loss, and the only cure is time."

My temples pounded. "What do I do

meanwhile?"

"Take her home."

I glanced up. "Hers or mine?"

"It's a tough call, Eric. If you're going to come out and tell her the truth, be gentle. She's under the impression that you two are couple of the year."

NINE

Southern Haven magazine once described Everson, Virginia, as a "charming little town with big city appeal." Today, it seemed like nothing more than a scaled-down version of New York minus the taxicabs and Brooklyn accent.

Too many hurried motorists on too few roads guaranteed a long, tension-filled commute home. Even though it was well past the morning rush hour when we left Batten Falls, the thirty-minute trek home had managed to take us nearly an hour, and we were still a mile away from Rolling Springs.

For a change, Kyra didn't complain about the traffic. No amount of blaring horns or tailgaters were going to ruin her uncharacteristically good mood. She said the horror of having her husband taken from her — or rather believing I was — had made her realize what was worth worry in this life, and what was not. Her giddiness only added to my misery.

Cool spring air wafted in through the open window, carrying with it the thick stench of exhaust. I could feel my wife's suddenly love-struck eyes on me as I held my breath, stared ahead at the back of a dusty produce truck, and waited for the traffic light to blink from red to green.

She laid her hand on my leg and smiled at me. It should have been a welcome change to see her teeth instead of fangs, but under the circumstances, it just unnerved me.

"Is the embarrassment of me being in that place what's bothering you?" she asked.

I snuck a glance at her before staring ahead at the road again. Her long red hair lay draped over her shoulders, sunlight intensified the blue of her eyes, and with the exception of the small blue circle in the center of her forehead, her skin was flawless. Why did she have to be so pretty? "Of course not."

"What, then?"

"I'm just worried about you." It was the truth, but not, of course, the whole truth. The light flashed green and I punched the gas. The sudden velocity thrust her back in her seat.

She let out a nervous laugh. "Easy there, Jeff Gordon."

84

Without commenting, I eased off the accelerator and turned on the radio. Five For Fighting sang, "If God made you, He's in love with me." It was the last song we'd danced to together. I jabbed the radio back off.

She frowned at me, but I pretended not to notice. A horn blared behind us. I glanced in the rearview to see some goofball in a white pickup riding our tail. I mumbled a curse and slowed to a crawl.

She touched my shoulder. "Just let him get by, babe."

Anger welled inside me — at the man for risking his and our lives just so he could get wherever he was headed a few seconds earlier, at myself for blowing my second chance with Kyra even before I knew I had it, but mostly at her for being so nice to me. Her disappointment and disgust I'd learned to live with, but this resurrection of affection was just too cruel.

I tapped the brakes a few more times. After a moment or two of riding our bumper so close anyone passing might assume we were giving him a tow, the man finally got the message and fell back. Satisfied at the growing distance between us, I sped up again to fifty-five.

Kyra leaned over and kissed my cheek. I'd

forgotten how warm and soft her lips were. She buried her nose in my lapel, inhaled, then gave me a funny look and sniffed again.

It occurred to me then that I was wearing the same suit jacket I had the night I'd spent with Danielle. I hadn't yet had it dry-cleaned. I jerked away from her. "What are you doing?"

"You smell like watermelon."

Every red-blooded man knows that the best defense is a good offense, and I was no exception. I made an annoyed face as I turned onto Macabee Avenue, our street. "And you smell like a psychiatric hospital."

I felt bad hitting below the belt like that, until I remembered all the times she'd verbally cut me down in the last few months. Her memory might be fried, but mine was just fine. I brushed off my jacket as if wiping off Danielle's scent was as easy as getting rid of a little donut powder. If only it were that easy.

Her smile returned as she leaned her head against me. "Tell those ladies you sell cars to that your wife would appreciate it if they'd keep their hands to themselves." There was a wink in her tone, but I found no humor in the words. I had learned over the years just how treacherous this line of joking could turn.

I pulled into the driveway of our house.

Kyra let out a satisfied sigh. "Well, look at that. The dogwoods are in bloom."

So they were. *So what?* I thought.

"They make the place look a little homier, don't you think?"

What was I supposed to say to that? She hated the house. I knew it and she knew I knew it. "Glad something about our home makes you happy."

A crease formed between her eyebrows.

I started walking up the driveway before realizing she hadn't gotten out of the car. I looked back over my shoulder at her through the closed window. Was she waiting for me to open the door? I'd stopped doing that years ago. Probably about the same time she started taking it for granted. Begrudgingly, I went back and yanked open her door.

"I can't believe you forgot me." She stepped onto the pavement. I couldn't tell by the odd look on her face if she was amused, hurt, or needed to use the bathroom. I barely looked at her as she kissed my cheek and thanked me. "It's good to be home."

For how long? I wondered.

As I ushered her up the sidewalk, she turned suddenly, startling me, and threw her arms around my neck. "You're alive!"

My knee-jerk reaction was to push her from me and tell her she'd lost the right to touch me this way when she kicked me out. Instead, I gently unwrapped her fingers. "You know this means no insurance money."

"That's okay." She gave my neck a quick peck before I could get away. "You're worth more to me alive than dead anyhow."

She was right, though I doubt she knew it. I'd changed my life insurance policy the week before to be paid out to Benji instead of her in the case of my untimely demise. If I wasn't good enough to share her bed, then she wasn't good enough for my insurance money. Besides, I couldn't stand the thought of her driving men around in a shiny new convertible that my death paid for.

As she followed me up the walkway, I felt her hands trying to smooth away a wrinkle from the back of my suit jacket. "You might want to get that dry-cleaned. Not only does it smell like your customers, it looks like you either slept in or on top of it."

I threw a perturbed look over my shoulder. "Don't start."

She grabbed my hand, forcing me to stop and look at her. "Baby, are you okay?"

I pulled away. "I'm fine. I'm just thinking about something at work."

"You work too hard," she whispered.

"What else is new?" I started walking again. There was a certain amount of comfort in settling back into one of our regular arguments. Hurrying in front of me, she blocked my retreat to the house. "You're not dead. That's new." She bit her bottom lip and gave me what may or may not have been bedroom eyes.

"Kyra! Eric!"

We simultaneously turned to face the yuppie neighbors I referred to as *D.I.N.K.s* — double income, no kids.

Neighbor Brenda Harrington laid her pruning shears beside the boxwoods in front of her house and tugged on the sun visor framing her pasty forehead. Her husband, Bram, pulled off suspiciously dirt-free gardening gloves. They both wore jeans that were made to appear worn, with deliberate factory-made tears and uniformly frayed cuffs.

The Harringtons met us at the end of the walkway, wearing grins that looked as fake as mine felt. "Kyra, Eric," Brenda cooed. "It's good to see you both."

"Good to see you, too," I lied, trying to nudge Kyra up the stairs by her elbow before these two phonies could say more than her mind could safely process.

Instead of appreciation, Kyra ripped her arm away from me and scowled.

Brenda shifted her weight to one leg and tilted her head to the side like a dog. "I can't remember the last time I saw you two together. We were really worried that you'd be selling soon and we'd be getting new neighbors." She looked at her husband. "Isn't it nice to see them together, honey?"

As usual, Bram had pasted his hair with too much gel and hairspray, giving him a Ken-doll appearance. "It really is."

If they said *together* one more time . . . I cleared my throat and tried, once again, to encourage Kyra up the stairs.

She batted my hand away and scowled harder. "You know Eric works a lot." There was an unmistakable defensiveness in her tone.

Both Bram and Brenda tucked a thumb into their front pockets at the same instant as if they had choreographed the move. I wouldn't have been at all surprised to learn they had. Their whole life seemed choreographed to me.

I stepped in front of Kyra like a human shield. "If you'll excuse us. My wife was in an accident and —"

Kyra stepped out from my shadow just as the couple gasped. Bram's eyebrows fell in an exaggerated dip while Brenda's hand flew to cover her mouth. "Oh no! Are you okay?" Her gaze jetted over Kyra's body, searching for evidence of injury.

"She's fine," I said, "but she has a concussion, so her memory is a little hazy. I'm sure you understand that I want to get her inside and lay her down."

Kyra nodded solemnly, looking relieved for the out.

"Oh, of course, of course," Brenda said. "I just wanted to remind you that our godchild, Adel, is competing with her pony club this Friday evening. Kyra, you had said you'd try to make it, but now that you two are," she paused, giving Bram a private look, "well, it sure would be nice to have you both there."

"We'll look at our schedules," I said, knowing we'd both have something, anything, to do that night.

"Fair enough, neighbors." Bram took his gloves from his back pocket and slid them back on.

I waved a good-bye, but the couple just stood there.

"Well, okay then," Kyra said, waiting, like me, for them to get the hint.

When they didn't, I ushered her inside, leaving them standing alone on the sidewalk.

I shut the door and peered through the peephole. They were still standing there staring up at the door as if they expected it to fly open and be invited in. I shook my head and turned around.

Kyra rolled her eyes. "Why do they think we would want to spend an entire day watching that spoiled brat — not only of no relation to us, but of no relation to them — prance around on her stupid pony with her nose stuck up the sky's butt?"

Heading for the kitchen, I heard her footsteps following behind me. I poured myself a glass of water from the tap and leaned my back against the counter. "They're something else," I said between sips.

She pressed her body against mine and played with a button on the front of my shirt. I would have backed away if the counter weren't preventing me. Instead I cleared my throat and gave her a dull look, hoping she couldn't feel my heart pounding.

"I thought you said you wanted to lay your wife down." She trailed her hand down the front of me, giving me no room to misinterpret her intentions.

I turned around to get away from her, giving her my back, and refilled my glass. I tried to gulp down a swallow of water but inhaled it instead. My body convulsed as my lungs tried to force the liquid out through violent coughs.

"You okay?" She backed up to give me room.

After a moment, my coughing subsided and I was able to catch a few breaths. "Wrong pipe," I choked out. My glass clanked as I set it on the granite counter. "So, I guess I'll be getting back to work if you'll be okay."

She frowned. "Already? I thought you, we, might . . . I mean, you don't know how much I've missed you."

"Well, um," I stuttered, probably wearing the same look I did when I was trying to get away from the Harringtons. "Mr. Thompson was kind enough to let me off two mornings to deal with this whole . . . but . . ."

Her shoulders drooped. "Rain check, then?"

I looked at the floor. "Sure."

"When will you be home?"

I paused so long she probably wondered if I'd fallen asleep with my eyes open. What was I supposed to say? Maybe her memory would return while I was at work and I'd get an angry phone call. Sadly, that was really the best I could hope for. I decided to bide my time for now. "I guess it'll be late. I need to take care of some business and catch up. You go on to bed."

She combed her fingers through the ends of her hair like she did when she was nervous. "Okay," she said. "Maybe I'll invite Marnie over."

She didn't remember her sister was out of the country on business, and I wasn't sure if I should tell her.

"I'll see if she can do dinner tonight," she said and opened the refrigerator. It was nearly empty except for a few Styrofoam takeout containers, a head of browning lettuce still in its plastic wrapping, and a jar of dill pickles. She unscrewed the metal lid, dipped her fingers into brine, and lifted one out.

As she crunched into it I thought of Marnie and wondered if she would already somehow have heard about her sister's little adventure in Batten Falls. I didn't see how. She'd been in France for a month and it wasn't like they had any family besides one another to spill the beans.

No, she probably didn't know yet, but surely Kyra had called and told her that we were separated. I needed to get to her and let her know what was up before she got to

Kyra. I wanted to believe my motivation was just following Hershing's orders to protect her, but I knew that wasn't entirely true.

With Kyra's cell phone in my pocket and my heart in my throat, I backed out of the driveway of my once-more home. By the grace of God, ingenuity, or sheer luck, I'd successfully navigated my way through the land mines of my wife's spotty memories and unpredictable emotions.

I slid her phone out of my pocket, feeling a little guilty about leaving her without one, especially since we'd dropped the landline. But what was the alternative? She'd have called Marnie. Then what? The gig would have been up.

I turned off Macabee and parked in front of a white colonial. A black cat perched in the window, watching me as I checked Kyra's text messages. All were deleted except one to Marnie, which just said a simple, *"Hurry home. Be safe."*

I dialed her number and pressed the asterisk. When it asked me to enter the password, I didn't really expect it to work, but surprisingly, it did. I couldn't believe that she hadn't thought to change her voice mail password since we'd separated. I could have been listening to her private messages this entire time for all she knew. There was one message from Bill Parsons, our youth pastor, asking about Benji, and one from Marnie, asking Kyra to pick her up from the airport that evening. Apparently her fashion-scouting trip had come to an end. Since I had to get to Marnie before Kyra did, I had no choice but to meet Delta flight 8319 at five fifteen.

I set the phone in my empty ashtray and shifted into drive, watching the cat watch me drive away. Thinking of the convoluted web I was weaving, I was more unsure than ever how to proceed with the medically-prescribed charade, or even if I should.

Nothing had prepared me for the raw pain of being thrust into the past. Of being looked at once again by my wife with eyes of love. Over the years her feelings for me had seeped out in such a slow trickle, the leak was hardly noticeable, until the pool lay completely dry. Seeing it full again made me desperate to dive in. I hadn't realized just how much I missed those waters. How much I missed her. But that wasn't my motivation for keeping her in the dark. I wanted to protect her. She was vulnerable, and I was still her husband. At least for a little while longer.

If only her accident had happened a year

ago, or even a few days ago, how differently our lives might have turned out. I never would have believed how quickly she could stir up the old feelings in me with just one bat of her lashes.

Maybe she could forgive me too. A spark of hope ignited inside me as I turned left out of our neighborhood — until words spoken long ago echoed in my ears: "Samurai, I'll give you everything, forgive you anything . . . except that."

Had she considered for one second that someday it might be *her* in need of forgiving?

Bloomless crape myrtles lined the side of the road, their multistemmed trunks reaching from the ground like gnarled fingers. I pulled along the shoulder and stopped beside them. A truck flew past, making my SUV tremble in its wake. I draped my arm over the steering wheel, lay my head down, and did what I had not allowed myself to do since my marriage fell apart. I cried.

What was I going to do? I had to tell Kyra the truth before someone else did. Of course, no one — not even her sister, Marnie — knew that I'd gone to bed with Danielle. Sure, Marnie might remind her of our e-mails, either unknowingly or, in her case, probably knowingly, but she couldn't fill her in on what she didn't know herself.

Kyra obviously had no recollection of the damage either of us had caused. What if she never did? I tilted the rearview mirror and checked myself. My dark eyes were puffy and red-veined, but they'd clear up on the drive to the dealership. After a Mazda Miata shot by, I adjusted the mirror, then eased onto the road.

I lowered the window, letting the morning air lap my face. How had I gotten myself into such a mess? Maybe it would turn out to be a blessing in disguise. Stranger things had happened. Maybe Kyra would never remember what I wished more than any- thing I could forget.

The double yellow lines splitting the road blurred into one as I stared at them. Even if she never figured out how far we'd strayed, I still had Danielle to contend with. I knew all too well how unpredictable a woman scorned could be. If I could explain things, make her understand the delicate situation and how sorry I was, maybe . . . just maybe . . .

TEN

"Danielle, you have a minute?"

Her pouty lips curled into a sly smile, reminding me why I had been attracted to her. Part cheerleader, part sex kitten, she did have a way. I motioned for her to come in. Her gaze traveled the length of my body as she sauntered past. I eyed the windows making up the far wall of my office. Nothing like trying to have a private moment in a fishbowl. Even if the showroom staff could see our every move, at least they couldn't hear what we said.

Danielle touched her neck, drawing my gaze to the creamy hollow beneath her ear I'd focused most of my kisses on the other night. "I hear Kyra's doing okay."

Word certainly did travel fast. I forced my eyes off her skin. "She's back home."

She threw a quick glance over her shoulder at the windows. The staff appeared busy and unaware. "That's good news. Hey, if you don't already have plans later —" she inched toward me — "I was thinking maybe I could buy *you* dinner this time. Soho's downtown is supposed to be amazing."

It had suddenly gotten uncomfortably hot. I pulled at my collar and stepped back. "See, the thing is —"

Before I could finish the sentence, Larry busted in. "Hey, ladies." Beneath his glasses, his gaze barely brushed Danielle before taking on a hardness and settling on me. "Sorry to interrupt, but I need boss man here to okay a deal so I can close."

With her back to Larry, Danielle fingered the top button of her silk blouse, trying to draw my gaze to her cleavage. "Yea or nay on my proposal, Mr. Yoshida?"

Perspiration dampened my hairline as I fought to keep my eyes off her intended target. Uncertain whether to dismiss her or Larry, I settled on the less volatile choice. "Larry, give us just a second."

He crossed his arms and leaned against the doorjamb.

Trying my best to intimidate my friend into saying *uncle* and leaving, I stared him down. The mule didn't budge.

I turned my attention back to Danielle. "Okay, we'll talk then."

Relief filled her smile. Red lipstick boldly

framed white teeth. "Wonderful."

Larry watched her leave, then turned around. "Man, what's wrong with you?"

I walked to my desk and sat down. "Back off, Larry. I'm trying to let her down easy."

With lips pressed so tight they puckered, he shook his head. "Let her down, eh? I thought you were innocent on all charges?"

Out in the showroom, someone tested a car horn with two annoying beeps.

I opened my desk drawer and rummaged through the pens, papers, and miscellaneous forms, pretending to search for something. I found an old Post-It with the work number of a client we'd sold an LS 600 to weeks before. Remembering that I'd already transferred the number to my computer database, I crumbled it and dropped it in the mesh wastebasket next to my desk. "I'm not in the mood."

"Good. Make sure you stay out of the mood."

I slammed the drawer shut, catching a paper in limbo. I yanked the knob and shoved the paper all the way in. "I thought you came in here to run a deal by me?"

With arms still crossed, he now stood with his legs spread in a wide stance, looking like a nightclub bouncer. "You think you're the only one around here who knows how to make things up?"

Why wouldn't he give it a break already? "What do you want?" An untouched copy of the *Everson Times* lay on the corner of my desk. I slid it over as though I intended to read it. After staring at it a moment, I realized it was upside down. I flipped it over and snapped it open.

Naturally, he didn't take the hint. "I'm just looking out for you, man. Someone has to since you're doing such a sloppy job of it." His tone softened. "How's Kyra?"

I lowered my paper and stared at a patch of razor burn dotting his cheek, unsure how to answer. *She's great except she doesn't remember that she hates me.* "Confused."

"I know she *was,* but I thought that doctor said she got her memory back."

Not having read the first page of the paper, I turned to the second. The headline stated, *Children of Broken Homes More Likely to Try Drugs.* I folded the paper and tossed it on my desk. "Not all of it."

When Larry uncrossed his arms, I was hit by just how much weight my friend had gained since his divorce. Though I saw him every day, he normally wore larger clothes that hid it a little better. The small white buttons of the dress shirt he sported today looked about to pop against his protruding gut. His ex-wife, Tina, might have been an unfaithful nag, but she did make sure his diet consisted of more than pork rinds and pop.

"At the risk of sounding like a girl, you want to talk about it?" Larry asked.

I squinted at him. "At the risk of sounding like your boss, buy a shirt that actually fits you, and get back to work."

Glancing down his chin at himself, he flipped up his striped tie and gave it a quick sniff. He scraped off whatever he'd discovered like he was working on a scratch-off ticket. He let the tie fall back to his shirt. "How about lunch?

The phone rang. Thankful for the escape, I picked up.

Larry glared at me. "I asked you a question, brother."

Pressing a hand over the receiver, I mumbled, "Yeah, whatever." I uncovered the phone. "Eric Yoshida."

Whoever it was hung up.

I shrugged and set the phone back in its cradle. "Must have been something I said."

Larry looked at his watch and grinned. "Hey, whadaya know? It's lunchtime now."

Looking up at the wall clock, I felt my whole body sigh at the thought of an hour-long interrogation over burgers and fries.

Larry was so much easier going before he'd found God. One little altar call had turned Dr. Jekyll into Mr. holier-than-thou Hyde. He was a good guy, but some days the religious routine was just a little too much, even for other Christians.

I searched for an excuse that would let me out of the lunch date, but exhaustion had dulled my mind.

Feeling like a prisoner being led to my cell, I followed him to his Jeep and slid into the passenger seat. "You sure you don't want me to drive?"

Larry sucked his teeth. "You just can't stand not to be the one in control, can you?"

The unexpected jab caught me off guard. "What? I just asked if you wanted me to drive."

As soon as we turned off the lot onto Main, he adjusted the rearview mirror. "Chill, dude. You've got control issues. So what? We all have something. Look at me." He waved a hand over his stomach. "I eat too much."

Heat crept up my neck. "I don't have control issues."

"Yeah, you do."

Where was this coming from all of a sudden? We had been friends for six years, best friends for five. I'd have thought it would have come up before now if he had a problem with me. "For example?"

He flicked on his blinker and passed a wagon. "Never mind."

"You can't even give me one."

"I could give you a hundred. How about this being only the third time in a year that you didn't insist on driving."

I made a face. "*That's* your example? I'm just a better driver."

"And you always have to pay."

"I make more money."

"You rearranged the furniture on the second day you moved in with me."

For crying out loud. "Your stupid couch was blocking the front door. What if there was a fire?"

Larry glanced at me sidelong. "And you always insist on picking the golf course we play at."

"Please," I said. "You picked the very first course we played together. Remember that? 'Cause I do."

Sudden recognition washed over his face as his skin mottled. "So tell me what's going on."

Oh sure, *now* he wanted to change the subject. Typical. "That course catered to ninety-year-olds who'd never played a day in their life. Even the caddies used walkers.

I was growing old just waiting for the hearse to drive them to the next hole."

Larry's nostrils flared as he sped up, passing a Buick. "Fine. Let's just drop it. Spill what's up with you and blondie."

Staring at the back side of his inspection sticker, I said nothing.

Larry shook his head. "You slept with her, didn't you? I knew it."

I looked out the window, watching strip malls and fastfood joints blur by, as I fogged up the glass with my breath. I braced myself for the inevitable lecture that was sure to follow.

"Does Kyra know?" he finally asked.

I swallowed the lump in my throat. "Man, she doesn't even know we're separated."

"What do you mean she doesn't know? How does she not know?"

The traffic light ahead changed from green to yellow. An old Ford Ranger sped up, catching the red light half-way through the intersection. Lucky for him no cops were around to cite him. Larry slowed to a stop and looked at me, waiting for an answer. "The concussion."

"You're kidding."

I frowned. "Do I look like I'm kidding?"

When the light flashed green, Larry passed through the crossroad, then pulled into the

Wendy's parking lot. He turned off the engine and faced me. "Let me get this straight. Your wife not only doesn't know you've been playing doctor with Danielle, she doesn't even remember you two aren't living in the same house?"

Over his shoulder, I watched a silver-haired man open a car door and help his wife out. I wondered if the woman took him for granted the way Kyra had me. When our eyes met, I nodded, then focused on Larry. "That's right."

With hands the size of a small continent, Larry rubbed his temple. "What are you going to do?"

It was a fair question. One I wished I knew the answer to. "No idea. I was hoping you might have some advice."

"Seems to me I gave you advice a few weeks ago, not to move out of your house. Then I gave you advice to stop flirting with Danielle. And then just yesterday, I gave you yet —"

I felt my blood pressure rise. "You know very well Kyra made me move out."

A dull look met me. "She make you go to bed with Danielle, too?"

The condemnation of a friend cut deep, but not deeper than my own guilt. "I screwed up, okay? I don't need an 'I told you so.' "

He pushed up his glasses. "What *do* you need?"

The sun stabbed through the windshield. I laid my hand over my brow like a visor, shielding my eyes. "To figure out how to fix this mess." I couldn't remember the last time I'd asked anyone for help, and it made me feel weak and off balance, like trying to stand upright during an earthquake. Maybe I did have control issues. If I did, I figured they were probably the least of my problems.

Larry laid one of his paws on my shoulder. "The truth shall set you free, my man."

I shrugged him off. "Oh, come on. Don't start with the God crap. I need help, not saving."

Larry studied me. "Pretty sure you need both."

I rolled my eyes. If he only knew how obnoxious he sounded.

It was getting warm with the windows up and the sun bearing down on us. Larry seemed to feel it just as I did. With a touch of a button our windows descended, letting in the smell of French fries. The vehicle was the only thing that cooled off.

Larry took his glasses off and pinched the bridge of his nose. "At the risk of ruining our friendship, I don't know how you can call yourself a follower of Christ and do what you have. I'm not saying you're not, I'm just saying you may want to reevaluate your faith sometime. As far as Kyra goes, you need to tell her the truth. Since you asked, that's my advice."

I sat there dumbfounded. Did the man who knew me as well as my own family just accuse me of not being a Christian? Kyra and I had been the ones to invite him to church the first time, for crying out loud. I felt my mouth screw up as I pointed a trembling finger inches from his nose. "You can call me a cheater, tell me I'm a terrible boss, but you don't get to question my faith. You don't know what —"

"You're right." He held his hands up in surrender. "I'm sorry."

My anger eased with the apology. I supposed if the shoe had been on the other foot, I might be coming to the same conclusion. "Listen; forget it," I said.

He gave me a weak smile. "I think you're just asking for my help so you can prove you're not a control freak."

"Is it working?" I asked, glad the tension had broken. We both stared ahead at a young couple walking into the restaurant with their hands in each other's back pockets. I wanted to yell out the window for the man to enjoy it now. Twenty years from now the woman would be more concerned with a clean stove than touching him. "She kicked me out over an innocent e-mail. What's she going to do when she finds out about the real thing?"

Larry continued to watch the couple, and I wondered if he was thinking of his early days with Tina. I remembered him saying that no matter whose fault it was, a breakup always felt like an amputation without painkillers. "I doubt the e-mail was all that innocent," he said.

Having nothing in my defense, I didn't argue.

The couple disappeared behind glass, and Larry opened the Jeep door. "It don't look good."

I took his lead and got out. "Yeah, thanks. You're a wealth of help."

We started toward the restaurant. Larry stopped suddenly, blocking a car from getting into the drive-through lane. The man raised a hand in annoyance and honked.

Stepping back, Larry let him pass. "All I can tell you is just take it one step at a time. Do the next right thing and say a whole lot of prayers. That's all you can do."

I wasn't sure if the next right thing was what I was about to do or not, but I didn't have much choice. "In order to do that, I may need your help."

"Name it."

"I need you to close shop for me tonight so I can leave early."

He pressed his lips together and studied me. "Is this to help your marriage or so you can be with Danielle?"

"Believe it or not, both," I said.

ELEVEN

As I wove my way through hurried travelers, it occurred to me how disproportionately good-looking people at the airport seemed, compared to the general public. Many of the women could pass for models, and a fair number of the men looked like they stepped off magazine covers from *GQ* to *Backpacker.*

Perhaps attractive people were more likely to have married well and could afford to travel. Of course many of those who had to fly for business probably worked in sales. Salespeople did much better if they were easy on the eyes.

Even at Thompson's Imports, the best-looking men closed the most deals. An unfair fact that had served me well. My above-average looks certainly hadn't impeded my becoming salesman of the year five times in a row and eventually landing a promotion and nice income. Of course it had also brought temptation over the years, which until recently I had been strong, centered, and in love enough not to succumb to.

I ran a hand through my hair as I scanned the small crowd gathered around baggage claim C, searching for the short blonde. As usual, I heard Kyra's sister before I saw her. Marnie had a boisterous belly laugh that made those around her laugh too.

I stood waiting, remaining anonymously behind her as a businessman at least ten years her junior flirted. She wore a fitted blue dress that showed off her toned forty-five-year-old body. When the man yanked a leopard print suitcase from the conveyor belt, she stepped back.

His gaze slithered over her tanned legs as he set the bag beside her. She thanked him for his help by giving his cheek a motherly pinch and warning him of the hazards of drinking from plastic bottles. His boyish face turned shades as he laughed. Like many others before him, he'd mistaken her obsessive paranoia for a quirky sense of humor.

Her hair brushed her shoulders as she turned around, looking directly at me. It took a few seconds before recognition washed over her. Her arched eyebrows dipped in confusion. "Eric, were you on my flight?"

I took a deep breath and smiled. "No, I'm here to give you a lift."

She looked around. "I thought my sister was coming."

"I wanted to pick you up myself."

Frosted pink lips curled into a suspicious smirk. "Why?"

Without answering, I glared at the businessman, or more accurately — boy, still ogling her. This guy had some kind of nerve. For all he knew she and I were a couple, and here he was undressing her with his eyes right in front of me. When he noticed me staring daggers at him, he snatched up his briefcase and moved farther up the conveyor belt.

I grabbed the hard plastic handle of my sister-in-law's suitcase and started walking. The click of her spiked heels followed.

I looked back over my shoulder. "You look well, Marnie. How was your trip?"

"It was good," she said from behind me. "I met a man."

This wasn't exactly earth-shattering news. She was always meeting someone or other. It was another of her not-so-little eccentricities. "Who's the lucky guy this time?"

"You say that like —"

"Like you're a serial dater? You are."

"Don't make it sound so sordid. His name is Adrian. He lives in Paris . . . for now."

I asked no questions. For one, I figured she would tell me all about this flavor of the month whether I did or not. For two, I already knew the basics. He would be attractive, dark, blind to her eccentricities, and rich. Marnie had a pretty good case of obsessive compulsive disorder, among other things. She only dated men with money because, despite her successful fashion career, she was deathly afraid of being poor. The only thing she feared more was actually walking down the aisle. That, meteorites, and even numbers.

"I can pull up front if you want, but I'm parked pretty close," I said.

Appearing on my right, determinately keeping stride, she smiled. "I wouldn't want you to go to any trouble. Besides, 76 percent of accidents involving pedestrians occur right outside the front door."

Even though I felt fairly confident she invented the statistics she often quoted, it did no good to argue with her. "Besides hooking another live one, how was France?"

She tossed her hair theatrically. "Fabulous while *I* was there. Everywhere I am is fabulous, Eric. You know that." Anyone hearing our conversation would assume she was conceited, but I knew her well enough to know she was both kidding and as full of self-doubt as a person could be.

"Keep telling yourself that and then at least one person will believe it." I turned and winked to show I was teasing. To Marnie, being ribbed was equivalent to being hugged.

She had no jovial retort, for a change, as she followed me the short distance to my parking spot.

I loaded her suitcase in the back of the SUV, and she climbed into the passenger seat. We sat silent while I drove and she texted back and forth on her BlackBerry. Though her behavior would be considered rude for anyone else, I knew it was just her OCD at work. She had to know that everything was in order or it would drive her over the edge she constantly teetered on. Anyway, I was glad to have her distracted. The ride to her house was too short for a meaningful conversation, and I would need her full attention.

Two traffic lights, three stop signs, two rights, and one left later, we pulled into the driveway of her Victorian. She finally slid her phone back into her purse. I parked beside her Mercedes, while she glanced behind her at the stack of my suits and dress shirts — still on hangers — piled on the seat behind us.

Sunlight caught the diamond pendant dangling from a delicate chain against her collarbone. Sparks of prism color flared in every direction. I wondered which in her long line of disposable suitors had given her the expensive gift and how long it took him to regret it.

She scrunched her nose, humor gleaming in her eyes. "Let me guess, you cheated on Larry too, and now you're living out of your car." She covered her mouth in mock dismay. "Oh no, you're not going to ask to move in with me, are you?"

I turned off the ignition. *Not when there's a perfectly good bridge I could jump off just down the street.* "Actually, I'm moving these things back home."

She couldn't have looked more surprised if I'd just claimed to be Princess Diana reincarnated. Her mouth dropped, making her look like a teenager who was about to say, "No way."

I let out a deep breath that I felt like I'd been holding for days. "We need to talk."

Her eyes turned into tiny brown slits. "What have you done to my sister now?"

Shadows darted along the dashboard cast

by swaying leaves from a nearby maple tree. I focused on them rather than her. "May I come in?"

"You may want to tell me out here. Inside, there won't be any witnesses if I kill you."

"I'll take my chances."

A waist-high iron fence outlined the perimeter of the yard. The gate squealed as I pushed it open, rolling her suitcase behind me. She strutted ahead, stabbed the wooden stairs with her spiked heels, and unlocked the front door. I followed her inside, squinting as my eyes adjusted to the stark contrast between spring sunshine and the dimly lit home. I set her bag by the front door as the room slowly came into focus.

The place seemed even drearier than I remembered. The ceiling painted deep green, heavy drapes, and an overkill of dark wood was to blame. The hardwood floor was stained the color of pecan; so were the doors, the trim, and even the round table perched in the middle of the foyer. Despite being set against the backdrop of bright floral wallpaper, the room still managed to make me feel like we were deep in the woods, hidden from the sun under a thick canopy of branches and leaves. Adding to the rainforest effect was the musty smell permeating the room.

Marnie lifted her chin and sniffed the air. "Do you smell that?"

"What?" I lied.

"That terrible mildew smell."

Knowing where this could lead, I shook my head.

"You're a terrible liar." She moved to the table resting atop a thick, wool rug and slid her hands under it. "Come on and grab an end. I had this carpet shampooed before I left. I guess the stupid thing never dried all the way. It's probably full of mold now. I'll be dead by morning if we don't get it out of here."

I looked at my watch. I was supposed to meet Danielle in half an hour. I didn't have time for Marnie's melodrama, but I knew if I didn't help her, she'd end up giving herself a hernia trying to go it alone. I grabbed one end of the table, and together we lifted it off the rug. For a piece of furniture that looked so solid, it was deceptively light. Probably made of pine but stained to impersonate hardwood. "Kyra thinks you're picking her up for dinner soon."

Her mouth twisted. "Who told her that?"

"You're a smart girl. Who do you think?"

"I think that's the nicest thing you've ever said to me." Together we carried the table into the adjacent kitchen and set it on the tile floor.

Creases left by the ridges under the table marked my hands. I rubbed at them. "That you're smart? Well, you are."

She walked back into the foyer. "No, that I'm a girl."

I followed. "And you said I was a terrible liar."

"Good one." She wiped her brow as if she'd worked all day, then motioned to the rug. "Would you mind dragging that thing outside so it can air out?"

"Sure," I said halfheartedly. I grabbed the end of it and began to pull. It weighed more than I could have imagined. By the time I'd hauled it outside and left it on the brick patio, I was sweating.

When I came back in, Marnie stood in the dining room, counting the flowered teacups sitting atop a hutch. "There's one missing."

Yeah, like someone would break into her house and steal one stupid cup. "No, there's not; count again," I said, but she was already in the process.

"You're right, there's seventeen after all." She gave the hutch one last look, then opened the French doors, which led to a sitting room. It was the one cheery place in the entire house. A large, arched window looked out over a generous yard. The sun poured in on white wicker furniture and the three prancing horses posing along the far wall. Each had been painted in vibrant, fanciful colors and speared in the center with a pole that once held them to their carousels.

Marnie motioned for me to sit on the wicker couch. It creaked under my weight.

She took the chair across from me. "You want something from me. What is it?"

My sister-in-law might be compulsive, but she had a way of cutting to the chase. I picked up a magazine from the glass table before me, glanced at the list of America's richest on the cover, and tossed it down. "What makes you think I need your help?"

She played with her diamond studs. "Don't you know I can smell even the smallest amount of blood in the water? Why do you think my friends call me the shark?"

"I think you mean the shrew."

"Well, at least you're thinking. That's an improvement. So, tell me what you've done." Though she smiled warmly at me, there was suspicion in her eyes. Although I knew she loved me and wanted to see Kyra and me work things out, she loved her sister fiercely, and her loyalty would always lie with her first.

Wringing my hands together, I recounted Kyra's accident and Dr. Hershing's advice.

Marnie wore a strange look through the entire recounting, but for a change she didn't interrupt. When I finished, she bobbed her crossed leg up and down as she studied me. "So, let me get this straight: my sister has forgotten that you cheated on her, and you want me to not remind her?"

I pinched the bridge of my nose, partly as a reaction to stress, and partly to not have to look at her. "It was just an e-mail," I said for the hundredth time. And that was true as far as she knew. "I'm not going to beg you. I don't even know if it's the right thing to do myself. I'm just telling you what the doctor said."

"I'd like to speak with him myself."

I wondered if she already knew him. After all, she'd been to every other shrink in town. "Of course."

"I'll need his number."

I slid my wallet out of my back pocket and searched through the array of credit and business cards. Not finding Hershing's the first go through, I filed through them again. I knew the fact that I couldn't find it looked suspicious.

Marnie ran her hand over the mane of the carousel horse beside her chair. "Eric, is there anything else you're not telling me? Now's as good a time as any to come clean."

I thought of Danielle and what I'd done, but of course I couldn't tell her that. She'd freak, kick me out of her house, and then what? I needed her help, for Kyra's sake.

I finally gave up on finding his business card and put my wallet away. "It's probably listed," I said lamely.

She squinted at me.

How was I ever going to get through the night? I was already feeling completely spent in round one, and I still had two rounds to go. "Look, I'm telling you the truth. I don't know what to do. Take Kyra out to dinner and see for yourself. She's acting like she's madly in love with me. She doesn't remember the discord between us. It's . . ." I began to choke up.

She leaned forward, pity shining in her brown eyes. "Okay, calm down. I won't say anything until I talk to her doctor."

"Dr. Hershing says she'll probably remember anytime now on her own."

"And if she doesn't?"

I sighed. "I know it's crazy, but I'm kind of hoping she won't. Not everybody gets a second chance like this."

Marnie narrowed her eyes. "A lie is like a rotting body, Eric. Eventually the stink always gives it away."

I wasn't sure what her metaphor meant exactly, but I got the gist of what she was getting at.

"I'm assuming you'll wait until I have her out of the house before you try to sneak your clothes back in?" she asked.

I nodded. "Hopefully she hasn't already been in my closet."

"It's too bad there's nothing in your closet to hide," she said.

TWELVE

All smoke and shadows, the Speak Easy Lounge lived up to its name. I lagged behind Danielle, my dark mood mirroring the dreary atmosphere. As though mocking me, Sade's "Smooth Operator" played. I gave the dimly lit surroundings a cursory glance, relieved to find no familiar faces.

The young hostess we followed stopped and laid down two plastic menus on a table in the center of the dining room. I shook my head and pointed to the corner booth at the back of the restaurant. With an eye roll, she plucked the menus back up and headed for the booth. I started to thank her, but she was off.

Under normal circumstances, I'd be a gentleman and gesture for my date to sit first, but today anonymity won out over chivalry. Brushing past her, I quickly claimed the seat that put my back to the door.

Danielle frowned as she slid into the booth after me.

I made a deliberate point of looking her over. "I figured looking as lovely as you do, you should be the one people see."

Wearing a blue strapless dress and matching shawl, she did look pretty, but embarrassingly overdressed. She had wanted to go to Soho's, but with that being one of the hottest and busiest spots in town, being seen there with her would have been suicide.

She tightened the shawl around her shoulders and looked around. "Well, this is, um . . . nice."

I knew of course she was disappointed. She had dressed to be seen, not to hide out in this hole-in-the-wall. I winked at her. "Wait til you taste their crab cakes."

She picked up a menu. "I'm allergic to shellfish, remember?"

I didn't recall her ever offering up that information and felt fairly certain I wouldn't have asked, but saw no benefit in saying so. "That's right." I picked up my menu. Its plastic jacket wore a tacky coating of grease and alcohol.

Rubbing her finger and thumb together, she wrinkled her nose at the one she held. When she noticed me watching her, she faked a smile.

I closed my menu without having read it and set it down. It didn't matter what I ordered. My nerves would make it impossible to eat.

Wisps of blonde from her upswept hair cascaded down the sides of her face and neck, falling on bare shoulders. "It's so good to be away from work. I can't tell you how much it means to me that you took off just to —"

Before she said anything we would both regret, I blurted, "Danielle, we need to talk."

Her hand froze as panic flashed in her eyes. The waitress appeared before she could question me. She wore all black, a small amber stud in her nose, and a look that made it clear she would rather be elsewhere. "Can I get y'all something to drink?" She tapped the point of her pen on her pad, waiting for Danielle to answer. *Tap-tap. Tap-tap.* It was all I could do not to grab the pen from her hand and fling it across the room.

Danielle ordered the house red. The waitress's eyes lingered on her a moment as though debating whether or not to card. Finally, she directed her attention to me. I regretted my new resolution to abstain in Danielle's presence. A nice stiff drink would do wonders to help me stomach the emotional bloodbath I was about to inflict. "Coke, please."

After the waitress traipsed off, Danielle touched the turquoise charm dangling from the thin silver chain around her neck. "What do you want to talk about?" Her voice was barely a whisper.

My original plan had been to take her to a public but low-key place where if she decided to hurl drinks and accusations, at least there'd be few witnesses, hopefully none of whom would recognize us. My intent was to be direct and tell her how I'd made an awful mistake, that I tried to put a toe tag on a marriage that was apparently still breathing.

"What is it?"

Before I could plunge the knife, an idea to spare us both came to me. I gathered her hands, soft and shaky, into mine. *Please let this work.* "I have some good news."

Fixed on mine, her eyes had never looked so green . . . or vulnerable.

"We haven't posted it yet, but there's a job for a senior sales associate in Leesboro. It pays almost double what you're making now." My enthusiasm sounded manufactured, even to me.

The waitress reappeared with our drinks on a round, cork-lined tray. She dealt us two cocktail napkins printed with a vodka logo, before setting down the glasses.

I gave her a quick glance. "We're going to need a minute."

Danielle's troubled eyes never left mine. "Leesboro? That's like three hours away."

Perspiration dampened my undershirt. I slid my suit jacket off and laid it over the back of the booth. "I know it's far. I was going to be selfish and not tell you, but that wouldn't be right." I hated myself at that moment and kind of hoped she'd hate me too. It would make this all so much easier.

Her fingernail scraped my thumb as she snatched her hands from me. I rubbed at the mark she left. "I'm just thinking of you."

Her expression hardened. "Me?"

It was all I could do to keep my hand steady as I sipped my soda, peeking over the rim at her. "You're young, beautiful, and smart. You ought to be moving up."

Her chin quivered. "I'll move up at Thompson's."

I lay my hands palms up onto the table, inviting hers back into them. "It's a man's world there. You've got to know that by now."

She looked at my hands but made no move toward them. "Are you implying the management practices sexual discrimination?"

"Look, I'm just being honest, as your friend. Off the record, Thompson will never let you get far there. It's a boy's club all the way."

She lifted her head, looking both defiant and hurt. "You're not saying that as my friend."

I felt like the world's biggest jerk but reassured myself that the job really was an upward move for her, and a promotion beat getting dumped any day. "Of course I am."

She touched her fingertips to her forehead. "You want me to move away?"

"Of course not. I just want you to be successful." It was hard to believe that just a year ago I prided myself on being an honest man. On going against the stereotype most thought of when they heard I was a car salesman. Still, what I was doing here wasn't exactly lying. I really did want her to be successful.

"What did I do wrong?"

I wrapped my hand around her wrist, trying to offer what comfort I could. "It's nothing like that."

The waitress passed by, slowed to consider us, then kept going.

Danielle covered her mouth, as though

she were about to be sick. "I thought things were good between us."

I knew this was going to be difficult but had no idea she would take it this hard or how contagious her pain would be. "Things were fine."

Anger ignited her eyes. *"Fine?"*

Panic coursed through me as I scavenged my mind for the words to make my last ones right.

Her mouth spread as though she were about to smile, but when she scrunched her eyes I knew she was on the verge of tears, not laughter. "Just fine? Just the other night you told me I was amazing; now, I'm just *fine.*"

"You're reading too much into what I'm saying."

When she crossed her arms, the shawl slipped from her shoulders. "I don't think so."

A woman cackled nearby. I threw a glance over my shoulder, relieved to discover her amusement was directed at her male companion, not us.

Danielle reached out, took my face in her hand and turned my head so that I was looking at her. "Since I've known you, you've been miserable with Kyra. For the last six months you were together, all you talked about is how she changed. How she doesn't want you. How lonely you are."

I took a sip of my drink, but the bitter taste in my mouth remained. "Things have changed," I whispered.

Her eyes welled again. "They sure have."

THIRTEEN

Though I'd never admitted it, I had always dreaded the night. I didn't mind the ominous shadows, the eerie stillness, or the feeling that the world, like the sun, had deserted me, half as much as the silence. On my occasional day off, while it was still light, there were enough dogs barking, car doors slamming, and ambulance sirens to distract me.

Nighttime was a different story. After all the domestic chores were done, the lawn mowed, bills paid, and phone dormant, the house became obscenely quiet — hushed enough to hear every last one of my rampant thoughts. Worse still, I had all night to entertain them.

I thought about my father, work, my IRA, but mostly about Kyra. When and why had she stopped loving me? Why couldn't I do the same, so her rejection wouldn't hurt so much?

I tiptoed up the stairs to check on her,

hoping I'd stayed out late enough that she'd gone to bed without me. Deep, rhythmic breaths came from the partially closed door. I inched it open and peered in. Dressed in a lace-rimmed nightgown, with her hair draped over her shoulders, she looked angelic.

Folds of silk fell in gentle waves across her contours, while the comforter lay in a heap at the end of the bed we once shared. I glanced at what used to be my side. Next to it stood a square mahogany table that my father had made. Besides my black hair, angled eyes, and last name, it was the only thing I'd inherited from him. He left us when I was four and died two years later. "What goes around comes around," my mother had said. Most days I felt the same. Others . . . well, I just wanted to know him.

The small table looked naked without one of my books resting on it. Usually, it would be holding some volume on the history of the world, Japan, or World War II, along with a pair of reading glasses that no one except Kyra was allowed to see me in.

Beside her side of the bed sat a round glass table, on which rested two candles, that stupid romance novel, a bottle of lotion, and something that hadn't been out this morning — a four-by-six framed photograph of the two of us in front of Niagara Falls, taken on our fifth anniversary. Even though I couldn't make out the details in the dim lighting, I didn't need to. I knew the picture by heart. We were sunburned, disheveled, and tired, but there was something about the way she lay against my chest, grinning at the camera that made my heart ache every time I looked at it.

I slid her cell phone just under the bed to make her think she'd dropped it. As I pulled back the top sheet to climb in, the oil painting above the bed caught my eye. I'd looked at it a million times, but tonight, I actually saw it. The painted mother kissed the rosy cheek of a little girl whose pigtails spilled from her bonnet.

I'm not sure why, but the child made me think of Benji. I hadn't heard from him since the other night and hoped that was a good sign that things were going well.

I looked down at Kyra one more time, fighting the urge to touch her face. Her lips were slightly parted, and her eyelids fluttered. I'd give anything to know what she was dreaming about.

Careful not to wake her, I climbed into bed, cringing as the mattress leaned under my weight. She moaned softly and turned on her side. I held my breath until she settled again. As I lay there looking at her back, feeling the warmth of where she'd just been, I let my mind wander with possibilities of the way things might go from here and found myself hoping for the hopeless.

I must have fallen asleep because a noise jolted me awake. Confused, I blinked open my eyes and waited for the fog of slumber to lift. I felt for Kyra, but my fingertips touched only cool sheets. Across the room, the alarm clock numbers were blurred, red streaks atop the dresser.

Rubbing the sleep from my eyes, I threw back the sheet. My ears strained to catch any movement. Maybe I hadn't heard anything after all. Maybe it had been a dream.

Slowly, I stood. Kyra was probably in the living room, reading or watching TV, but until I knew for sure, trying to sleep would be futile.

As I tiptoed down the hall, I cupped a hand to my ear trying to decipher the muted television voices, to make out what she was watching. Knowing her, it was either one of the music channels or a decorating show. The noise was too low and muffled to tell.

I peered around the corner, hoping first that she was there and second that she wouldn't see me. On the couch, she lay with her head propped on one of the fancy round pillows I was forever picking up off the floor. Her face glowed and dimmed with the flickering light from the TV. When I shifted my weight from one foot to the other, the floorboard squeaked beneath me. My stomach dropped, and my gaze flew to meet hers.

One side of her mouth curled up in what looked more like a grimace than smile. "Hi," she said dully. Gone was the spark in her eyes that had burned so bright earlier in the day.

Unsure what to do, I just raised my hand in a sort of half wave. She patted the couch, inviting me to join her. I sat beside the place her knees bent. She pushed herself back into the cushions to give me room.

"How was your day?" she asked with an expression I couldn't read. Before I could answer, something on TV caught her attention. When I turned to see what she was looking at, I felt a little slighted to find it was nothing but a shampoo commercial. After a few seconds, she turned back as though suddenly interested in my answer.

"Eh," I said.

"Now I know where Benji gets it."

"Gets what?"

"Remember when he would come home from school, and we'd ask how his day was?"

I shrugged one shoulder and hummed an

"I don't know" like he used to. We'd endured that maddening response for years.

She gave me a tired smile. "Really, baby, tell me about your day."

"Much better now," I said.

Staring at the television, I zoned out as I considered my options. I startled out of it when something touched me. I looked down to see Kyra's hand sliding up my T-shirt. Her touch sent jolts through me.

"You're awfully jumpy. Are you sure nothing happened at work today?"

I took her hand from me and kissed it. "The only thing about my day that matters is sitting here with you now."

Her expression hardened. "If you don't want to tell me, fine."

I sighed. "What's that supposed to mean?"

She sat up, aimed the remote at the television, muting it, before turning back to me. "It means I'm interested in your day."

"Since when?" I asked wearily. She was as interested in my day as I was in who was who in Scandinavian politics. I took the remote from her hand and pointed it at the TV. The room went black.

An annoyed voice rose from the darkness. "What's with you today?"

Her arm brushed against mine as she bolted up. I sat there numb, listening to her stomp away. After a few minutes, I made my way to our bedroom, wanting to fight but needing to make up. I crawled into bed beside her and — even though I knew I shouldn't — molded myself into the familiarity and warmth of her back.

I'd learned from experience that sometimes the right words had no syllables, but then again I guess sometimes the wrong ones did too.

After a moment she whispered, "Samurai, what's happened to us?"

Everything, I thought. "Nothing," I said.

She flipped over so that we were face to face. Her warm breath fell on my lips, and I wanted to kiss her at that moment more than I'd ever wanted anything.

"Something's really wrong, isn't it?" Her eyes searched mine. "Tell me."

But how could I explain to her what I didn't understand myself? "Tomorrow's a big day for me," I said. "Let's try to get some sleep."

FOURTEEN

Tired from not sleeping well, I was even more drained than usual when I left the weekly sales meeting the next morning. Numbers were low, which meant so were the team's spirits. Mr. Thompson made sure of that by playing the "If this group can't produce, I'm going to have to start looking for one who can" card . . . again. All of his unnecessary bluff and bluster was getting more than a little old.

The man began his career pushing metal just like the rest of us. He knew as well as anyone that a bad day, week, or even month in the car sales business was bound to happen no matter how good you were or hard you worked.

Thompson waddled down the hall, a scrap of sales sticker flapping from the heel of his shoe like a backward flipper. As soon as he disappeared behind his office door, I yanked on my tie to loosen it. Even with it now dangling against my collarbone, I could still feel the phantom knot strangling me.

Turning the corner, I spotted Larry bent in front of the watercooler filling a paper cone. He gulped down the drink, crumpled the cup in his fist and made a two-pointer into the already-full garbage can.

When I slapped him on the back, he started coughing.

I grimaced. "Sorry."

Catching his breath, he said, "I'm fine," and wiped his mouth with the back of his hand. "Hey, what'd you think of Thompson's little pep talk?"

We both already knew what one another thought of it, what we always thought of anything our boss had to say, but still we played the game. "Wow," I said. "You know, I can't remember the last time I was this inspired. How 'bout you?"

He pulled a receipt from his pocket, examined it, then stuffed it back in. "Words are inadequate. I don't know what pumped me up more, being called lazy or having him compare me to a corpse." He patted the side of his face. "My cheeks still red?"

To me, his face always looked a little ruddy. "Is that because you're mad or from all the hot air he blew on us?"

Larry nodded a *good one.* "You know,

working with you makes this job almost tolerable."

I gave him a tired smile. "Feeling's mutual." He had a way of finding the humor in just about every situation. Without him, I would have snapped long ago, or at the very least, had to find a new profession.

Larry ushered me into my office and closed the door.

I groaned. "Please tell me it's not time for another lecture already."

He pressed both palms on the edge of my desk, looking as serious as I'd ever seen him. "I saw Danielle this morning. Her eyes were red. You two need to talk."

I crossed my arms, mentally preparing myself for an argument. "We already have."

"You told her it's over?"

"Yes."

He jerked his head back in surprise, giving himself a double chin. "Oh, well, good. Good job."

"Yeah, thanks. We through here?"

Looking solemn, Larry leaned his shoulder against the wall and buried his hand in his pocket. "Does Kyra know yet?"

The mention of her name made my stomach feel like it was full of battery acid. "She doesn't know about Danielle."

"No, I mean that you and she are — were

— separated."

Perspiration started to trickle down my back. I leaned over and stuck my hand in front of a wall vent. Sure enough, hot air met my palm. Thompson was so cheap, it could be a hundred degrees outside and rather than turn on the AC, he would insist on using the fan. As if circulating the same hot air would magically cool things off.

I slipped off my jacket and laid it across the back of my desk chair, feeling the dampness on my back and armpits. "Not yet. She's starting to remember. I think the doctor was right, and she's figuring it out on her own."

Larry rubbed beads of sweat from his forehead, giving the vent a perturbed look. "Can I give you some advice, chief?" He paused like he was waiting on my answer. As if it mattered what I said.

When I raised my eyebrows, he said, "Come out with it. All of it. It's like one of those stupid TV sitcoms, where everyone's being goofy and covering up something when they could have saved themselves a mess of trouble if they just told the truth up front."

I stared at him. Was he really comparing my failing marriage and infidelity to a poorly executed comedy? This wasn't some stupid TV show. This was my life. And it was more than a few laughs at stake; it was my marriage. My heart . . . and Kyra's.

"My point is, just tell her. It's bad no matter how you look at it. Rip the tape off fast. It's going to hurt either way, so why drag it out?"

I chewed on this a minute. He was right, of course. It would be bad, no matter what, but Kyra would probably remember in a day or two. Maybe figuring it out piece by piece on her own would make it easier for her to swallow.

But maybe she'd never remember just how bad things had gotten . . . or find out about Danielle. Then what? We'd live happily ever after. Why not? I'd never have believed a week ago that my wife would so much as look at me again, let alone gaze at me with that spark back in her eyes. I'd already been given a miracle. What was one more?

Larry licked his lips. "Can I ask you something?"

Looking into his grave eyes, I knew the question was going to be a heavy one.

He studied me. "Why wasn't she enough?"

I knew that what he was really asking was why he wasn't enough for Tina. "It wasn't her . . . and, man, it wasn't you. I mean, she's great and, Larry, you're great. It's just . . ."

He pulled the chair away from the other side of my desk and sat. As he studied me, it was no longer my friend's pain I was looking at, but Kyra's.

I pushed pens around in their coffee cup holder. "It wasn't her, but it wasn't exactly not her either." I glanced up at him.

He pulled at his goatee, looking deep in thought.

"She stopped wanting me to touch her but wouldn't even tell me why. It was always a different excuse. Besides that, everything I said or didn't say irritated her. Nothing I did was right. Nothing. I stopped feeling like I was good for anything but bringing home a paycheck and taking out the trash. I stopped feeling like a man. You know?"

The truth will set you free.

"Yeah. Yeah," I answered.

"Yeah, yeah, what?" Larry asked.

"The truth will set me free."

He smirked. "Your conscience finally talking to you?"

"What?"

He laughed. "You're losing it, man."

"Whatever. Listen, I'm going to do like the doctor said and see if Kyra will figure it out on her own."

145

"The separation. But what about the affair?"

Affair? I cringed at the word. It wasn't an affair. It was a one-night stand. A lapse in judgment. A thing. "One problem at a time." I flipped through my desk calendar, looking for nothing in particular.

"You have to tell her."

I said nothing.

Larry's face mottled. "Dude, you *have* to tell her. I've been on the other end of the stunt you're pulling, and it bites. I don't know, maybe if Tina had come clean herself rather than being found out, maybe I could have forgiven her."

As I thought about what he was saying, I could practically feel the ulcers forming. What I needed was a guarantee. If only I could play out what would happen if I did tell her, then compare it to what would happen if I didn't. How was I supposed to gamble with our lives this way? But then I knew, of course, that I already had.

FIFTEEN

Before I stepped through the front door, I had one thing on my mind: to get to bed and fall asleep as quickly as possible. After Kyra greeted me in the foyer wearing a bedroom smile and long silk nightgown, soft wisps of hair brushing against her face, that mission became all the more imperative. If I laid a hand on her tonight, not only would Marnie let me have it, but it would add fuel to Kyra's anger later when she found out what I'd done.

When she leaned in to kiss my lips, it took everything in me to turn away and give her my cheek. Although she had to interpret my reaction as rejection, if I'd hurt her feelings, she managed to hide it. Her smooth, painted fingernails softly scraped my palm as she scooped the car keys from my hand. She set them on the table by the door, then took my hand and led me through the dining room, out to the screened porch. As we passed through the house, I caught a whiff of steak, asparagus, and something freshly baked.

Both excitement and dread filled me as I realized that my wife might be trying to seduce me. It had been years since she'd taken this kind of initiative. I knew what I should do if she indeed was, but the feelings she stirred in me made me afraid of what I actually would do when and if the time came.

The door squealed as she pushed it open. There, in the shadows, stood our patio table set for two. She'd adorned it with a tablecloth and the silverware she only dragged out on holidays. Cloth napkins fanned out from empty wineglasses, which were paired beside crystal goblets of water. Candlelight flickered up from the center of the table and the iron sconces that hung on the brick wall behind us. Balmy night air wafted in through the screen, making the flames bend and bow.

Candlelight danced in Kyra's eyes as she gazed at me for the longest time.

My heart lodged in my throat. "What's all this?"

She smiled at me, then the table. "Happy anniversary, lover."

My mind raced. What was today? It was

April. We weren't married in April. Were we? No, it was definitely October. The mistake was hers, not mine. "We were married in October. October twentieth," I added, now confident. "You're a few months off."

Her smile grew as she sauntered toward me. The hem of her nightgown swayed around the ankles I could only catch glimpses of, leading down to pretty, manicured toes.

A sudden realization hit me like a sucker punch. I was just as in love with her tonight as I'd ever been. When she reached out to touch my cheek, I fought against the urge to draw her body tight against mine. Instead, I stepped back. She flinched, looking unsure. I wanted to tell her that I wasn't rejecting her. That I wanted her more at this moment than I ever had. Of course, I couldn't. I'd lost that right. I'd lost everything.

Recovering, she pulled the chair out for me. It was all I could do to keep my eyes off the silk clinging to her curves. She waited for me to sit, then disappeared back into the house, quickly returning with two plates of romaine topped with pieces of bloodred tomatoes and dollops of blue cheese dressing. She set a salad before me. "You'll need your strength tonight. So you'd better eat up."

I grew warm at the truth of this statement. I would need every bit of my strength all right, but not for the reasons she implied.

As she plucked her napkin from the glass before her and slid it across her lap, I did the same. She picked up the wine bottle and tilted it over my glass.

I put a hand up to indicate I didn't want any. If ever there was a night to keep my inhibitions, it was this one.

She gave me a questioning look. "Since when don't you want to share a glass of wine with your wife?"

"The last time I drank that stuff it gave me a terrible hangover." One I'd be paying for the rest of my life.

She wrinkled her nose. "I don't remember you ever drinking enough to get a hangover."

"There's a lot you don't remember," I said, hating the sound of my own voice.

She handed me a goblet of water from the table and picked up her wine, then clinked our glasses together. "To remembering . . . and our anniversary."

I started to remind her of what I'd already said, that it wasn't our anniversary, but she spoke first.

"Listen, baby, I know you've been under a

lot of stress, and I know a big part of that is because of me and the accident." She looked so contrite when she said it that I wanted to reach out and comfort her, but I figured it would only make matters worse.

"Maybe I don't remember everything, but I remember what you did."

A surge of panic shot through me and my mind raced with confusion. If that were true, why would she be dressed so sexy and behaving this way? Though it wasn't really her style, I wondered if maybe she'd just been setting me up to knock me down. I searched her face but didn't find hatred or even a glimpse of anger, which told me that she didn't remember the e-mail. Even if she did, she couldn't remember what she had never learned. She couldn't know about my night with Danielle.

"I know you left a life you loved at Braddy's Wharf to give me and Benji everything money could buy. I know we've fought about your long hours and me wanting a job, and I've probably seemed ungrateful when you're obviously doing your best. I'm sorry for that. I appreciate the love that gets you out of bed six days a week to go to work."

Suddenly she beamed at me. "You know what though? I'm alive and you're alive and as long as that's the case, we've got everything we need." She reached across the table and held her palm out to me, inviting me into her grasp.

I knew it was wrong to accept her touch, but it seemed worse to leave her hanging out there thinking she was unwanted. And so, reluctantly, I placed my hand in hers. Her skin felt softer than ever.

"We have a good life, Samurai. Let's not let the stress of my accident, your job, what's going on with Benji, and everything else make us lose sight of that."

I probably looked like a simpleton sitting there with my mouth open, not knowing what to say. I certainly felt that way.

"Let's make tonight the first anniversary of the rest of our lives. Can we?"

For reasons I didn't stop to question, the intense longing and regret I felt looking into her eyes gave way to a tidal wave of conflicting emotions — doubt, anger, pain, and a myriad of other feelings I couldn't name. Her rejection came flooding back washing ashore once again all the loneliness and begging for answers as to why she no longer wanted me. I couldn't breathe, knowing that now was the time to tell her everything, but how could I?

The glow of the candle flames painted her

face in hues of gold. She picked up her glass again and held it out to me. "Wish me a happy anniversary, baby. Let this be the first day of the rest of our lives. Just say it and let's start over. I don't want to lose what I thought we had. What I know we can have again."

Part of me wanted to hold my glass out to hers and part of me wanted to smack hers from her hand and ask her how it felt to want something she couldn't have. I knew I had to tell her the truth about Danielle. Maybe she'd still feel the same way once she understood why I'd done it. Maybe her glass would still be extended.

It was now or never.

"Kyra, I love you," I said, "but there's . . ."

Before I could continue, her face scrunched up as she set her glass down. She dropped her head into her open hands and began to sob. Her shoulders heaved as she fought to take a breath.

Not knowing what else to do, I pushed away from the table and went to her. I wrapped my arms around her and laid my head against her trembling back, feeling her warmth, inhaling her scent, wanting her in a way that overwhelmed me. "I'm so sorry," I said over and over until at last she quieted.

And I was sorry. Sorry for her, sorry for

Benji, and sorry for me.

When she finally turned around to look at me, she wiped at her eyes and let out an embarrassed laugh. "You must think I'm crazy, but, baby, I didn't realize how much I needed to hear those words until you said them. 'I love you,' I mean."

And as if she had finally given a name to what I had felt all along, I realized that was exactly what I needed too. What I had needed all along maybe. Not just to hear them but believe them. "Do *you?*" I asked, feeling emotionally naked.

"Love you?" She stood, took my face in her hands, and began kissing it all over, her soft, damp lips pressing against my thirsty skin. She whispered, "I love you," again and again, until our lips met.

As soon as I tasted her, I pulled away, but like a magnet that was too strong to resist, my mouth found hers again. And then, before my mind could catch up with my body, I was carrying her upstairs.

I stood before our bedroom, like I had so many times in our early years, with her in my arms. The door stood shut, forcing me to pause to consider how I was going to get it open without dropping her. When I did, reason finally caught up to desire.

"Kyra, there's something . . . I . . . Baby, I

love you, but there's . . ." My head swam trying to find the right words, knowing none existed. There would never be a better time to come clean than right now. If I could just conjure up the nerve to tell her everything. One more day may as well be forever, but when I opened my mouth to speak, she kissed me again, and before I knew it I was setting her on the bed. As she smiled up at me, I knew this would be the last woman I would ever make love to, even if this was the last time she'd let me.

Any remnant of self-control left me as she began to unbutton my shirt. She hadn't made it past my sternum when the doorbell rang.

Out of breath and flushed, Kyra gave me a questioning glance. With a groan, she climbed out of bed and followed me down the stairs. I pulled back the curtain on the front window, and together we peered outside. Marnie stood under the porch light, swaying back and forth with her arms wrapped around herself and her eyes smeared with black.

Sixteen

I eased down the stairs trying not to wake Marnie, whom Kyra had set up the previous night on the couch. She'd shown up on our doorstep hysterical in one of her phobia-induced panics, convinced the mold from her carpet was of the dangerous black variety and had spread like cancer throughout her house. She needed a place to stay until the antifungus SWAT team could comb the place millimeter by millimeter and annihilate every last trace. Try as we might, we could not convince her of the ridiculousness of abandoning her home over a musty carpet.

We had three empty bedrooms upstairs, but she found fatal flaws with each. The guest room turned her eyes into saucers when she considered the canopy bed. "What if that thing falls on me and I suffocate?" she asked. Kyra and I both assured her this would not happen. That in the fifteen years we owned it, it had never fallen on anyone. Even if it did, it surely had no more potential to suffocate her than a standard bedsheet.

No go.

The spare bedroom beside the guest room, thankfully without canopy, housed a waterbed — a relic from my bachelor days. This was no good, of course. The mattress might puncture and kill her. After all, she said, it was common knowledge that a person could drown in as little as a teaspoon of water, and she was a sound sleeper.

Like Goldilocks, we led her to the next room — Benji's bedroom. Although she eyed the sports posters with apprehension I didn't understand, it was the various trophies lined up on shelves around the room that made her deem it unsuitable. Naturally, one or all of them could fall and crush her skull.

When we'd offered to take the trophies down, she shook her head. It was the shelves themselves which were the real danger. They were built into the wall, which meant unless the whole wall tumbled, the shelves could not. This law of physics didn't convince her, and neither could Kyra or I.

The last possibility was the sleeper sofa in my office. When I pulled out the hidden mattress, she hyperventilated. "Let me guess," I said wearily. "It might magically fold itself up during the night with you in it and you'd suffocate." And so, in a house full of empty bedrooms, Marnie slept on the couch.

As I descended the stairs, my view of the ceiling gave way to the living room below and Marnie, dressed for success, sitting on the sofa where Kyra left her last night. The blanket she'd given her lay neatly folded over the armrest.

When she saw me, she set down her mug and blew a strand of blonde from her face. "Oh, good, you're up.

I sniffed at the java-scented air.

She pointed toward the kitchen. "I just made a pot. Want me to fix you a cup before we talk?"

I looked forward to the coffee, but the conversation, not so much. "I really have to get to work," I said.

"Sit down." Her voice was soft, but tone unyielding.

I sat in the chair beside the couch, not knowing exactly what was coming but having a pretty good idea.

She wrapped her manicured fingers around the ceramic cup she held, speaking at it instead of me. "I have a confession."

I raised my eyebrows.

"With Kyra's permission, I spoke with Dr. Hershing. When I told him about your little tryst with that girl, he was miffed that you didn't tell him so he could have all the facts when treating her. He's reconsidering his decision for you to let her remember on her own. He said it might end up hurting her more if you don't tell her before she finds out herself."

"She's my wife, not his," I said, now feeling defensive. Something lumpy pressed into my lower back. I reached behind me and grabbed the small, round pillow and set it on my lap. "I love her more than anything, Marnie. I'm doing everything in my power not to hurt her. Hershing doesn't know her like you and I do. He's only speculating on what he thinks is best for her. She's doing fine. Better than fine. She's happier than she's been in years." I leaned forward locking eyes with her. "You know I'm right."

As she spoke, I saw something in her I'd never seen before — the mother she might have been. "I *am* my sister's keeper, Eric. Just like she would be mine if the situation were reversed."

"Maybe I will have that coffee," I said, cringing inside. I loved Marnie, I did, but there were days I wished I had married an only child. Her heels clicked in rhythm against tile as she followed a few steps behind me.

She pulled a stool from beneath the kitchen island and sat as I poured myself a cup of Colombian. Still standing, I held my warm mug, wishing I was anywhere but here.

Marnie combed her fingers through her hair. Even though she was adopted, the look on her face right then reminded me so much of Kyra. "She remembers the chasm between you two. Did she tell you that?"

I took a sip of the coffee that was almost as strong as espresso. I tried not to choke on it as I forced it down. "She alluded to it, yes."

She nodded as if she already knew this much. "I don't think she remembers just how long it's been going on, and she definitely doesn't remember your affair."

My face caught fire. "It wasn't an affair. It was a stupid e-mail!"

She cleared her throat. "Whatever you say. She doesn't remember it. I would have told her, Eric, but after talking with Hershing, I'm just as afraid to do it as I am not to."

My gut cramped at the confirmation of what I had already known in my heart of hearts. I wasn't as forgiven as I had hoped.

Marnie continued, "Do you know they had her on suicide precautions the day she went into Batten Falls?"

I simply nodded.

"Even as bad as things had gotten between you, thinking you had died about killed her."

Unable to look at her, I studied her leather boots bobbing up and down under the counter.

"Even though she deserves to know the truth, I don't think I can be the one to tell her."

I tried to smile. "Thanks."

"Don't thank me. I'm not doing it for you."

Relief filled me. "I won't let you down."

Fruit rested in a wicker basket in the middle of the granite-topped island. Her fingers traced the peel of one of the oranges. "You already have."

SEVENTEEN

A waffling customer who finally decided to buy right at closing time kept me at work even later than usual. The house was dark and quiet when I arrived. The only sound was the creak of a loose floorboard as I walked into the foyer. I started to toss my wallet and keys on the hallway table, as I always did, until I remembered Marnie. Instead, I laid them down softly.

I slipped my shoes off and left them paired along the wall of the entryway. Tiptoeing into the living room, I found my sister-in-law snoring softly on the couch, a blanket covering everything but her head and toes.

Walking as light-footed as I could, I headed up the steps, the carpet a cushion beneath my stocking feet. Thankfully, the bedroom door had been left cracked open. I held my breath and slowly pushed it, cringing as it squealed. I'd been meaning to oil it the better part of a year, but who could really blame me for wanting to spend the one day a week I didn't work relaxing instead of playing handyman?

Poking my head through the doorway, I peered inside at blackness. The only light was that which stabbed in from the hallway behind me. I opened the door wider to allow more of it to enter the room. The light fell across the floor like a golden road leading right to her. I opened the door further still, causing the path to widen until it covered most of the floor and part of the bed, killing the illusion.

I exhaled when I saw her long silhouette motionless on the mattress. My eyes hadn't yet adjusted enough to make out her features, but even cloaked in shadow, she looked beautiful, lying there in her customary position — one leg bent, the other stretched out — with her hair fanned around her face like rays of sunshine.

Just the top sheet covered her. The blanket lay in a heap on the floor beside the bed. She was forever kicking that thing off, then accusing me of stealing it in the night. With a smile, I shook my head at the achingly familiar sight and bent to pick it up.

It was then I heard the mattress shift under her weight. "Samurai?"

I stood. She leaned over and turned on

the reading light. Gold washed over her face, revealing puffy, red-veined eyes. My stomach dropped. She'd been crying, which meant . . . she knew? Danielle told her. Or maybe Larry, thinking he was doing the right thing. The Christian thing.

"Listen, Kyra," I whispered.

"Did he call you?" she asked, wrapping her arms around her bent legs. She wore my Dallas jersey as a nightshirt. I'd seen her in it at least a dozen times, but I couldn't remember her ever looking so good in it. Even with my stomach full of worry, I couldn't take my eyes off her. "Larry?" I finally asked, unsure.

Her eyebrows dipped. "No, our son."

My head swam trying to decide how to answer this question. "He called?"

Her eyes filled with tears, and her words were barely decipherable. "He's being medically discharged."

Feeling light-headed, I sat on the edge of the bed. "Over ant bites?"

"You knew?" Her question was more inquiry than accusation.

"He called while you were in the hospital and told me it was a possibility."

She wiped her eyes. "Why didn't you tell me?"

"He wasn't sure yet; didn't want you worrying over nothing."

She looked down at her wet fingers, then at me. "Nothing?"

"He didn't really think . . . I mean, ant bites . . ." My voice trailed off as I lost myself in thought, considering the magnitude of the bombshell I'd just been dropped.

We sat there so silent that Marnie's snores sounded like they were in the next room rather than downstairs.

Finally she said, "He's devastated."

An unexpected surge of jealousy bit me. "I'm surprised he called you instead of me."

"Why should that surprise you? When a boy's hurting, of course he wants his mother."

Of course, I thought. Hadn't he always? I slid closer to her.

"He sounded so broken, Eric. I've never heard him that way."

I kissed her forehead and pulled her against my chest, taking in her warmth and vanilla-almond smell. I began to wonder if somehow this was my fault. If my family was being punished for my sin. I shook the thought off and peeled Kyra from me.

I kissed the salty tears from her face and did my best to smile. "He'll be okay," I said, trying to comfort myself as much as her. "It's his biggest disappointment in life, but it won't be his last. God has other plans for him; that's all. Better plans."

Fresh tears replaced the ones I'd just kissed away. It was obvious that she wanted to believe in that. To believe in me. I felt like I could puke.

"I know you're right," she whispered, "but it's going to be a long crawl through darkness before we see that light."

"It's going to be tough," I agreed. "For all of us."

She laid her head back down on my shoulder.

I wrapped my arm around her waist and rubbed her back. "Did he say when he'd be home?"

She shook her head. "He didn't know. Whenever they get him processed, whatever that means."

I started to explain, but she cut me off.

"Being a sailor was all he ever wanted. It's not fair."

"I know."

She took my face in her hands and looked at me so long and hard, it felt like she could see right into my soul. "Make love to me, Eric."

I doubted it was right to oblige her, but the vulnerability in her eyes made it impossible to say no. And so I closed my eyes, found her mouth, and allowed myself to forget what I hoped she would never remember.

EIGHTEEN

"Let me get this straight. You're pretending that what your wife forgot about really didn't happen?" My mother played with the end of the long white braid draped over her shoulder and gave me the look that had been curdling my blood since childhood.

"I know how it sounds," I said. "But what are my options?"

"You might try the truth."

I pulled a chair from the dining room table, turned it around, and straddled it. Her apartment was the only place I sat that way. I guess it made me feel a little more like a man riding a Harley and a little less like a child sitting at his mommy's table. "You want me to remind her that our marriage is falling apart right after she gets out of a psychiatric hospital and finds out her son is in the worst crisis of his life? Against medical advice?"

She cleared her throat several times, the

way she always did when she disapproved but didn't want to come right out and say so. "That must have been some e-mail." She ran the tip of her braid back and forth against the small mole on her cheek as though trying to sweep it away.

"Not all of this is my fault, you know." An iron rooster glared down his crooked beak at me from behind glass. I looked away from the strange bird and the rustic hutch.

Mom let go of her braid and began to pick instead at the dried flower arrangement in the center of the table. Flecks of tiny leaves and petals crumbled down onto the quilt serving as a tablecloth. "I'm just not getting how one sneaky act is rectified by another."

"I'm up for other suggestions," I said and meant it. No one had a problem telling me I was digging myself a hole, but did anyone throw down a ladder so I could climb out?

She lifted a dainty porcelain teacup that looked like it had no business belonging to such a robust hippie of a woman and brought it to her mouth. "You sure you don't want any? It's fennel. Excellent for digestion." My mother, the self-described granola, was all about natural remedies, holistic healing, and karma.

"Have I ever said yes to your potions?"

"No. And I'll bet your colon is a mess."

"I'd drink a gallon of the stuff if it would help, but digestion isn't my problem. Got anything to help an ailing marriage?"

She looked to the side as if racking her brain. "I'm not sure they make a tea for that."

"Baah!" Alfred yelled.

"Someone should tell him that makes him sound like Ebenezer Scrooge," I whispered.

"He knows. Where do you think he got it?"

My mother and I glanced down the hallway where the voice came from. My stepfather emerged, wearing bleach-stained jeans sagging off his flat butt, a comb-over that wasn't quite long enough to fully cover his bald head, and lips pressed tighter than Thompson's wallet. He held a yellow tape measure.

Mom blinked at him. "You got something to say, old man?"

"I could hear most of the conversation, and for the record, keeping something like that a secret is a bad idea."

She stared him down. "Instead of eavesdropping, you should have been hanging that shelf. I've only been waiting six months."

Alfred held the tape measure out toward her like it was a yo-yo he was about to launch. Turning to me, he yanked on the metal lip of the tape measure, pulled it out a few inches, then pressed the button that slurped it back in. "Tell me how lying to your wife is helping your marriage?"

"Like I told Mom, I'm not lying to her. I'm just letting her keep forgetting something that was best forgotten anyway."

My mother's cup clanked as she set it back in its saucer and scowled at Alfred. "Why do you have to have an opinion about everything?"

Rows of wrinkles formed on his brow.

I was beginning to feel claustrophobic "Ma, Alfred, please. If this is going to cause a fight, I'll leave. One marriage in ruins is enough."

"Bah." Alfred waved his hand at her "Your stupid shelf is up, woman. You can dry your herbs now." He shook his head and disappeared again.

My mother smiled lovingly at where he'd been standing. "He's something, don't you think?"

That went without saying.

Alfred reappeared, this time holding a bunch of what looked like dried ragweed. "Did you give him the picture you found of Ren?"

Here we go, I thought. My mother could

not hear my father's name without a rant.

"He walks away from his wife and baby, and we're supposed to frame his mug and hang it on the wall like he was a stinkin' hero?"

"He might have regretted what he did," I said, surprising myself. I'd never defended him before. "You don't know."

She crossed her arms. "People don't change."

Though I suspected she was right, I prayed she was wrong.

Alfred whipped his bouquet of flowers at her as though it were a club. "Oh come on, Beatrice. Let the man rest in peace. That was forty years ago. If people couldn't change, you'd still be smoking two packs of Pall Malls a day and setting your boulder holders on fire."

Her face turned red as she jumped up.

Before I had a chance to tune her out, she dug a hand into her waist and pointed a plump finger at him. "That is no *man* you're talking about. A man does not leave his wife and child with no job, two months behind on the rent, and not so much as a bus ticket to their name."

His eyes grew large, and he tried to say something.

But Mom wasn't finished. "Where was he

when I didn't have anyone to drive Eric to Little League because I was pulling another night shift? Where was he when Eric broke his arm? Where was he . . . ." She stopped midsentence and closed her eyes. Slowly, she opened them again.

She left me sitting alone at the table and took a seat on the same couch she probably had since the day my father left. I'd long since stopped wondering what the thing looked like without its layers of mismatched afghans.

I stood and turned my chair around. "Forget my father for a moment."

"Your father?" Hatred flashed in her eyes. "This man —" she pointed at Alfred — "was your father. Ren was nothing but a —"

"Okay, forget Ren, Ma. I've got to go meet one of the guys to pick up Kyra's car." I turned to Alfred, who was nibbling a flower off the end of the bunch he still held. "Can I help you before I go?"

He waved the bouquet at me. "You go on; I've got this."

"Mom, we good?" I asked.

"Fine." She flipped on the small television set she kept on wheels so she could hide it quickly should any of her hemp-loving, anti-boob-tube friends pop in.

173

I looked around the crowded apartment that smelled of incense, chamomile, and brownies and sighed. If it was this hard explaining the situation to my parents, how would I present it to Benji? He would be home soon, and not only would I be worried about Kyra remembering, I'd be worried about Benji helping her remember. My only hope was to make Kyra so in love with me again that even if her memory returned, she would forgive me.

"You're delusional," my mother said.

Panic-stricken, I thought maybe I'd spoken my thoughts out loud. When I looked at her, I was relieved to find her bickering with Alfred, not directing the statement at me. Even if she had said it to me, she'd be right. But I could live very happily in the land of denial, so long as Kyra shared the address along with me.

Nineteen

It had been beautiful the day I'd first brought Kyra to Macabee Street. The smell of flowers and mulch scented the warm spring air. Her face lit up when I parked the car, and I suggested we take a walk. Hand in hand we strolled by enormous houses, pristine yards, and couples walking designer dogs along tree-lined sidewalks. As we approached the biggest poodle I'd ever seen, a ball of sculpted fur wagged hello. The animal sniffed Kyra's hand but was quickly distracted by a teacup terrier across the street.

Kyra looked back over her shoulder as the dog's owner led her away by a studded pink leash. "Fancy neighborhood," she said.

What my wife didn't know was that I'd already been down this sidewalk a dozen times without her, window-shopping and daydreaming about the day I would surprise her with the keys to our dream house.

With my promotion, we were moving up in the world, and I felt our home ought to reflect our success. The old craftsman's cottage we lived in was fine, of course, and Kyra seemed content there, but I'd never been one to be satisfied with status quo. Maybe it wasn't right, but it kind of annoyed me that she settled for so little back then. Like playing Rat Pack songs at Francesca's, when she was good enough to be a concert pianist with the New York Philharmonic.

With Kyra's hand in mine, I stopped in front of a large stone colonial and grinned at her.

Staring up at it, she wrapped her arms around herself as if she were suddenly cold. "What would a family need with so much space? They could spend entire days without so much as bumping into one another." Her gaze fell on the Sold sign, and a dark look passed over her.

I felt sick to my stomach. I'd spent almost everything we had on the down payment, believing she'd be a little miffed that I hadn't consulted her, but secretly thrilled at my chivalry and provision. Women were always saying they wanted a man to take charge. I was beginning to think that was just in theory. I knew she hated moving from Braddy's Wharf as much as Benji and I did, but we'd both agreed taking the job at Thompson's was necessary if we ever hoped to pay for our son's college education and our retirement.

"Is it a done deal?" Her tone was cold enough to freeze molten lava.

I told her we had thirty days to back out if she really hated it, and I promised not to be mad if she did, but to please, please wait until she did a walk-through to decide. We'd been here ever since.

I sat in my SUV across the street from that dream house chain-chewing sticks of gum.

The sun hit my rolled-up windows in such a way that every speckle of dust and dirt showed up like organisms under a microscope. In dimmer light, it had looked clean as a pin. The more I stared at the smudges and flecks of grime, the more irritated I became. I looked around for something to wipe them off with but found only a box of lotion-infused tissues. I spit my latest piece of Big Red back into its wrapper, added it to the small mound of silver in the ashtray, and looked through the blemished windshield.

Just a few feet ahead, a towering pear tree cast a shadow on the road. With a turn of the ignition and a little bit of gas, I inched into the shade. The car looked clean again and I was happy to pretend it was. After another stick of gum and a long, deep breath, I decided it was now or never.

I felt like an intruder when I turned the knob of my own front door without first knocking. Would things ever feel normal again? At the moment, that possibility seemed like anything but.

Kyra met me in the foyer wearing sweat-pants and a frown. "Where have you been?"

"Your car was ready." I pulled her ring of keys from my pocket and dangled them before her.

She took them from my hand and set them down. "Great."

You're welcome, I thought.

"Oh, and I stopped by Mom's." I dropped my own car keys on the foyer table next to hers.

Her expression softened. "Is she okay?"

"Of course."

She gave me a funny look.

"I visit with them every other Wednesday, remember?"

Her lips curled into a smirk. "Ironic, isn't it?"

"What's that?" I said.

"That you seem to keep forgetting that

my memory's gone bad."

A few months ago, I would have bantered with her, but I guess I'd left my sense of playfulness on Danielle's pillow. I walked to the window and looked out at Bram Harrington, who was helping his wife into the Volvo I'd leased him twenty-four months ago — or maybe it was thirty-six. I needed to check on that tomorrow. It might be time to put him in a new one.

She walked behind me and wrapped her arms around my waist. I didn't deserve her, but I needed her. Her warmth. Her love. Her vanilla-almond smell. "Marnie's leaving," she said. Her warm breath tickled my ear.

I turned and gave her a questioning look.

"Her boss asked her to fly to Milan. Another buyer had an emergency and had to cancel."

"She didn't mention anything to me about it."

"It was last-minute."

Pressed into my back, I felt her chest rise and fall as she sighed. "I wonder what it would be like to just run off to Europe," she said, "or Asia, or Africa, any old time you wanted."

And then the perfect idea hit me — an opportunity to make me a hero in my wife's

179

eyes instead of the villain I felt like. "You should go with her."

She scrunched her nose. "What?"

"Yeah, I mean you've always wanted to go with her on one of those boondoggles. I've been pretty busy at work. Benji said it would be at least a week or two before he gets to come home. Go. Have fun. Get your mind off things for a while."

"Milan?" she whispered. "Really?"

"Sure, why not?"

A shadow crossed her face. "I had my appointment with Dr. Hershing this morning."

I didn't know she had an appointment. My heart quickened, but I reassured myself that she must not have had any major memory breakthroughs or she wouldn't be still standing here. I pulled her hands gently from my waist and turned around. "Feel like going out for dinner?"

The sun streamed in through the window igniting her hair in golden red. Love overwhelmed me. "That's your question?"

"We've got to eat sometime."

"I'm thawing chicken." The look on her face told me that I'd asked the wrong question. Seemed I'd been doing that all my life.

"How'd the appointment go?"

She sighed. "Weird. I keep feeling like that

movie where the guy thinks he's living a normal life but he's really the star of a TV program, and everyone knows it but him."

"The Truman Show," I said. "Jim Carrey. We watched it together the night Benji took that little brunette who used to live down the street to dinner. We were trying to pretend we weren't waiting up for him, remember?"

A sparkle lit her eyes. "I can't believe you remember that."

"Her name was Doris Lipscomb," I said, pleased to have done something right, "and he wouldn't ask her out again because he said she gave him a heart-shaped balloon."

Kyra gave me a sheepish grin. "I remember you did your infamous yawn and stretch move on me that night."

I couldn't help but laugh. "I did that on our second date, not a decade and a half into our marriage. Your memories are jumbled."

"You did it that night too." She sounded so sure.

"I did not."

When she raised an eyebrow at me, she looked just like her late mother. "You most certainly did."

"You're my wife; I don't have to do the yawn and stretch."

She crossed her arms. "Is that right? Once the ring's on the finger, it's all in the bag, huh?"

I shrugged.

"So, you think you could have me any old time you want me?" Her tone had become playful, sexy.

"Woman, I've got you wrapped so tight around my finger, it's turning purple."

She laughed. "You're awfully cocky."

"And awfully lucky." I pulled her against me, wondering how long that luck would hold out.

TWENTY

Being locked overnight with a bunch of teenagers and holy-roller types was the worst possible way to spend an evening I could have imagined, but Larry was convinced that I was a danger to myself if left unattended while Kyra was out of the country. So he'd corralled me into helping him chaperone the youth group lock-in on Friday night.

The last time I was in church had been with Kyra. Sitting beside me, she tried to hold my hand, but I kept my fingers flaccid so that hers slid right out. When hurt flashed in her eyes, I felt the ache too. Causing her to suffer was the last thing I'd wanted, but how else could I make her understand how she'd made me feel? My mother would say I was being passive-aggressive; to me it was just trying my best to show her what I couldn't seem to say.

She rejected my advances again that night,

and the next, until I became like a lab rat shocked every time it reached for the piece of cheese. After enough electrical burns, I finally concluded that starvation was the less painful option.

That Sunday at Faith International had been the final occasion I'd made it to church that year. When I'd accepted the promotion at Thompson's, even though I bemoaned having to work Sundays to Kyra, I secretly considered it a fringe benefit of the job. Having to work that day was the perfect, unarguable excuse not to go. I hadn't wanted to be in church then any more than I wanted to be here now.

Still, by eleven or so, I found myself resigned to my fate and even laughed once or twice at Larry's stupid jokes.

The kids got along remarkably well, playing board games and stuffing themselves with pizza and junk food. Only the occasional disagreement surfaced and was quickly buried again by the chaperones. For that, I and my blood pressure were grateful. By midnight, the girls split off to perform makeovers on each other in the bathroom, while the boys gathered around the two TV sets for a video game marathon.

The carpeted sanctuary had been emptied of most of its chairs and was now lined with sleeping bags that would probably not be slept in. I leaned against a wall beside the snack cart. I'd just wolfed down several handfuls of chips and was pouring myself something to wash them down when I noticed a teenage boy sitting by himself on the edge of the stage.

Despite wearing a nondescript T-shirt and jeans, the kid would have stood out even if he hadn't sequestered himself. He looked Hispanic, which made him the only non-Caucasian besides me among the otherwise lily-white group. No wonder he felt like an outcast.

Larry patted a couple of the boys on the back on his way over to me. Two shrieking girls ran by the doorway in hot pursuit of something, someone, or each other. I stuck my head out and called for them to stop running.

When I turned around, Larry was standing beside me. "This ain't so bad, now is it?"

I took a sip of my drink, thinking about Larry's question. Flat, lukewarm Dr Pepper slid down my throat. "No comment."

He took off his glasses and rubbed the indent on the bridge of his nose, then slid them back on. "Admit it. You're having fun."

I set my thin, plastic cup on the table

beside me littered with empty pizza boxes and board games. "About as much fun as that time my mother maced me."

"Your mother maced you?"

"She was trying to force one of those keychain pepper sprays onto the ring, and it went off."

"Some would argue that there's no such thing as an accident."

In front of one of the television sets, a boy wearing a knitted cap over shoulder-length hair started having words with another boy. As the two exchanged insults, they began to play a not-so-friendly game of tug-of-war with the remote.

Larry's gaze darted from me to them and back again. "Want to take this one?"

"You go ahead." I nodded toward the kid on the stage. "I was just on my way to talk to Lone Ranger over there."

He glanced at him. "His name's Angelo. He turns eighteen tomorrow."

I made my way over and leaned against the stage beside him. The kid gave me a brief side glance as he pulled at the end of his hair as if trying to cover his face so I couldn't see him.

His awkwardness must have been contagious, because suddenly I felt self-conscious too. "Hey there," I said. "I hear it's your birthday tomorrow."

He didn't respond.

I cleared my throat. "Eighteen, huh? That's a big one. My son's just a year older than you."

His dark eyes settled on me for just a second before moving back to watching the group. It hit me then that the kid might not even understand what I was saying. I'd never been very good at Spanish, though. In high school, it was the one class that kept me from making A–B honor roll. After repeating it a second time, I'd at least learned the basics. *"Me llamo Eric. Como estas?"*

Angelo turned and glared at me. "Dude, I'm third-generation. You can cut the Spanglish."

I felt warm as I tried to recover. "Sorry. You were just looking like you . . . Never mind."

Wearing a look of disgust, he clicked his tongue. "You look like you came over from Ho Chi Minh City, but you don't see me speaking to you in Vietnamese."

"I'm half-Japanese," I offered, knowing he couldn't care less.

He went back to watching his peers.

I wanted to leave the kid alone with the gargantuan chip on his shoulder, but Larry watched me with an attaboy grin. It had been a long time since I'd done anything noble in his or anyone else's eyes. Although I'd never admit it to him, it actually made me feel good to win his approval again. Besides, what else did I have to do for the next — I checked my watch — six hours?

"Why don't we start over? I'm Eric." I put my hand out.

After staring at it for an uncomfortably long time, he finally took it. He had a good grip, not overbearing, but not wimpy either. His hand was small and cold. "Angelo."

I leaned back and pressed my palms against the polished surface of the stage. Before hoisting myself up, I asked, "Mind if I sit?"

Predictably, he shrugged.

My shoulder muscles pulled and burned as I lifted my own weight. More and more, I was starting to feel my age. I sat there beside him a minute or two in silence, hoping maybe he would start a conversation. When he didn't, I finally said, "I grew up in an all-white neighborhood." Not wanting to see him brush me off again with a shrug or blank stare, I kept my eyes fixed straight ahead at the boys laughing and punching each other's arms. Everyone but Angelo and I seemed to be whooping it up.

Since he didn't walk away, I continued, "There were only two Asians in my school and I was one of them. I was your age before I met another person who was half-Japanese like me, and she was an old lady." I thought about that woman, then added, "Well, she was probably younger than I am now, but back then she seemed older than Moses." I smiled at the thought. "I'll bet that's how old I seem to you."

"I'm not sitting here by myself because I feel some ethnic stigma."

So, the kid had a brain. Good. "Then why are you?"

He nodded toward the group. "Bunch of hypocrites."

"Who, them?"

The look he gave me made it clear he thought the question was a dumb one. "No, my mother." He banged the heels of his black and red Pumas against the stage one after another in an annoying rhythm.

I had been right. He and I did have something in common. Neither of us belonged here, and not just because of our race. I understood where he was coming from better than he knew. "Believe me," I said, "I get how Christians can come across as hypocrites. Pretending to live one way and trying to get everyone else to live another, but —"

"Who's a Christian?"

The question caught me off guard. "What?"

"Who here is a Christian?" He raised his eyebrows like he already had the answer. "Show me one."

My tired mind was probably not working as quick as it should be, but I just couldn't grasp what the kid was getting at.

Pointing at the group to the right, he said, "You see that kid with the skateboarder hair?"

I followed his line of vision to the boy with straight black hair swooping down into his face and nodded.

"He was baptized last month and gave a testimony in front of the whole church that brought tears to my mother's eyes."

I waited for the punch line.

"He was still dripping water when he hit on my sister. He's dating one of her friends."

"Not everyone —" I started to say.

He cut me off. "See that kid over there with the glasses?"

I looked over at the one in the John Lennon specs, lying on the carpet, propped up on an elbow.

"He got a girl pregnant last year."

I gave the boy another look. He couldn't

190

be more than seventeen. "How old is he?"

Angelo ignored the question. "That one, with the hair . . ."

I turned my eyes to the boy with a mop of curls, sitting cross-legged among the group.

"He sells weed so he can buy video games."

They're just kids, I wanted to say, feeling as defensive as if he'd accused me personally. Instead I asked, "How do you know all this?"

"People tell my sister everything. She tells me. The worst part is that it's not just the kids. The pastor we had last year resigned because he had an affair. The *pastor.*" He shook his head. "They're not Christians."

Dozens of verses I'd had to memorize when I joined our church swirled through my head, from the Ten Commandments, to "judge not lest ye be judged," to "all have fallen short of the glory of God."

"What about you?" Indignation rushed blood to my temples. "Are you so perfect that you can cast stones at them?"

He crossed his arms and huffed. "I'm not perfect, but I go to sleep with a clear conscience. I'm not stealing stuff or taking anyone's virginity or cursing my parents out on the way to Sunday school." He turned to me with a look of defiance. "That's the difference."

"No," I said, "you just think you're better than them because you're justifying your sins, just like they've justified theirs. Christians are sinners like everyone else. The real difference is grace."

He twisted his mouth but looked less certain. "People use grace as an excuse to sin."

"And you're using the law as a way to negate grace. Are *you* a Christian?"

"Yeah," Angelo said defensively. "Yeah, I am."

Who is this man preaching to this kid? I wondered. I had no idea I had this in me, but what I was saying seemed right even if it was coming from my own sorry lips. "We're all sinners. That pastor who had to resign is no better or worse than me or you. The Bible says if you're guilty of one sin, you're guilty of all. Remember when they were about to stone that woman accused of cheating on her husband?" I didn't wait for an answer. I felt driven to make this kid understand, maybe so I could too. "What did Jesus tell them?"

He shrugged, not like he didn't know, but like he didn't care. I knew better.

"Being the judge and jury over everyone, you need to read the book so you know what the rules are. Jesus said the one who was without sin should cast the first stone."

He looked down at his dangling legs. "Did they still stone her?"

I felt the zeal start to seep back out of me. I hadn't been that worked up since, well, ever. "No, they dropped their rocks. He told the woman, go and sin no more. Just like that he forgave her, and she was given a fresh start."

Angelo stilled his legs. "What if that woman left and just did whatever she pleased, kept on sinning and all?"

As I considered the question, I imagined Kyra giving me that kind of pardon, and I knew just how that woman must have felt. Who in their right mind would ever pick up a burden that heavy again after someone finally took it off their shoulders? "She didn't," I said, surer of that than anything in my life. "But that wasn't the point of the story, anyway. The point was —"

"Don't throw stones if you live in a glass house?" he offered, the angry edge gone from his tone.

"Don't throw stones," I said, more to myself than to the boy.

Twenty-One

In the distance, Larry stood on the lot with his back to me. As I made my way toward him, I looked up. The overcast sky appeared ominous — a sea of foreboding gray, but the breeze was soft and warm, which gave the day a not-unpleasant, surreal feeling. I hoped the clouds would finally give up their water. According to the *Southside Herald,* our reservoir was dangerously close to dry. I wasn't worried, though. It looked like rain. It felt like rain. And with a musty dampness in the air, it even smelled like rain.

Although I was beyond tired, having only gotten an hour, maybe two, of broken sleep on the sanctuary floor the night before, I still felt better than I had in a long time.

As I approached Larry, he jerked around, revealing too late that he'd been blocking my view of Danielle.

When she looked at me, I froze. "Hey,

there," I said. "Didn't see you behind Hoss here."

Larry took off his glasses, puffed on each lens, and cleaned them with the end of his tie. "At the rate I'm gaining, just be glad you can still see the sun." He slid his glasses back on. Bags hung like hammocks below his bloodshot eyes. "Of course, there's not much sun to see today anyway." He looked up at the sky. "Hope that rain comes though. We sure need it."

Danielle wore an uncharacteristically conservative navy suit that ended at the top of her knees. "Hello, Eric." Her words were clipped and careful. "I hear your event went well last night."

"Yes," I said hesitantly.

Larry put a hand on my shoulder. "You should have seen this guy. He was breaking up fights, fielding life's unanswerable questions, and turning an angry misfit into the life of the party. Just goes to show you there's hope for anybody."

"Angelo's a good kid," I said. "He just needed a little push in the right direction."

He squinted at me. "I was talking about you."

He was trying to be funny, but the truth of it hit too close to home for me, so I let it blow by without comment.

Danielle looked from Larry to me with a dull expression, and I'm sure she must have been thinking about what a hypocrite I was, ministering to teenagers when I was nothing but an adulterer myself. "Well, good. Good for you," she said without emotion.

Larry looked back and forth between us. His gaze landed on me, and I knew him well enough to understand the wide-eyed look was an implied warning. He cleared his throat and turned to Danielle. "Good luck with that interview, hotshot."

Her smile looked as natural as one painted on a corpse. "Thank you, Larry. I appreciate that. And your advice."

I wondered what interview she had and what advice he'd given her, but of course I couldn't ask without her thinking I cared more than I did. I watched him walk past a row of SUVs as a string of colored pendants flapped above us.

When he disappeared into the dealership, Danielle turned to me. "You don't look as tired as you ought to, considering how little sleep Larry said you got."

I buried my hand in my pants pocket, scooped out the loose change, and jangled it around in my fist as I fought for something to say. I finally settled on a simple, "Thanks."

She tucked a strand of hair behind her ear. "I have an interview today."

"Who with?" I asked, trying not to sound too interested. If she left for another position, it sure would make my life a whole lot less complicated. Hers, too, I imagined.

"That job in Leesboro you told me about. The manager's in town, so he agreed to interview me over lunch. Don't tell Thompson."

Knowing what thin ice I stood on, I kept my expression as neutral as I could manage.

"So," I said, speaking slowly, weighing each word, "was Larry able to give you some good interviewing tips?"

When her eyes filled with tears, I knew the ice had cracked. "He was very helpful. He's a good guy. I wish there were more of them in this world."

I let the insult go. I deserved it, and then some. A late-model, silver Camry pulled into our lot in one entrance and back out the other. People were always using the dealership for U-turns. It made Thompson curse every time he saw it, unless of course they slowed to eye the merchandise. I watched them drive away, then faced Danielle again. "So, what advice did Larry give you? Maybe I can add to it."

"He told me people treat you the way you let them." Her eyes glazed over as if she were pondering this. After a moment, she looked at me again. "So, what words of wisdom do you have for me?"

I couldn't bear the intensity of her gaze and looked at the two-door behind her with its gleaming black paint, brand-new tires, and inflated sticker price. The second it was driven off the lot it would depreciate ten thousand dollars. Did customers care when they came to buy one though? No. They just wanted the instant gratification of something pretty and new. "My advice would be to be yourself and trust that what's supposed to be will be."

A soft whimper escaped her lips. "Is me leaving what's supposed to be?"

I looked around the lot to see who might be watching us. There were a few guys moving about on the showroom floor, but they were too far away to worry about.

She grabbed my chin and jerked my face toward her. "Why do you keep looking around? You think anyone cares about us?" Her face twisted with anger as she let me go. "No one cares, Eric. No one cares." Covering her face, she began to cry.

I pulled her to my chest. Her body trembled against me as she dampened my shirt with her tears.

After a few seconds, she pulled back and wiped at her tears. Her lips were quivering and streaks of mascara marred her mottled face. "You never did tell her, did you?"

Of course I knew what she was talking about, but instinct took over. "Tell who what?"

"Doesn't pretending to be stupid ever get old?" She sucked in a breath and looked out at the bumper-to-bumper cars lined up at the red light. "Doesn't matter. Larry's right. The worst punishment I can give you is to let you live with your lie." She rubbed at her nose. "I just can't believe I let you make me cry again."

Good old Larry still had my back after all.

"You know, I honestly thought when I told you I was applying for that job that you would ask me to stay." She laughed without humor and hugged herself as a fresh stream of tears ran down her face. "How pathetic is that?"

I felt like the world's biggest jerk, but I didn't know how to make her pain go away. Meeting her gaze, I hoped somehow she could see in my eyes just how truly sorry I was. "I guess we'd better get back in there," I finally said. "It's got to be about show-time."

She wiped her eyes again. "And all the world's a stage. Isn't it, Eric?"

I felt so tired all of a sudden. Tired enough to curl up right there in the parking lot and sleep for a month. "Dani, I really am sorry." Maybe Larry was right. Would the truth really set me free from this guilt and all the pain I'd caused?

She pressed her fingers against her eyes. "Do you still love her?"

After a moment, she wiped her eyes and looked up again. "I know you're not ready right now, but maybe once the divorce is filed . . ." Her voice trailed off as though she'd lost her thought. She now stood close enough for me to hear her quick, shallow breaths.

She played with the necklace lying across her cleavage. It took everything in me to keep my eyes planted on hers, not because I wanted to check her out, but because flesh always drew my eyes like metal to magnet. If my bearded Aunt Ethel showed skin, I'd have to look, whether I wanted to gouge my eyes out after or not. It was a reflex I could not afford at the moment.

If my gaze deviated even for a second, she'd assign meaning to it. She'd done enough ad-libbing with my intentions as it was. I stared at the green of her despondent eyes, trying not to look as rattled as I felt. Larry poked his head out the showroom door, pointed at his eyes, then at me.

Trying to ignore him, I looked back at Danielle, who now played more frantically with the charm, dragging it back and forth on its silver chain. "This is the last time I'm going to throw myself at you, but let me just say this. I love you. She doesn't."

Love? I thought back to the e-mails, the texts, the couple of late-night calls I'd made to her from the front porch while Kyra slept, and shame filled me.

What had started as mutual loneliness turned into a little flirting, some sexual tension, and then before I knew it I was on a runaway train that nothing short of a derailment could stop. Now that the train was smoldering on its side and we were all lying there beside it dazed and bleeding, I realized that Kyra hadn't been the only victim.

"If Kyra divorces you — I mean in the future, not now — maybe . . ." She stood up straighter and crossed her arms across her stomach, as though bracing herself for whatever I might throw her way. "Just tell me the truth. If Kyra wasn't in the picture, would we still be together?"

All the vulnerability of a lost little girl waved over her like a banner. I wondered if it had been there all along. More than anything, I just wanted to look away from the pain I'd caused. But I wouldn't let myself. Not this time. Nothing was worth this. Nothing.

"Please tell me," she repeated.

It would have been the easiest thing in the world to lie to her then, but for the first time in a long time, I saw her as the friend she'd been to me before she'd become both more and less. If I didn't tell her the truth now, maybe no one ever would. Maybe she'd never get off this Ferris wheel she rode. Even though I didn't care about her the way she wanted me to, I cared about her more than that.

"In all honesty," I said, lowering my voice, hoping to soften the blow, "even if I didn't still love Kyra, and even if she decides to divorce me, I'd always know that you were the kind of woman who would sleep with a married man. How would I ever trust you?"

Her face tightened into an angry ball. "You're a married man who slept with *me*. How could I ever trust *you?*"

"Exactly," I whispered.

She turned on her heel and headed for the building, leaving the shards of her self-esteem at my feet. The enormity of what I'd done hit me once again, and I wondered if

Kyra could ever forgive me. I didn't see how when I couldn't even forgive myself.

Twenty-Two

It had been almost a week since Kyra had gone to Milan with her sister. I called her every day on my lunch break, which was every night her time. I always started the conversation the same way, and today was no different. "Hey, lover, how was your day?"

"Incredible," she said. "You wouldn't believe what we did."

"Do I want to know?"

"Probably not."

"Does it involve other men?"

I took her pause to be playfully deliberate. "Yes. Lots."

"Were they good-looking?"

Another pause.

"Were they straight?"

She laughed. "I didn't ask, but all except one were awfully effeminate."

"What about the straight one? Was he attractive?"

"In an old-guy sort of way, I guess."

I chuckled. "Tell him if he touches you, I'll kill him."

"I don't think it would do any good."

"He can't be swayed away from your charms, eh? I can't blame him."

"No, he's deaf."

"He's what?"

"Very funny."

"Hey," I said, "you're coming home in a few days."

"Don't remind me," she said.

"Don't sound so thrilled."

"It's just there's so much to see here."

"There's lots to see here, too," I said. "We've got the freeway, Piggly Wiggly, the science museum, and that pool on the corner of Arlington and Sherwood with the green water."

"And the handsomest man in the world. Don't forget about him."

"Who is he? I'll kill him, too."

"Be sure to leave me a suicide note if you do."

"Come home now," I said, missing her so much it hurt.

"You come here."

Sometimes we talked until she fell asleep like when we were dating. Sometimes she was on her way out to some fashion gala or another with Marnie and her entourage of Italian designers, and I had just enough time to tell her how much I missed her. Boy, did I miss her.

With each passing day, I fell more and more in love with my wife and more and more terrified she'd remember the incriminating e-mail. I knew the right thing to do was to tell her the truth, the whole truth, and nothing but the truth. After all, I'd finally leveled with Danielle and survived to tell the tale. But Kyra was a different story. I wasn't completely oblivious to the fact that my rationalization was pathetic, but my heart didn't care.

Danielle didn't get that job in Leesboro, and I doubt she even really applied, but Thompson had decided to take care of her in his own way. Somehow he got wind of what had happened, and to placate her — or just to remove her from my sight, I'm not sure which — he bumped her up to the finance department. She seemed content now that her cubicle, title, and paycheck were all larger. Even though she still wrinkled her nose like she smelled roadkill every time our paths crossed, she at least wasn't sulking anymore. She'd moved on, and with my son coming home tomorrow and my wife the day after, I was anxious to do the same.

If Benji and Marnie could both be persuaded not to remind Kyra about my betrayal, we might just be okay. Surely I could get them to see that reminding her of what I'd done would punish more than just me. Did the entire family have to be ripped apart because of my mistake?

Maybe not, hope whispered. Hopefully not.

Thompson called me into his office to tell me he was leaning toward handing the reins to me when he retired next year.

"You know, I was seriously considering Larry," he said. "He's a good worker and a heck of a salesman, but not many men would be willing to give this job what you and I would."

I looked down at his left hand and saw that his wedding band was missing. That would make this, what, divorce number four?

He looked me over, as if considering livestock he might purchase. "You're one of the only men I've known in my life, besides myself, who understands that getting what you really want in life requires a little sacrifice. Heck, a lot of sacrifice."

I was only beginning to realize the extent of what I'd sacrificed for my job. And that I wasn't sure whether the payoff was worth it. Of course I didn't feel that I needed to share that particular information with Thompson just yet. I figured there would be time enough to sort all that out once things were squared away with Kyra.

Though he still seemed to be considering Larry for the promotion too, I didn't worry. The old man was just hedging his bets. Like he said, no one would give the job what I would.

You wouldn't know that Larry and I were not only competing for the same job, but rooting for opposing teams as we split a bag of Doritos and six-pack of PBR, watching basketball on the big screen in my basement rec room.

As usual, my team was winning. They were on fire this season. Even if there was a major upset and they didn't win this game, they'd still go on to the finals. We both sat on the edge of the couch as my favorite player, Jay Johnson, pump-faked the opposing point guard, then drove the ball to the free throw line. I held my breath and stood as he shot, hitting nothing but net.

"Yessss!" I punched my fist into the air, feeling as if I'd made the jumper myself.

Larry leaned back, took a swig from his can, and pointed the remote at the TV. It went black. "Game over."

"Oh, come on," I said. "Your guys still have a whole period left to make it up." I was egging him on, of course. No way was his team coming back from a twenty-five-point hole.

He stood like he was leaving. "Whatever."

"Someone's a poor loser." Waiting for his retort, I saw something on his face that wiped the smile off mine.

"You really think that, don't you?"

"Think what?"

"That I'm a loser."

I looked around like maybe there was a candid camera pointed at me. How did we go from having fun to fighting in two seconds flat? Kyra and I had no problem with that kind of acceleration, but Larry and I? Never. "What are you talking about?"

"Forget it." He pushed past me and headed for the stairs.

"What's your problem?"

He stopped and turned around. The look on his face was one I'd never had aimed at me before. I pushed my mind's rewind button but couldn't replay a single thing I might have done to earn his anger.

"I'm going home," he said looking past me.

"Are you ticked?"

"Maybe."

"Is it the game?"

Halfway up the stairs, he stopped and looked over his shoulder. "Yeah, genius, I'm mad because my lame team lost to the best in the league."

"What, then?"

He walked back down and stood at the foot of the stairs a few feet from me. One of the empties he held spilled a drip on the carpet. "I'm not supposed to tell you."

I eyed the leaking can. "Tell me what?"

"Nothing."

I took all but the full can from him and walked them to the garbage behind the bar. "C'mon, man, spill it," I said as I put the lid back on.

"Spill what? That you're a winner and I'm a loser? You don't do anything wrong, and I don't do anything right."

I tried to take a mental step back and analyze what was happening here before reacting. There had to be a logical explanation for his strange behavior. Larry was the one person I could count on when the whole world was against me. I didn't want to lose that, especially not over . . . well, whatever this was over. "C'mon, Lar, don't do this. I can't defend myself against accusations unless I know what they are."

"If I tell you and you tell Thompson I told you, I'll kick your —"

"Easy," I said, putting my hands up. "Listen to yourself. You're threatening me."

He rubbed his face. "Just don't call me a loser because I'm not. I may not do things the same as you, and I may not want to take over the world, but that doesn't mean I don't have aspirations."

"I know that," I said. "I know you do."

"Do you?"

Now that the imminent threat of being beaten up had past, I dropped to the couch and looked up at him. "Just tell me what's got you so worked up."

He pointed his kielbasa-size finger at me. "You better not tell Thompson we talked about this."

"Never."

He sat in the recliner beside the couch and leaned forward with his elbows on his knees. "Thompson told me you said my gross is lacking. I'm laying over too easy, huh?"

Blood rushed to my face. That was something I said to our boss when he pressed me to find something about Larry that could use improving. Nobody was perfect, he'd said, and a good leader needed to see the positives and negatives even in their best friends. "He pressed me to give him one thing you could work on."

"You just can't stand to lose, can you?"

"Lose what?"

"Thompson told me he was leaning toward me for the promotion."

"That's funny," I said, "because he told me he was leaning toward me."

Larry crossed his arms. "When?"

"Today." I figured that answer ought to shut him up. He didn't look bothered, which freaked me out.

"What time? Because he pulled me into his office right before he left."

The blood drained from my face. What was that slob pulling?

"You look kind of ticked. I was hoping you'd be happy for me."

I shook my head. Was he for real? "How happy can I be? That's supposed to be my job."

He sneered. "Says who?"

"Sales manager is next in line for general manager. You're next in line for my job. You don't leapfrog over your boss. That's not the way it works."

He looked up at the ceiling and shook his head. "Let me ask you something. Why do you even want this promotion?"

"Because I deserve it."

"You seem to think you deserve a lot of things."

I stood. "What's that supposed to mean?"

"I'm just speaking the truth. You might want to try it sometime."

"Where's all this coming from?"

"I'm sick of you getting everything a man could ever want and just throwing it away for nothing."

"Is this about Kyra?"

"Yeah, it's about Kyra. What do you think I'm talking about? You had it all and you blew it, for what? A stupid promotion and a girl who still sleeps with stuffed animals? I still can't wrap my mind around that." It was Larry's turn to stand. He dwarfed me by several inches and close to a hundred pounds. His face twisted with anger. "Why would you do that?"

"This isn't about the job or Kyra. It's about Tina."

"No, it's about why you would throw your whole life away for nothing. And look, at the end of the day, you're not going to end up with anything. Which is exactly what you deserve. I thought you were turning things around when you finally leveled with Danielle, but I guess I was wrong. You're just as big a jerk as you ever were."

I shoved Larry, but bounced right off him

onto the couch. Before I could get my footing, he had me turned around and in a headlock. I could hardly breathe with my throat jammed in the crook of his arm.

"Just tell me why you'd do something so stupid? You had it all. Great job. Big house. Beautiful wife. What's your problem?"

Somehow I managed to push him off me. "Stop making this about Kyra and me. Just forgive Tina. She's not even with the guy anymore."

Red-faced and breathing hard, Larry took a few steps back, watching to make sure I wouldn't pounce. "I forgave her a long time ago, but what good would it do to take her back when I can't even stand to look at her? You may get this stupid promotion, and you may get your bride back, but someday your lies are going to catch up with you."

"If the promotion's so stupid, why do you want it so bad?"

"I don't have a wife to come home to. I don't have anything but a broken-down TV and a best friend willing to sell me out for a corner office. That's why."

Dumbfounded, I just stared at him. "I didn't know you wanted it so bad."

"Does it make a difference?"

I looked down at the Berber carpet beneath my feet. Did it? It was true that I wasn't used to losing. "You want me to throw the fight?"

His laugh was cold and mirthless. "I'm not asking you to throw the fight, *friend*. I'm just asking you to fight fair."

TWENTY-THREE

"I can't believe you're here." Kyra wrapped her arms around my neck and kissed me. The cashmere of her sweater didn't feel half as soft as her lips against mine. When she retreated, the disturbed look in her eyes betrayed her true feelings. I'd caught her off guard and apparently not pleasantly so.

Drained from the twelve-hour flight from Virginia to Italy, I stood in the hallway waiting to be invited into the hotel room.

"You don't look happy to see me," I said, as much to her as Marnie, who glared at me from the bed she sat on.

Kyra stepped aside and let me into the room. Two full-size beds took up most of the space with a claw-foot table, two chairs, and a chest of drawers occupying what was left. Though tastefully decorated, it was a small room by American standards. On the edge of my wife's unmade bed sat a silver tray holding a plate with a spoonful of tomatoes, a crust of bread, and a fork in the center of it.

"Of course I'm happy," she said. "I'm just surprised. Why didn't you call? It would have been terrible if you flew this whole way and we weren't even here."

That possibility practically gave me an ulcer on the flight, then taxi ride over, but I didn't think the leading man I was trying to play would admit that. "Sometimes in life, you have to take chances." I pulled the bouquet of roses I'd picked up on the way over from behind my back and held them out to her.

She gave them a strange look as she took them from my hands. "That's really sweet. Thank you."

Her hesitancy made me wonder if her feelings for me had changed overnight. I brushed the dampness from my hands, wondering if it was from the flowers or my own nervousness.

She walked over to the bathroom and disappeared inside it with them. I heard the water turn on, which Marnie took as a cue to finally say what she'd been trying to convey through scowls.

"What are you doing here?" she whispered.

"Trying to win my wife back. What else?"

217

"Shouldn't you be doing that *after* her memory returns?"

She was right, of course, but I was more and more convinced that a preemptive strike at redemption seemed my best and only hope. If and when Kyra's memory returned, she might weigh this moment against what I'd done and maybe I'd earn a little leniency.

Her eyes narrowed, and she was about to say something else but stopped and turned. Kyra emerged from the bathroom holding the flowers, which leaned awkwardly inside their makeshift, ice-bucket vase. Petals rained down like snow. In my mad rush to get to the hotel, I must have overlooked the fact I'd bought a bouquet of half-dead flowers.

Decaying roses. Real romantic.

Embarrassed, I squatted down and began plucking debris from the carpet. "These are already on their last leg. I'm sorry. I'll take them back and get you fresh ones."

She stooped beside me to help. Our hands brushed as we reached for the same petal. "Don't you dare. I love them. It's just that . . . the only time you bring me flowers is when you've done something wrong."

Laughing nervously, my gaze jetted from her up to Marnie, hoping she'd save me.

Knowing she wouldn't.

Instead, she sat there on her bed, arms and legs crossed, wearing a stony expression and her workout clothes. "He's a man. They've always done something wrong." She tapped her sneakered foot against the carpet. "Where are you staying?"

"Nowhere. I'm just in for the day," I said.

"What?" both women said simultaneously.

I shrugged as if it were no big deal. "Hey, I missed my wife, so I decided to fly in and spend the day with her." Somehow that line I'd rehearsed at least a dozen times on the flight over sounded more Pee-wee Herman than the John Wayne I'd intended.

In my fantasy, Kyra was supposed to lay a hand across her heart as tears sprang to her eyes. Looking at her now, staring me down with that unreadable look of hers, I began to wonder if maybe I'd accomplished nothing more than inconveniencing her.

I stood and brushed my hands together, knocking off the last bit of dried leaf. "I thought you might think it was romantic. You know, the man you love flies across the globe just to spend a day with you in one of Europe's most amazing cities. I thought women liked that sort of thing." My face grew warm. "I thought, well, you know . . ."

"You should have called," Marnie said.

"We have plans for tonight."

I licked my lips. "Oh, well, I . . ."

When Kyra's mouth turned upward in that Mona Lisa way of hers, I knew it was going to be okay. "It's true, lover, we do have a party to go to."

"Not a party," Marnie interjected. "A gala on a yacht with the biggest names in fashion. Probably the most important networking opportunity I'll ever get."

Kyra turned to her sister and tilted her head to the side. "He flew in just to spend the day with me. How awesome is that?"

Relief filled me. "So, you're not mad?"

She laughed. "Yes, I'm furious that a handsome man flew all the way across the world just to take me on a romantic excursion. What girl wouldn't be?"

I extended a hand down to her and she took it. Bracing myself against the pull of her weight, I helped her stand.

Marnie pouted. "You can't do this to me."

Kyra sat beside her on the bed and leaned into her shoulder. "What are you sad about? You'll rub a lot more elbows if you don't have to babysit your little sister."

Looking on the verge of tears, Marnie said, "Please don't make me go alone. What if I fall over the side of the boat? Who would even know? I could be treading water for days until I died a slow, horrible death of thirst. Do you know what saltwater does to your insides if you drink it?"

Kyra raised an eyebrow. "You're not going to fall off the side of the yacht."

"You don't know that."

I could see Kyra's resolve melting away with each quiver of her sister's lip. "Fine, but he's coming too."

My heart sank. I had our evening planned. I'd reserved a table at the most romantic restaurant in all of Milan — according to Google, anyway — and a horse and carriage to take us there. I even arranged for a violinist to serenade her over dinner. I haggled the guy down to one hundred and fifty if he learned Rod Stewart's "Broken Arrow" by then.

A boat party with Marnie and her snooty fashion friends was not on the menu.

She squinted at me long and hard, as though deciding if I was yacht-gala worthy. After a moment she rolled her eyes. "You need to call the concierge and tell him you need a tux."

Kyra must have seen the disappointment in my eyes because she set her soft hand on my cheek and gave me the sweetest look. "You are the kindest, most romantic husband in the entire world." When she kissed me, I realized my plans weren't nearly as important as her happiness. What really mattered was that I was with the woman I loved, and we had an entire day together.

"Can I at least have you to myself until then?" I asked. I'd really hoped to see da Vinci's *The Last Supper* while we were here, knowing neither of us would likely ever get the chance again.

Marnie frowned at me. "We couldn't possibly. I've got a meeting across town in an hour."

"Who's got a meeting?" Kyra asked.

"I do." Marnie sounded perturbed.

"Who?" Kyra repeated.

"I . . . do," Marnie said slow and loud as if Kyra were deaf and stupid. A knowing look finally washed over her. "Fine. Go. But remember, it's a two-hour drive to the party."

Kyra glanced at her watch. "We've got enough time to catch one or two attractions and get a quick bite."

Marnie lit up. "Oh, you've got to take the tram tour. Catch number twenty. It's the one with the big Ciao Milano sign painted on the side. The whole tour just takes about forty-five minutes, but you'll learn so much about the city. Then, you can catch a taxi to Golden Quadrilateral. It's one of the absolute best places to shop in Milan. Most of my inspiration so far comes —"

"Don't you have to get ready?" Kyra said, grabbing her purse.

Marnie rolled her eyes and mumbled something about a cultural vacuum and Mc-Donald's.

TWENTY-FOUR

"So, where we headed?" Kyra said as she walked beside me down the dimly lit hotel corridor. "I'm guessing it's not Milan's shopping district."

"You probably don't remember this," I said with a smile in my voice, "but you hate to shop as much as me. I'd like to take you to see da Vinci's *The Last Supper*. Is that okay?"

She slid the long leather straps of her purse crossways over her shoulder, letting the bag fall across her stomach. I'd never seen her wear it that way before, but from everything I'd read, tourists couldn't be too careful in Italy. I guess she'd heard the same thing.

Keeping stride, she slipped her fingers into mine. "A great choice. You'll love it."

"You've already seen it?" Disappointment filled me. I'd just assumed we would experience it for the first time together.

"The day I arrived. It's the one thing I didn't want to chance missing."

A stocky man with thick blond eyebrows and matching ear hair ducked out of one of the rooms and looked at us as if expecting someone. When our eyes met, his face turned red, and he retreated back inside his room and closed the door.

"We can do something else, then," I offered, hoping she'd insist we go.

"I'd love to see it again." She gave my fingers a squeeze. "You know you can't buy the tickets at the door, right? They only let twenty or so people in at a time and they're always sold out."

I gave her a *you should know me better* look, which made her laugh.

"Guess I forgot who I was talking to."

On the ancient-looking streets of Milan, catching a taxi was easy enough, and to my relief, our driver spoke perfect English, albeit with a heavy Italian accent. The ride to the church was short, so when he told me I owed him forty-two euros, I about choked. Kyra gave him a tongue-lashing like I'd never heard, and by the time she was through with him, he was apologizing for everything from dishonest drivers to the global economic decline. I was just glad I wasn't on the receiving end of her rant.

225

Watching the cab speed off, we stood on cobblestone streets just a few hundred feet from the large brick church that housed the world's most famous painting.

"Here it is," Kyra said. "Santa Maria delle Grazie, home of Leonardo da Vinci's masterpiece."

From the outside, the church was plainer than I'd imagined. "For some reason I thought the place would be more cathedral-like."

She stared ahead at the large brick building with a look of affection. "If you look at it from the back, it looks ten times bigger, but if it's a cathedral you want, let's hit the duomo next. It's one of the most magnificent in the world."

"Do we have time?" I hated that we only had the afternoon to fit in our little Roman holiday when there was so much to see here.

"Plenty," she said. "It's not far and there's a restaurant close by that has great pizza."

"Little Caesars?" I asked.

She gave me her *you're not funny* look as she took my hand and pulled me gently toward the church.

I glanced at my watch. "Our viewing starts in about ten minutes."

"We better head right back there then. Those guys wait for no one."

The church was so much more on the inside than its outside alluded to. Our feet clicked along the tiled floors as we explored the magnificent frescos hanging between massive columns. The place even smelled old and impressive — a combination of linseed oil, incense, and time. Soon, we were joined by a group of a dozen or so other tourists and ushered back like sheep.

We all grew reverently quiet as we stepped into a white, rectangular room. Rows of generic spotlights pointed toward the main attraction, with the only natural light in the space coming from a line of small windows at the top of one wall. Those windows were outlined with chipped, multi-colored tiles that looked every bit as old as I suspected they were.

The rest of the room looked rather blasé except for the arched ceiling. The floor was made of simple brick, and the white plaster walls had been patched here and there. The room itself was not worthy of the rest of the church, but the nondescript backdrop only made the two frescos stand out.

On the wall behind us loomed a magnificent painting of the crucifixion. I knew nothing of this artwork and wondered why it got so little attention when it seemed to me to be every bit as well done as its more famous neighbor. Directly across from it, spanning the space of an entire wall, was what we'd come to see. We were allowed only so close, and while cameras were forbidden, it didn't stop the onlookers from blatantly snapping pictures with their cell phones.

Kyra and I stood with our hands touching on the railing that kept us from getting too close. "Can you believe they built a door in the middle of it?" she asked.

I looked at the arch in the center of the painting, which had been sealed shut. "Guess they didn't realize what they had."

"I can empathize with that."

"Me, too," I said, wondering if she intended the same double meaning that I had.

"Look at the detail," she whispered.

"They all look miserable," I said, referring to the disciples gathered in front of the long table.

"Wouldn't you be, if Jesus just told you that one of you was about to betray Him?"

I stared ahead at the painting, considering what I would have thought if I'd been warned by God Himself that I would cheat on Kyra someday. I wouldn't have believed it. "Which one's Judas?"

She pointed to the man who was reaching for the same piece of bread as the One he would betray. "Isn't it poignant the way they're both reaching for the same thing?"

As I studied the onetime apostle, thoughts of what he'd done spun in my head. I tried to make sense of what might have caused such a blatant betrayal — greed, pride, insecurity? Nothing more than every man wrestled with at one time or another in his life. "Do you think maybe Judas got a bad rap?"

She turned to me, looking surprised. "How's that?"

"He messed up, but it's not like he's the only one. Thomas doubted Jesus when He'd come back from the dead, and what about Peter denying Him three times? How horrible was that? So how come Judas is synonymous with betrayal and not Peter?"

She gave me an incredulous look. "This from the same man who blames Adam for the fall of all humanity?"

"Yeah, well. I've been rethinking . . ."

Thankfully, I didn't have to finish the thought because the guide told us our time was up.

I followed Kyra out of the room. "That wasn't very long."

She ran her fingers through her ponytail. "They're supposed to give you fifteen minutes, but it sure didn't seem like it, did it? You got to see it though. That's the important thing."

"No," I said, pulling her toward me, "getting to see you is the important thing."

She blushed. "We're in a church, Eric."

"What could be holier than love?"

She laughed. "Who *are* you?"

"The man who adores you."

Pulling away from me, she lifted a camera out of her purse and held it in front of us.

"Smile," she said.

Right before the camera flashed, I kissed her cheek. She turned the camera around, looked at the small digital screen, and grinned at me. "We're adorable."

I took it from her and looked for myself. We really did look good together. "Not adorable — sexy."

"Well, we better take our sexy selves over to the duomo before it gets too late."

The Milan cathedral, aka the duomo, was everything Kyra had said it was. It looked like an enormous, gothic castle with its elaborate points aimed at heaven, carved in the likeness of saints, angels, and crosses. The inside was an elegant mass of marble, ordained with painted tiles, hand-carved statues, and intricate stained glass windows.

As I looked around, I felt as though I was committing a sin just by being in there.

Despite its beauty, I couldn't wait to get out of there.

"So, what'd you think?" Kyra asked, as she intertwined her arm into mine and led me onto the street and back into daylight.

A tall stick of a woman knocked into me as she strutted by. She threw a look back at me as if I'd been the one to run into her. No excuse me, *scusi,* or anything. She looked more Swedish than Italian, and I guessed she probably was one of the many models employed by the fashion capital of the world.

"It's certainly amazing but I felt so small in there. So insignificant. Do you know what I mean?"

"I think so." She leaned into me. "That's how I feel when I'm looking up at the stars at night. Sometimes it scares me to think of just how small I am compared to God." She pointed to a row of shops down the street. "There's the place Marnie and I ate when we came here. You up for real Italian pizza?"

"You sure you don't want something a little more fancy?" I said, still thinking about the cathedral.

"We're doing fancy tonight. Besides, you can't come to Italy and not have pizza."

"I can eat pizza at home."

"Not like this," she said.

On a brick sidewalk, we sat under an umbrella as tourists and locals alike filed by. Sipping bottled water, we waited for our meal to be delivered and people-watched. Two shops down, a palm reader sat outside at a small, cloth-covered table. Even from a distance, it was obvious she was toothless. She wore a hideous purple-sequined top and rimmed hat. With her long, gnarled fingers, she petted the surface of what I guess was supposed to be a crystal ball. It looked more like a bowling ball to me. Whatever she said to the young woman in her chair made the girl grin and fork over a handful of euros.

Smells of garlic and basil wafted past me, and I looked over to see a waiter carrying a plate of half a dozen or so different foods, from potatoes to chunks of meat all covered in some kind of red sauce. My stomach grumbled right as our own waiter set down a round metal tray with a pizza in the center of it. It looked enough like a regular pizza except that the cheese was melted in chunks rather than spread evenly over the pie, and whole basil leaves garnished the top. Kyra pulled a slice from it and laid it on my plate, then took one for herself. "Taste," she said with obvious anticipation.

Slowly, I took a bite. The crust was thinner and crunchier than I was used to, but the sauce was superb, especially mixed with the basil. I smiled and nodded at her.

"Isn't it amazing?" she asked.

"Amazing," I agreed, gazing into my wife's eyes on a sidewalk in Milan.

Twenty-Five

After an hour of the girls primping and another two-hour drive, I found myself on the deck of a yacht. I'd never been on one before, but I suspected this was a high-end model.

We stood on the upper deck, letting warm night air comb through our hair and across our faces. It smelled of a pleasant blend of expensive perfume, saltwater, and roasted peppers. Evening painted the sky the same shade of inky blue as the ocean, making the perfect backdrop for the stream of white lights lining just about everything from the gleaming wood deck under our feet to the metal railings outlining the perimeter of the ship. Even the sky sparkled. As I glanced up at the stars twinkling happily above us, I prayed for the first time in a long time.

I know I don't deserve to be here with Kyra. I probably didn't deserve her even before I did what I did, but, God, if You'll let me off the hook just this one time, I promise . . .

What could I promise that God needed? Nothing, of course. I was the only one who needed something and that something was grace.

Although we were surrounded by beautiful people wearing beautiful things, none of them could compare to Kyra. Her hair fell in ringlets over her creamy white shoulders. She wore an emerald dress that Marnie had designed specifically for this party. It hugged her in all the right places and cinched at the waist in a string of multicolored jewels that looked as real as the diamonds around her neck.

As I studied her freckles, the upturned corner of her heart-shaped lips, and her silhouette, I was struck for the hundredth time just how far above myself I had married. I'd give anything if I could just deserve her again.

Soft light fell across her lightly made-up face and hit her eyes just right, making them sparkle. She'd never looked more beautiful. All around us laughter rang out, champagne and wineglasses clanked together, and live jazz rose up from the lower deck.

Couples danced wherever they pleased, while others simply ate from tiny plates or people-watched.

"Are you cold?" I asked my wife, just to have something to say.

She shook her head. "It's warmer tonight than it has been."

"I could get your shawl if you need it." I hadn't been this nervous the night I'd proposed.

"No, really, I'm fine."

"I thought Cello would be here," Marnie said from behind us.

It startled me to hear her voice. I'd been so wrapped up in the moment, I'd forgotten she was even there.

Kyra mumbled something in reply but her eyes never left mine. "You look so handsome in that tuxedo."

I looked down at the penguin suit. The concierge had done well. It was a perfect fit and finer than anything I'd ever worn before. "Thanks; you look pretty amazing yourself."

She bit her bottom lip, managing to look both girlish and all woman at the same time. I couldn't stop myself from leaning in to kiss her.

Marnie grabbed my wrist. "Eric, may I speak with you a moment alone?"

Kyra's eyebrows dipped, and her gaze passed between us in question before she excused herself to find the bathroom.

While we waited for her to get out of listening range, Marnie wiggled her fingers over my shoulder at someone.

"Ciao, bella!" A man called to her. I didn't care enough to turn to see who.

She pressed her fingertips to her lips and flung him a kiss before turning her attention back to me and lowering her voice. "Flying in for the day just to see the sights with your wife. What have you done with the real Eric?" Her eyes roved around the crowd, whether looking for bigwigs to impress or doing one of her OCD compulsions, I wasn't sure.

I sipped from my champagne glass, wishing I had a Coke instead. Sickeningly sweet bubbles filled my mouth and made my nose itch. I rubbed at it discreetly. "I should at least get credit for trying."

A server passed by, dressed an awful lot like me. He held a platter of stuffed mushrooms and paused to offer us one. They smelled wonderful, like olive oil and fried onions, but before I could grab one, Marnie shooed him along. "This is the sort of thing you should have done years ago. Not now."

"Sometimes it takes losing something before you appreciate what you had. And I do."

A woman with short dark hair laughed so

hard she stumbled backward, bumping into Marnie. Champagne trickled over the side of her glass and onto the wood floor. *"Scusi,"* she said, still laughing in her friends' direction.

Marnie dismissed the incident with a wave of hand, and the woman was absorbed back into her group.

"That dress is beautiful," I said, hoping to butter my sister-in-law up, but it was true. Her blue, one-shouldered getup made her look the epitome of high fashion.

She touched her gown. "Audrey Hepburn inspired this one."

I raised my eyebrows, trying to appear interested.

Her expression darkened as she opened her small, sequined purse. "She's going to remember." She stared into the bag and then snapped it shut again, looking reassured by whatever she'd seen in there.

"People make mistakes," I said. "I made a mistake."

She sniffed. "I know that you love her. If you didn't, I'd have paid for her divorce lawyer myself. But love or no love, she deserves to know the truth."

"She deserves to be happy, too," I said. "Can we just be happy until she remembers?"

Something like sympathy shone in her eyes. "You know, when you two first started dating, I thought it wouldn't last a week. She's too good for you, you know."

"I know."

"But you're the only man she's ever loved. Why couldn't you have been the one guy most women swear doesn't exist. Is it really that hard to be faithful to a gorgeous woman you're in love with?"

"There's more to it than you know." Shame filled me when I realized that once again I was trying to blame Kyra for what I had done. "If I could take it back, believe me, I would."

She gulped down the rest of her champagne like a shot of tequila. "It's going to take a lot more than a trip to Italy and an apology to make up for what you did."

"I know," I said miserably.

"You know what?" Kyra asked.

I jerked around.

Men all over the boat had their hungry eyes glued to her. I felt jealous and proud at the same time. I suspected even with the diamond ring and matching wedding band perched on her left hand, if I hadn't been there, she'd have been converged upon faster than a rabbit in a foxhole.

Marnie threw me a glance. "He knows if

239

he doesn't ask you to dance soon, he's going to be waiting in line."

"Eric doesn't dance." The look on Kyra's face was unmistakable disappointment. She was right; I didn't dance, but not because I didn't enjoy doing it. I just didn't enjoy feeling like I might be making a fool of us. But other than Marnie, I didn't know these people. What did I care what they thought? "I do tonight." I took her hand and brought it to my lips.

I don't know how many times I stepped on her toes, but if her feet were sore, her smile hid it well. After what seemed like minutes, but must have been hours, the wind began to blow harder and the temperature dropped. Marnie had excused herself long ago into the company of her earlier admirer, and guests disappeared in droves into the warmth of the lower deck. Before long, we found ourselves nearly alone.

"I've embarrassed you enough," I said, taking her hand and leading her to the railing overlooking the water. Finally, I felt like her knight in shining armor instead of the court jester.

She adjusted the straps of her dress. "Are you kidding? Fred Astaire couldn't have done better."

I laughed. "You're crazy."

"Crazy for you."

I wrapped my arm around her shoulders, feeling the gooseflesh which had risen across her skin with the latest gale. "You're freezing." I tried to rub her arms smooth.

She snuggled into me. "I didn't feel how cold it had gotten until we stopped moving. Ready to go below?"

"In a minute." My heart pounded as I realized the rareness of this moment, knowing we might not ever get another one like it. "Kyra, do you love me?"

She put a hand on each of my cheeks. They felt like ice, but melted me just the same. "More than my own life."

I couldn't have been more vulnerable. "Promise you'll never stop loving me."

She gave me a curious look as a smile glinted in her eyes. "I'll never stop loving you."

"And that you'll never leave me no matter what."

"Baby, are you okay?"

"Promise," I said, more sternly this time. Like Jacob tricking his brother out of his father's blessing, I knew I wasn't playing fair. It had worked for him though, and maybe it would work for me, too. I was willing to try anything. I couldn't lose her.

"You hold my heart, Samurai. Where else

could I go?"

I took her hand in mine, and together we looked out over the ocean and the small waves of foam the ship carved through the water, shimmering in the moonlight.

"When I get lumpy and wrinkly will you still love me?" she asked without looking at me.

"Of course," I said.

She turned to face me. "What if I get really fat, then lose a bunch of weight and my skin sags all over me like a pendulum. Would you still love me then?"

"Yes," I said. "Will you love *me* if I get man-boobs and nose hair?"

Her laughter rang out more beautiful than any music we'd heard that night. "I'd loan you my bra and buy a tiny Weedwacker. Will you love me if all the hair on my head falls out and grows back on my chin?"

"I'll love you all the more," I said. I turned and looked her square in the eye. "I'll love you no matter what, Kyra. The way you look has nothing to do with that."

She let out a deep breath as if exhaling all the fears I felt. "Will you love me if — ?"

"I will love you when you're old," I said. "I will love you if you're cold. I will love you if you're fat. I will love you and all of that. I will love you in a car. I will love you

242

on a star. I will love you, chili pepper, even if you become a leper. I will love you, wife of mine. I will love you for all time."

Her ear-to-ear grin told me I'd done something right for a change. She hugged our clenched hands to her chest. "I don't want this moment to end."

"But it will around the bend."

She looked up at me with wide eyes. "Eric?"

"Yes, my love?"

"Stop rhyming."

"Sorry." I pulled her tight against me and inhaled her smell, wondering if this would be the last time I'd ever get to do that. She tilted her head up, inviting me to kiss her, which I gladly did.

"Fireworks," she said.

"Always." I leaned in to kiss her again.

"No —" she pointed up at the sky — "really; fireworks."

I turned to find the sky exploding with a shower of color and a series of gunshot-like pops. The deck filled with people once again and just like that, our moment was over.

TWENTY-SIX

The flight from Milan to Virginia seemed twice as long as the way there, but the trip had been more of a success than I'd dared to dream, and knowing Kyra would be home soon at least gave me something to think about between in-flight movies. Even so, the last thing I wanted the day after returning was another trip to the airport.

I set the alarm for nine o'clock so I could be there a half hour before Benji's flight was scheduled to arrive. As I wiped shaving gel and bits of beard from the bathroom sink, a memory came to mind that I hadn't thought of in years.

It was a Sunday afternoon, and Kyra, Benji, and I had just finished church and then lunch at Sonny's by the Sea.

We stopped home to change into jeans and were walking along the beach, letting cool, foamy waves rush over our feet. Kyra slipped her fingers into mine and leaned her shoulder against me. "What are you thinking?"

"Just that I'm happy," I said.

I couldn't see her eyes behind the sunglasses she wore, but the upturn of her pretty little mouth told me that she was too.

She dropped my hand and jerked around. "Where's Benji?"

I whipped my head in the direction I'd last seen him. Fear filled me, until I saw him near the sand dunes, digging for something.

"Benjamin, you're not allowed to be on there," Kyra called.

"I found a crab!" he yelled.

She started toward him and I followed. "Benjamin Andrew, I'm not going to tell you again. Get off there now."

"He's not hurting anything," I said, staring at her sunburned back. Her shoulders were red in places I must have missed putting the suntan lotion on the previous day when we'd been here swimming.

She stopped and gave me a stern look. "It's illegal."

I waved my hand. "Oh, come on, no one's going to say anything to a little boy digging up a sand crab."

"Yes, someone is." She marched over to him and picked him up.

"Look, Mommy," he held the creature in front of her face. She bent her neck backward to keep from being pinched. "That's nice, sweetie, but don't go on those sand dunes again. They're here to protect us."

His expression grew somber. "I'm sorry, Mommy."

"Good," she said softly. "Then maybe next time you'll remember."

"Look, Daddy!" He held the crab out toward me.

"That's quite a critter you found there. Careful he doesn't get you with those pinchers."

Benji held him up in front of his face, examining him from every angle. "His name's going to be Benji Jr."

Kyra laughed as she set him back down on the sand. "I see the resemblance. He definitely has his grandfather's good looks."

"Ha-ha." I slipped my hand around hers again. "And your mother's intelligence."

Still holding him, Benji kicked at the sand. "Can I keep him?"

"No," Kyra said, without giving it a second's consideration.

I gave her fingers a squeeze. "Honey, every kid should have a pet crab."

She knelt down and set her hand on his arm. "Everything has a place it ought to be,

Benji. Yours is with me and your father. His is in the sand here on the beach."

His bottom lip pushed out. "I can get him sand."

"It's not the same," she said. "If something's not where it ought to be, it won't be happy."

Along with the sun, love warmed me. *This is my family,* I thought. *That's my wife, giving my son advice that he might remember someday when he's a man.* I knew I would. Or at least the way she looked right then with her red hair, lightened to near blonde from the summer sun and growing out of the pixie cut she'd let her sister talk her into.

I helped her stand. "What happened to 'bloom where you're planted'? That's what you're always telling me."

She brought my hand to her mouth and kissed it. "Yes, but he has a chance to bloom where he was created to. That's even better than blooming wherever the wind blows you, don't you think?"

Benji looked up at me with those angled blue eyes of his. "Dad? I could get him sea grass and water from the ocean. I'd —"

I let go of Kyra's hand to pick him up. "Your Momma's right, Ben. How'd you like it if someone took you from us and put you in a big glass cage? Even if they stick a bed in there and some french fries, it doesn't mean you'd really have what you needed, would it?"

"Can we get french fries?" he asked.

Kyra threw me a side glance. "We just had lunch."

Benji yelped and dropped the crab. He held his hand, looking at it like he couldn't believe what had just happened. Seizing his second chance at freedom, the tiny crab scurried as fast as his little legs would carry him toward the surf.

Benji's eyes filled with tears. Kyra examined his palm, then kissed it.

"Benji Jr, you're a bad crab!" my son called after his would-be pet.

"He's not a bad crab," Kyra said. "He's just a smart crab."

Benji gave her the evil eye.

"Honey," I said, "you don't always have to be right. If your son says he's a bad crab, he's a bad crab."

Kyra put a hand on the side of her mouth to help her voice carry and yelled, "Benji Jr, you're a bad crab!"

Benji cracked up and wriggled in my arms to be let free. Kyra and I each took one of his hands and swung him back and forth into the waves, letting his feet touch foam and listening to him howl with delight, forgetting all about his disappointment.

As I turned the bathroom light off, I heard the door open. Whoever it was made no attempt at stealth, so I figured a burglary was unlikely. "Hello?" I called.

"Hey, Dad," Benji answered.

I laid the hand towel on the counter and hurried out. Despite being dressed in civilian clothes, my boy looked every bit the sailor, with his chest muscles clearly defined beneath a fitted T-shirt and black hair buzzed tight around a face that had lost any last trace of baby fat we'd sent him off to Illinois with. I couldn't get to him fast enough.

I caught him in a bear hug. Between the Old Spice and a tinge of diesel I was probably just imagining, he even smelled like a sailor. As I held him, his arms hung loose at his sides until finally he gave my back an unenthusiastic pat and pulled away. It hurt my feelings a little, but I understood. The kid just had his lifelong dream crushed — he was entitled to a little grief.

Undeterred, I grabbed him by the shoulders and pulled back, looking him in the eyes — slanted like mine, but as blue as mine were brown. It never ceased to stun me that the toddler who threw himself on the floor with a blood-curdling scream when

I tried to wean him from his Pooh Bear was really a man now. A handsome, smart, hard-working, ambitious sailor — at least for a little while longer. I was the father of a man.

I looked him over. "I thought you didn't come in until —"

"I took an earlier flight." He pulled away from my grasp and set his canvas bag by the door. The thing was so bulky he could have been hiding a body in it.

I tousled what was left of his hair. The ticklish feel of it brought me back to summers past. I just couldn't get over him. "Looking sharp, squid."

He flinched. "Don't call me that. I'm not a sailor anymore."

"It's not over until it's over." It was a stupid and maybe even cowardly thing to say. The Navy wouldn't send him home unless the medical discharge was imminent.

He shrugged and walked past me. "Just because the coroner hasn't pronounced the corpse dead, doesn't mean it's still breathing."

"I'm sorry." I felt his pain as if it were my own.

"Yeah, me too." He headed for the kitchen, his boots clunking against the hardwood.

I followed. "You hungry?"

He opened the fridge, looked at the measly

fare consisting more of condiments than anything else, and closed the door again. "Not really. Just tired."

"Didn't you sleep last night?" It was a direct flight, so it wasn't likely he had jet lag.

"I haven't slept well since they told me I was being sent home."

"Maybe we can pick you up something to help until . . ."

When he looked at me, I knew no amount of Benadryl was going to give him the rest he needed.

"Mind if I go lay down?"

One of the things I was prepared for was Benji wanting to shut out the rest of the world and go into hibernation like he had when we moved here the summer before he started high school, then later when his first love broke his heart. Like Kyra, he was susceptible to wallowing in pity, and also like Kyra, a push and pull here and there kept him from it. "I kind of had a surprise for you."

"Can it wait until after I have a nap?" Not pausing for an answer, he trudged upstairs.

Two hours later, I was practically asleep on the couch myself when he made his way back downstairs, looking twice as tired as when he left. "All right, I guess I'm ready for my surprise." You'd have thought by the look on his face he expected me to give him a dead puppy.

"Up for taking a drive?"

He shrugged one shoulder. It killed me to see him so blue, but the trip would help. After an hour and a half of me trying to fill the silence with small talk and him giving me as many one-word answers as he could slide by with, we arrived at the marina. I'm sure he'd guessed our destination before now.

"Good old Braddy's Wharf," he said, sounding almost happy.

I backed into a spot in front of an old-time parking meter that still took nickels. We looked through the windshield at the rows of salt-washed stilt homes facing the cove. Except for their sun-faded colors, they all looked the same, more or less, with their wraparound porches bordered by patches of grass popping up in resilient tufts from the sand, that neither sea salt nor drought had managed to kill.

Mostly artists and fishermen lived in these houses, supplying the nearby restaurants and gift shops that catered to vacationing families. As everything built up around this place, somehow it managed to age unaffected.

"Remember the first time you took me flounder gigging?" He looked over at the spot near the shoreline that we'd started from.

"You were really good at it," I said. He was ten years old, and once I told him how to hold the gig and spear the fish between the eyes, he never lost another flounder. He took to fishing like Kyra took to music. Joining the Navy was the most natural thing in the world for him. I'm pretty sure he had seawater flowing in his veins instead of blood.

"I didn't even get to go out once." He stared at the sound side, which was as still as a mirror while we listened to the distant roar of waves.

I supposed he meant out to sea on a naval ship. I opened the car door. "Let's take a walk."

The smell of brine and fish filled the air. Benji opened his door and followed. It was early afternoon now, and the sun sat high above us. "You still think you can read the time from it?" he asked, squinting up.

"Is there anything I can't do?"

He gave me a half smile, which was 50 percent more than I expected. "All right, without looking at your watch, what time is it?"

I shielded my eyes and squinted up at the sun, then over at the shoreline, and back again. "Twelve ten," I finally said.

He looked at his watch and shook his head. "Twelve thirty; not bad."

"What makes you think I'm wrong and that thing is right?"

He held his wrist out and sunshine gleamed off the glass face. "This is a diver's watch. I bought it at the commissary with my last paycheck. The SEALs use these. They have to be accurate."

"The military makes mistakes just like everyone else," I said, realizing it sounded like I was being deeper than I'd intended.

"Yeah, they do. I'd have been a good sailor, Dad."

"You'd have been the best."

We hiked on awhile around a couple of small sand dunes and up the trail we'd been taking since Benji was old enough to walk. As we climbed higher up the large hill, the breeze finally began to sweep off the water — fresh, salty, and cool. Benji and I inhaled a lungful of it at the same time. "My word, I love it here," I said.

"So why did we leave?"

"Better opportunities," I said. "The economy was too seasonal here. Private school ain't cheap, Ben." I looked over the patches of red moss dripping down the sides of a nearby boulder like melted candle wax. Wildflowers bloomed all around us — purple, yellow, and orange — wherever the wind had scattered their seeds. "I'll bet your mom knows the name of every flower here."

Benji stopped walking. "What's going on with you two anyway?"

I didn't stop. "I told you about her fender bender, right?"

"You should have told me when it happened, and I wish you'd stop calling it that. A fender bender doesn't cause amnesia. The accident had to have been pretty bad to give her a concussion."

"It really wasn't much more than that." I picked up my pace, wanting to outrun the questions.

He caught up to me again, keeping stride easily with his long legs. "Whatever. Is her memory back?"

I shook my head and braced myself for the inquisition I knew would follow. Two seagulls circled overhead like a pair of vultures, then headed back toward the pier. "Not exactly."

I found a rock big enough for the two of us to sit on and caught him up to speed, leaving out the worst, of course. He picked a piece of tall, dry grass from the ground and chewed it, as he stared at three men on a fishing boat dragging in their net. It looked like a decent catch from where we were. "So, you're living at home, and Mom has no idea that you were separated? And no one's going to tell her?"

"The doctor says it's best for her to remember on her own."

"Why?"

"He said in her mind we were kinda like newlyweds. She doesn't remember the past few years and how bad things had gotten."

He pulled the grass from his mouth and wiped debris from his tongue. "I didn't think things were that bad between you."

I looked at him. "C'mon, Benji, don't act like you didn't know we had problems."

"I know you fought a lot, but lots of parents fight. I always knew you loved each other."

"Well, she does now."

"Wow," he said. "Does she remember me?"

I stood and brushed off the cold dirt from the back of my jeans. "Of course she remembers you."

His face turned red, which only made his eyes look bluer in the sunshine. "I mean about the Navy and all that."

"She knows," I said. "That's why I sent

her with your Aunt Marnie — so she wouldn't have so much time to worry about you."

He pushed off the boulder. "She's worried about me, and I'm worried about her." He looked off into the distance. "Hey, let's go see if Sonny's by the Sea is still there. Man, they had good oysters."

We walked back down the side of the hill, this time with me following him.

He looked back over his shoulder. "I'm sure Mom would have let you come home, eventually. You guys have been together forever."

"People split up every day," I said. "People who've been together a lot longer than we have."

"Not you and Mom."

I let him have his fantasy and hoped he'd let me have mine. "So, how long do you think it would have taken her to forgive me?"

He stopped, shielded his eyes, and looked up at the sun. "Three months and four days."

I tried to laugh but felt more like crying. He was probably right. She'd most likely have eventually forgiven me for the e-mail, and maybe with counseling and time we could have continued like we had the past few years, me on the guest bed and her in ours. But how long could I have gone on that way? The loneliness was killing me. I mean that in the most literal sense.

"What time is she coming home tomorrow?"

"I'm picking her and your Aunt Marnie up first thing in the morning," I said. "Why? You want to come?"

He scrunched his face, indicating he'd rather not.

A sudden gale blew sand at us. I turned to keep it from getting in my eyes and watched Benji do the same. After a second it died down, and we continued on.

Ahead, we saw the old restaurant overgrown with weeds. The wood siding was falling off in places, and a tear ripped through the roof. Rodents and seagulls now called it home. With a troubled look, Benji met my gaze. "What happened to it?"

"I don't know." Then I remembered my mother telling me about a hurricane a few years back that flattened a few of the older structures and took out part of the pier. "Hurricane Janey, I think. Remember that?"

He ran his fingertips across the splintered shingles and looked up at the neon sign that never did have all its letters lit at one time. "This place is like my childhood. I can't believe it's gone."

"Change is hard," I said, or maybe I just thought it.

"You know Mom always wanted to play the piano here."

"Is that right?"

"She thought that Sonny never hired her because he was prejudiced."

"Against redheads?" I asked, confused.

Benji made a face. "No. His father fought in World War II."

The truth hit me. "So the Japs were good enough to spend their money here, just not good enough to work here?" I thought back to how Sonny treated me. I hadn't picked up on him not liking me, but then Kyra always said I was oblivious to that sort of thing. I guess sometimes that could be a blessing. "She never told me."

"She didn't tell me either." He squatted and scooped up a handful of sand. "I overheard her talking to Aunt Marnie on the phone a long time ago." Looking deep in thought, he smiled and let the sand spill through his fingers.

"What?"

"I just remembered that I told her when I grew up I would buy it for her, and she could play anytime she wanted."

That was our Benji. "You sure do love

your mama."

He gave the restaurant a closer look. "Maybe I still can."

"In this condition I'm sure you can get a good deal, but that still doesn't make it free."

"I'll get a job. I just want to see us all happy again, like when we were here." He looked more defeated than when we'd left the house.

"Can we go now?" I asked. I was sorry I brought him. It hadn't been my intention to heap on more disappointment. Just to remind him of better times. Somehow I guess I'd managed to do both.

TWENTY-SEVEN

Benji and I exchanged unimpressed glances as Kyra prattled on about Marcello, a designer she and Marnie had met in Italy. I tried not to be jealous, but the way she talked about him, you'd think the guy walked on water. She picked up a roll. "Besides being an incredible designer — and I mean incredible — he plays the violin like an angel." She smiled between Benji and me as if this should amuse us somehow.

Happy day, a musician too, I thought. He probably was a great dancer, poet, and lover as well.

A kid shrieked in the booth behind us. The parents shushed her, which only made her shriek louder. Kyra threw a glance over her shoulder as she buttered her roll. "Get it? He plays the violin and his nickname is Cello."

Benji took a sip of his soda. "Cute." He looked about as thrilled as I was. I guess he didn't like his mother gushing over another man any more than I did.

Her smile faded as she looked back and forth between us. "I just thought it was funny that he played a string instrument."

"Yeah, we get it," I said, although I really hadn't until she explained it. "So, in a nutshell —" I cracked yet another crab leg I had no intention of eating — "you had a great time and Marnie found the next big thing."

She set the roll back down. "She's going to personally introduce him to a designer — Panachee, I think she said. Apparently this woman is a really big deal."

I pushed away my plate full of mutilated king crab legs. "I never heard of her. Why didn't you tell me about this guy when I was there?"

"I mentioned him," she said looking uneasy.

"No, you didn't. You sure you don't want me to drive you back to the airport so you can return to Milan and hang out with him?"

She shook her head at me like I was an insolent child. "He's just a nice guy. Sheesh."

I looked at Kyra's and Benji's barely touched entrees and said, "Since no one's eating, does anyone mind if we go?"

"Great idea," Benji said, a little too enthusiastically.

A neighboring patron pushed away from his table just as our waiter walked by with a full pitcher of tea. Before he could react, it sloshed over the side and right onto our plates. It missed Kyra and Benji, but I, and most of our food, ended up wearing it.

Cold liquid soaked through my shirt, and a handful of ice cubes slid down my front and landed in my lap. Dark amber pooled on my plate and Kyra's. The waiter grimaced. "I'm so sorry; let me get a towel."

I brushed the ice onto my hand as he rushed off.

The person who'd caused the mishap went on talking and laughing, oblivious. Shaking his head, Benji watched him leave. "Excuse you."

The waiter returned with some paper towels. I dabbed them against my shirt and wet hands and tried my best not to sound irritated. "We'll just take the check."

He said it was on the house and continued to apologize, but Kyra in her sweet, disarming way let him off the hook. By the time she finished, she had us all convinced that our meal being ruined was the best thing that could have happened to us.

As we made our way back to the vehicle, I pulled at the cold, wet fabric of my shirt so it wouldn't lie against my skin. With the window now whipping my hair around and drying my shirt, we drove along I-81 with eighteen-wheelers flying by us on all sides.

Kyra turned back to Benji. "Baby, I just want you to know how proud we are of you."

"Proud?" His tone implied he thought her statement ridiculous.

"Of course." I hit my blinker and passed an Accord that didn't understand the concept of a minimum speed limit. "You went after your dream, Ben. That's more than most people do."

I looked in the rearview mirror to find him staring out his window. I wondered what he was thinking, but Kyra went ahead and asked.

"I think it's finally hitting me," he said. "I'm not going to be a Navy man. I'm really being discharged. I couldn't even make it through boot camp. How pathetic is that?"

Kyra reached back and squeezed his leg. "Benjamin, you listen to me. You are the smartest, most kindhearted, loving, giving, God-fearing, wonderful boy I know. Don't you ever, ever sell yourself short. What happened wasn't your fault."

"None of that changes the fact that I'm

out." He let out a sound that was part moan, part whimper. "I'm out."

I glanced in the mirror again to see my son crying. When our eyes met, he covered his. Kyra unbuckled her seat belt, and before I could protest about how dangerous that was, crawled back beside him.

I snuck glances at them. He laid his head on her lap and sobbed in a way I hadn't seen him do since he was a boy. Kyra cried along with him.

When we arrived home, Benji opened his mother's door and helped her out before disappearing inside.

After changing into a clean shirt, I joined Kyra on the couch. "Where's Benji?"

"Upstairs." She laid her head against my chest. "I can't stand to see him this way."

"It's awful," I agreed. "But there's no way through it except through it."

"I just hate it for him."

I bent over her hair and inhaled.

"Are you sniffing me again?"

"You smell like pancakes."

"This is some kind of maple-based treatment Marnie made me try." She grabbed a handful of hair and held it under her nose. "I only did it to make her stop talking about what a wonder-serum it is. You know how obsessive she can be."

"That I do. I like your regular shampoo."

She kissed my neck. "The smell you like is actually my conditioner."

I kissed the top of her head. "Thanks for clearing that up."

Sitting there, with my wife nestled against me, it hit me that whatever it was we'd lost for so long, was actually back — the comfortableness around one another, the mutual respect, the playfulness. I'd forgotten how good it felt to just be with her without all the tension. There wasn't a place on this earth I'd rather be than right here.

I looked over her to the front window. Sunshine poured in as one of the neighbor kids whizzed by on his bike, wearing a baseball hat instead of the helmet he was required to by law.

An idea hit me. "I thought of something that might help Benji."

"What's that?"

"Batting practice."

"Batting practice?"

It wasn't an original idea, but I recognized it immediately as a good one. "It's a great stress reliever. Larry took me there when you and I —" I stopped myself, horrified by what I'd almost said.

She sat up. "When you and I what?"

Above us, something heavy scraped

266

against the ceiling. "Think he's rearranging his room?" I asked, trying to distract her.

"When you and I what?" she repeated.

"When you and I had one of those fights about work or something."

She searched my eyes. "That wasn't what you were going to say."

I picked up the remote off the table. "Yes, it was."

She laid her head back down. "So, hitting bats might make him feel better?"

"No, not hitting bats. That would just hurt. But hitting balls might."

"Maybe a little beer drinking, belching, and scratching too?"

"He's not old enough to drink."

"I was kidding," she said.

"Oh."

"When would you go?"

"Tomorrow."

"Why not now?" She glanced at the window. "It's still early."

Her eagerness to be rid of me hurt my feelings, but I'd always been sensitive that way. "I don't want to leave you the day you get home."

"I don't mind. You two have a guys' night. Take him to that sports bar with the wings you both like for dinner after. I can hang out with Marnie."

She started combing through her hair with her fingers. "She's taking Marcello to Ole's for dinner. If you two aren't going to be around, I'll take a nap, then join them."

"You want to have dinner with him?"

"Not with him. With him and Marnie. I had dinner lots of times with him in Italy, Eric. It's no big deal."

Jealousy bit hard. "You think that's acceptable? Having dinner with a man I don't know?"

A smile played on her lips, which only made me madder. "In this case, yes."

There was only one thing that would make this okay. "Is he gay?"

"If you mean happy, then yes."

"You know what I mean."

"He doesn't like to kiss other men, no."

"Does he like to kiss *you?*" The last remark was out of line, but I only realized it after it flew out of my mouth.

She stood. "I'm not even going to justify that with an answer."

"So it's true," I said.

"Since when did you get so jealous?"

"Is he ugly?"

"No, he's not ugly."

I pictured a young, buff, stallion of a man sitting across the table from my wife, telling her that her eyes sparkled in the candlelight, asking her to pass him the salt just so he could have a reason to touch her hand. I'd kill him. No, I'd kill her. No, I'd kill Marnie.

"Oh, so you're attracted to him. I knew it."

"You don't know jack."

"This is how affairs start, Kyra."

Her eyes narrowed. "Is that right?"

"That's right. You're not going to dinner with some Italian hunk." I knew how ridiculous I was being, especially in light of what I'd done, but I couldn't get my mouth or emotions to agree.

"Yes," she said, her eyes narrowing, "I am." She headed for the stairs.

"Kyra, I'm asking you —"

"You've got to be kidding me," Benji said from the stairs.

My gaze flew to where he stood. "I'm sorry, Ben. We didn't mean to wake you."

The elastic band of his sweatpants had worked its way toward his side, which told me he'd been tossing in bed.

"You guys aren't going to start this back up."

"Start what back up?" Kyra asked.

"I'll move out before I live with you two at each other's throats again."

I made big eyes at him, hoping he wouldn't say more.

He gave me an annoyed look. "Just keep it down, please. I'm gonna try and take a nap."

When he disappeared back up the stairs, Kyra turned to me, looking confused. "I knew things had grown stale, but . . . at each other's throats?"

I licked my lips. "You know teenagers. They love to melodramatize everything."

She looked dejected. "Let's not do that anymore. Benji's got enough to worry about."

"Agreed," I said. "So, you want us to pick you up for dinner after the batting range?"

She was halfway up the stairs when she turned around. "I already told you I'm having dinner with my sister and Marcello."

I figured when she said she didn't want us to fight anymore that meant this discussion was over. Staring up at her, I felt an overwhelming desire to hit something. "Fine. Maybe I'll have dinner with some of my female coworkers then."

"Or maybe you could just do lunch," she said. "Oh, that's right. You already do." A strange look crossed her face. "We've argued about this before, haven't we?"

My blood ran cold when I realized what was happening. *Maybe not,* I told myself. *Look at her face. She's unsure.* There was still time to convince her she was just imagining things.

I started to disagree, but stopped myself. Adding one more lie to the pile was something I just couldn't stomach.

She rubbed her forehead as if the newfound memory gave her a headache. "Why would we fight about you having lunch with your coworkers? Was I that jealous?"

"We've fought about a lot of things," I said. "But we've started over, remember?"

Looking dazed, she slowly nodded. I watched her retreat up the stairs and recalled the last fight we had before she'd found the e-mail. It had been about me having lunch with my female coworkers, one of which was Danielle. I realized two things then: one, that things were not as good between us as they once were, and the same old demons still lurking below would surface; and two, my wife was getting her memory back.

TWENTY-EIGHT

During the long hours Kyra was gone, I sat on the couch, flipping through channels, wondering why there were so many cleaning product infomercials and what my wife might be doing at that moment.

I'd offered numerous times to take Benji out for dinner or to the batting cage, but he maintained he wasn't up for it. I ended up just ordering us a couple of sandwiches from McCallister's down the street, and resigned myself to house arrest.

I raised the corned beef sandwich to my mouth, sniffed the mustard-coated rye bread, then set it down again in its wrapper without taking a bite. I knew I should make myself eat. The only thing I'd taken in all day was a brown-speckled banana, half a pot of coffee, and a roll at the Harbor Inn. Rampant thoughts about Kyra and what she might be doing with Mr. Italiano didn't exactly whet my appetite.

Despite the ridiculousness of it, I couldn't help picturing the two of them going at it like teenagers and eventually moving the party to his hotel room. He was probably loaded and would have one of those penthouse suites that took up an entire floor, a heart-shaped bed, and a giant Jacuzzi that just happened to have a chilled bottle of Dom Perignon and two glasses waiting beside it.

Drawing in a deep breath, I reminded myself of what Marnie had said. Kyra wasn't like that. She hadn't even let *me* get to second base until our wedding night. The front door opened and Benji walked in. Looking at him coming in, I felt disoriented. I hadn't even heard him leave. "Where have you been?"

He gave me the same one-raised eyebrow his mother was famous for and plopped down next to me. "You sure you weren't the one in the accident? I told you I was going next door to see the Harringtons."

"The Harringtons? Why?"

He smelled like hickory smoke. Bram was always grilling up something.

"Because they asked me to."

"When did they do that?"

"At boot camp. They wrote to me."

I was beginning to feel like the whole

world was off. "The Harringtons wrote to you?"

He sat beside me, unlaced his boots, kicked them off, and set his socked feet on the coffee table. Kyra would have a fit. Not because his feet were up there, but because the soles of his socks looked like he smeared them around in a pile of dirt. I wondered how long he'd been wearing them.

"You okay or has Mom's date got you all discombobulated?"

My cheeks grew warm. "Get your feet off the table, I've got food up here, and it's not a date."

"You'd deserve it if it was." He set his feet down. "Even I know you can't pull that macho stuff on the modern woman."

"You think your mother is a modern woman?" Was she? I never really thought about it. Just like the rest of women throughout history, she cooked, cleaned, and made no sense, so I doubted it. "Anyway, it's not a date."

"I know." He slid his hand up his T-shirt and scratched his chest. "I was just picking."

"Well, stop."

We sat there a minute staring at the TV, though if someone had asked me what I was looking at I wouldn't have been able to say.

"So, why were the Harringtons writing you?"

"Because they're nice people and they're interested in my life," he said.

"Yeah, they're nice," I said halfheartedly. *Phony and annoying, but nice.*

Benji eyed my sandwich even though I delivered one just like it to his room an hour before. "What did you get?"

"Same thing as you," I said.

He nodded to the overweight brunette throwing pizza dough in the air on the TV. "What are we watching?"

The woman caught the crust on her fingertips and said in a thick Louisiana accent that she'd be right back after a word from her sponsors. A fabric softener commercial blinked on.

I shrugged and held out the remote to him.

He didn't notice it, because his eyes were glued to the corned beef.

"Take it," I said, waving the remote.

"You sure you don't want it?" He picked up the sandwich.

I set down the remote as I watched my son tear into bread, meat, and Swiss cheese. Five minutes later, the only thing that remained of the sandwich was a smear of yellow mustard on the corner of his mouth.

I wondered if he'd put on a bunch of weight like he had when that girl broke his heart. If we didn't get him over this Navy thing soon, he'd look like Larry.

He ran his tongue over his lips as he flipped through the stations. He set the remote down when he got to what looked like a *Deadliest Catch* knockoff. Icy waves were beating a fishing vessel mercilessly.

"Those guys are crazy," I said.

"I don't know." He looked at me. "I can see the draw of that lifestyle. You know how much money those guys make?"

"You mean if they live?" I said.

"I could buy my own boat."

"You mean if you lived," I repeated.

Right on cue, one of the men caught his foot in a line the others were throwing over the side of the ship. It nearly dragged him into the water. Luckily another crewmember saw it, dove on him in the nick of time, and grabbed on to a thick chain. The other men shot right into action and freed the victim's foot as though they'd performed the move a million times.

Benji and I sat quiet watching while the man rubbed at his leg, choking up as he thanked them for saving his life. I'm sure Benji, like everyone else, saw it as a touching moment; I just saw it as scary. When a commercial came on, he said, "Well, maybe I could do something else to buy a boat."

I'd have thought seeing what we just had would have deterred him. "What's your sudden interest in boats?"

"I've always liked boats."

"What kind of boat would you want to buy?" I was thinking if it was a kayak or canoe I might surprise him with it to take his mind off the Navy.

"A troller. You know, one of those big commercial ones."

I about choked. "You know how much those things cost?"

"Forty-five to sixty-five thousand used from what I could find online. It's cheaper than a college education though, and it would pay for itself in time."

"You want to be a fisherman, Benji?"

He shrugged. "Maybe."

His whole life flashed before my eyes. This wasn't at all what I pictured when Kyra insisted we paint his nursery in bright colors and read to him every night to boost his intelligence. "You know how much they make?"

"I don't care."

"You should," I said. "About twenty-five grand if they're lucky."

He gave me the look all teens were good

at, that made it clear they thought their parents knew squat. "How do you know that?"

"Because before I took the job here, I thought about it myself."

He gave me a curious look. "You?"

"I thought about doing just about everything, just to get out of the car business."

"If you hate it so much why do you do it?"

I raised both hands. "To give you guys this."

His expression gave me the impression he thought I was a fool. Maybe I was. Moving here, making manager, buying into this neighborhood, none of it had brought us happiness in the end. Just a different set of problems. A bigger set.

Benji stared at the TV, watching the captain yell at one of his men. "Once I knew I was probably getting kicked out, I started thinking about what I wanted to be before I got the Navy itch."

I couldn't help but smile at the memory that conjured. "You wanted to be Popeye."

"I still want to be Popeye," he said. "Lots of people in Braddy's Wharf make a living fishing, you know."

I took a sip of my sweet tea, which was watered down now from the melting ice.

"It's a hard life, Ben."

He shifted in his seat like I was making him uncomfortable. *Well, tough,* I thought. *Better to be uncomfortable in your warm, paid-for house than laying in the gutter, penniless five years from now.*

"What isn't?"

"There are easier ways to make money. A lot more money. That's all."

He rolled his eyes. "Money isn't everything."

"You say that because you've never lived without it."

He let out a breath like I'd sucked the life out of him. Seems I was getting good at doing that to people lately. "I kind of thought you'd give college some more thought. You have a business sense about you like no one I've ever seen. The right school could really help you hone that."

He buried his face in his hands and ran his fingers through what little hair he had. "I thought we buried the college discussion when I left the first time."

"Okay, okay, just throwing things out there."

He turned to look at me. "Well, stop throwing. This is my life, not yours. You're the businessman, not me."

"Well, if you're going to make your living

fishing, you have to be one too."

"I just want to fish."

"Well, life doesn't work that way."

He turned sideways to face me. "How does it work, Dad? Tell me. I get married, sell out for a big house in a snooty neighborhood, fight with my wife while my kid listens through the wall wondering when the divorce is going to happen, then get a little something on the side so I can feel better about selling out my dreams?"

I clenched my jaw and felt short, angry puffs of air shoot from my flared nostrils. I wasn't about to discuss my alleged shortcomings with my kid. "You may be a man, but you're still my son. You'll show me respect as long as you live under my roof." I realized then that what made me so angry was that he was exactly right.

He snatched up the remote and flipped the channel, replacing the fishing show with a cartoon. He slammed the remote on the table, knocking the battery from it. It rolled off the table onto the rug. "You know what the Navy taught me? You want respect, you earn it."

TWENTY-NINE

Kyra stayed out so late with her sister and their designer-slash-musician friend that I had fallen asleep on the couch by the time they got back. Rather than take a chance on learning that my wife had remembered more of my indiscretions, I pretended not to wake up when I heard them come in. Although a person would need to have no sense of smell whatsoever to sleep through my sister-in-law's obnoxious perfume.

The next morning Kyra made an emergency appointment with Doctor Hershing, I'm sure to tell him what he already knew. Would she be angry at him for not filling her in, or would he even tell her that he knew? I certainly wouldn't. Not with her temper.

With Benji, Kyra, and even Larry mad at me, I was desperate for advice and, if I was being honest, a little sympathy. So I visited the two people obligated to give it to me.

"She said that?" my mother asked from the other side of her table.

Alfred took a sip from his cup, then shook his head like he'd lost his best friend.

I wrapped my hands around the warm mug Mother had just set in front of me. It smelled more like pumpkin pie than coffee. "I know it's bad."

She bent to pet the elderly Persian Alfred had rescued from the SPCA the week before. He looked like he had mange with his spotty shave job. Mom had finally given up on trying to brush out his knots. He purred like an engine as she stroked him. "Ya think?"

"Thanks, Ma, you're really making me feel better."

"Oh, I'm sorry, did you come here so I would make you feel better?" She pulled the cat onto her lap. "I got nothing." She turned to Alfred. "Hon, you have anything that might make this kid feel better?"

Much to both of our surprise, he said, "I think so, yeah."

She looked at him so long and hard it seemed to me she was trying to extract his thoughts through telepathy. Whatever she saw there seemed to satisfy her. "Why don't you two take a walk? It's a nice day."

"Bah," Alfred said. "Why don't you go

take a walk and leave us men here to talk?"

"With this hip?"

"Go shopping or something. Your hip's always good enough for that."

"I don't want to go shopping. Do we need anything? No. Do we have any money even if we did? No."

"Do you need money?" I asked, hoping she'd say no. It would only blow a hole in her pocket.

"Bah." Alfred stood and picked up his walking stick, the head of which had been carved into a face that looked suspiciously like his. I didn't know if the resemblance was coincidental or not.

He lifted his cardigan from the back of the chair and slipped it on. "Come on, junior."

My parent's apartment backed up to a walking trail that led to a park. As far as I could tell, they never used it. They seldom left the place except to shop.

Even though I had no desire to take a walk, we couldn't have asked for nicer weather. It was a perfect seventy-two, without a cloud in the sky, and the scent of flowers and mulch filled the air.

Alfred walked alongside me, leaning on his stick like a cane. As far as I knew, there was nothing wrong with his legs. I think he used it for the same reason he wore his hair long. He may have looked like a Grateful Dead groupie, but he was more conservative than most Republicans. I suspected he'd been every bit the child of the sixties back when he met my mother, but he'd grown out of that persona long ago. Since she hadn't, he probably decided when in Rome . . .

He stopped and pointed his stick to the brown grass to the right of us. "It's starting to all look like one giant pee spot."

It took me a second to figure out what he meant. "You mean how the grass dies from the dog's uric acid?"

He chuckled. "Uric acid — yeah, smart guy. I say pee, you say the chemical derivative."

"To-may-toe, to-mah-toe," I said.

He smacked his lips. "I'd like to have a big ol' ripe one of those right how. If mother nature don't cooperate, I don't guess we'll be growing any on the patio this year. Your township have y'all on water restrictions too?"

"I don't know. I think so." I waited for a jogger to pass. "What is it you wanted to talk to me about?"

"You Yankees always have to get right to the point, don't you?"

I was born and raised in what I, and everyone else who lived here, considered the tip of the south, but my southeastern Virginia wasn't as far south as his native South Carolina so it was all relative I guess. I wasn't in the mood to argue. If he wanted me to be a Yankee, so be it.

We came across a black metal bench with *Josh rules* spray-painted in white across it.

Alfred looked at the graffiti before he sat. "I bet he don't neither."

"I think that's safe to say." I watched a couple swinging their little boy along the path between them. His melodic laughter made my heart ache. *That used to be us,* I thought, *Kyra, Benji, and me, not so long ago.* I prayed that family wouldn't end up where we had.

A water fountain stood a foot from us, and I figured I'd get a drink while Alfred rested. It might have just been my imagination, but the water here seemed to taste so much sweeter than where Kyra and I lived.

As I pushed down on the pedal, cold liquid hit my lips.

"I ever tell you your mother cheated on me?" Alfred said.

Water spewed from my mouth. I wiped my chin and turned around. A man on a bike rode by, giving me a funny look.

"No," I said. "No, you didn't."

"That's because she didn't. She knows I would have killed her."

"Listen, Al, I'm too tired for nonsense."

He tapped his stick against the ground. "Shush and let me talk."

I sat on the bench beside him and we turned sideways to face one another. A sycamore tree cast a shadow over our feet.

"What happened to you two?" Alfred asked. His once-blue eyes now looked more gray from the cloudiness of age. "I remember the day you came home with this cheese-eating grin telling your mother and me that you met the woman you were going to marry. Your courtship was so fast it gave everyone whiplash. She and I both said it wouldn't last a year. Now, look at you."

I already felt miserable and he wasn't helping. "Yeah, look at us."

"My point is that you've been married twenty years. That's a long time in this day and age. How many of those years would you say were good?"

He was starting to sound like Doctor Hershing. "All of them up until maybe two years ago."

"So, eighteen — that's 80 percent. How many marriages you think last that long and are 80 percent good if they do?"

His math was off, but I decided it helped nothing to correct him. "I guess I should be happy with what we had, huh?"

"No, you should try to make it twenty more."

"She's going to divorce me."

He stopped and looked at me. "No, she isn't. You know how many times in our marriage your mother threatened to divorce me?"

I figured the question was rhetorical, but when he didn't continue, I finally shrugged. "A gazookin, at least. I've threatened it too. People say stuff."

"I don't remember you guys fighting."

A group of teenage runners buzzed past us like a swarm of bees.

"Our fights were more cold wars than nuclear ones." We sat in silence for a few minutes before he continued. "In our forty years together, your mother and I have gone through more than our fair share of droughts, but we always get back to where we need to be."

I began to wonder if maybe Alfred was right, that we were just cycling through and would eventually swing back around to contentment again. Still, years of resentment seemed like a little more than a simple dry spell. "Whatever love she had for me dried up years ago. This isn't a drought, Alfred; it's a desert." Yes, that's exactly what had happened. We'd both immersed ourselves in our separate lives. We stopped touching and talking . . . and until recently, even caring.

Alfred stabbed his stick into a fallen leaf. "Without the desert, an oasis is just another watering hole."

"What?"

"I've seen the way she looks at you, Son. That desert's about as dry as rain."

I thought about this a minute and decided he was either saying what he thought I wanted to hear or else seeing what he wanted to. "Judging by how dry our rain is lately, I'd say you're about right," I said.

I waited for his *bah.* Instead he stood, a piece of the leaf still clinging to the end of his stick. "The rain stays away for a while, sometimes a long while, but it always comes back." He turned his head suddenly. "You smell that?"

I sniffed the air. "Hot dogs?"

"Hot Dog Ronny's, baby! You bring your wallet?"

I patted my back pocket for the familiar lump and nodded. "I thought you were a vegetarian."

"Only when your mother's around."

He would have gotten a laugh out of me if I wasn't so miserable. We started walking along the narrow strip of asphalt again, heading toward the smell of meat. "What I'm trying to tell you, Eric, is hang in there. She'll come around. She loves you. I know that sure as I know that your mother loves me."

"Sometimes love isn't enough," I said, "like with my father. He claimed to love Mom and me, but actions speak louder than words. I'm sure that's how Kyra probably feels about what I did."

"Maybe so. You know, maybe if you forgive your father, karma will let Kyra forgive you."

It was all I could do not to roll my eyes. "I'm afraid I'm not much of a karma man," I said.

"There ain't a religion out there that don't preach karma in one form or another. Christianity included. 'Reap what you sow' ring a bell?"

"I don't think it works quite the way you're implying."

"Maybe it does, maybe it don't; but since we're on the subject, I think you should forgive your father either way. The people who need the most forgiveness ought to do the most forgiving. Your Bible say anything about that?"

"It talks about forgiveness," I said.

"Good."

When we approached the silver hot dog wagon with the Hot Dog Ronny's logo spray-painted on the side, I pulled out my wallet. "How many you want?"

Alfred looked at me like I'd lost my mind. "You know I'm a vegetarian."

After staring him down, I apologized to the vender and turned back to my stepfather. "You just said —"

"Bah, I just like to pretend. My being a vegetarian makes your mother happy. If I go and eat that delicious tube of heaven, how would I look her in the eye?"

"So, why did you ask me to buy you one?"

"I just like to pretend," he said. "Now pretend to be the man your wife married and go and give her the apology she's waiting for."

THIRTY

I actually felt hopeful as I drove home to Kyra. The more I thought about it, the more I realized that Alfred was right. She would be mad and hurt for a long time, but a flirtatious e-mail wasn't enough to make her divorce me. She just wanted to make me suffer, and be sure that I knew how much I had hurt her.

She still wasn't aware of the actual sex part, and she never had to be, as far as I was concerned. Danielle seemed to be over it, and the only other person who knew was Larry. He might hate my guts at the moment, but he, like every other red-blooded American man, knew the code — you didn't rat out another man to a woman, unless she was your sister or mother . . . or you wanted her for yourself. None of which pertained to Larry's relationship with my wife. At least it had better not.

So, all I had to do was give her a heartfelt

and sincere apology, do a little groveling, and convince her that the flirtation was just a symptom of our sick marriage, which was the absolute truth. I'd promise her counseling, that Holy Land trip she'd always wanted to take, or whatever else she thought would help us move forward.

I expected her to be mad. I expected her to get even. I did not, however, expect her to be leaving to go on a job interview.

"Why shouldn't I get a job?" she said as she looked at herself in the full-length mirror on the back of our closet door. She wore her hair pulled back into a fancy knot at the nape of her neck. Her white silk blouse dipped at the neckline, just enough to show off a few freckles and a shadow of cleavage.

"Why should you? It's not like we need the money. Do I not provide everything you could possibly need?"

In the reflection of the mirror she gave me a hard look. "No, you do not." Her voice cracked ever so slightly and I saw something in her eyes that told me she was bluffing. I knew that Alfred was right; she was going to forgive me.

She sat on the bed and picked up one of the heels sitting beside it. She slipped it on.

"So, where are you applying for jobs?" I asked, still trying to figure out how to launch into my confession-slash-apology.

"Tambourine's."

"Are you going to wait tables?"

She clicked her tongue in disgust as she stood. "No, I'm going to wash dishes."

"Was that a ridiculous question? You don't have a degree. You have no marketable skills, except playing the piano." The lightbulb finally went on. "But they already have a regular pianist. Besides, you don't want to work there."

"They fired him, and don't tell me where I want to work."

"I just think you could do better."

She headed for the bedroom door. "My mother thought that too." She turned and gave me a slow once-over. "So did my friends. Maybe I should have listened."

The jab was meant to hurt, but knowing her state of mind shielded me from the full impact. I'd need tough skin in the days to come. As soon as I came clean with her, she'd be shooting darts at me left and right hoping to draw a little blood. If we were going to weather this, I couldn't let her drain me dry or else I'd be the one wanting to walk. If we could get past it, we might just cycle back like Alfred said. I desperately wanted to get back to where we were just yesterday when I was still her samurai.

Sitting on the couch, I listened to her car back out of the garage. I hadn't seen Benji all morning, so I decided to make another attempt at father-son bonding. I went upstairs and knocked on his bedroom door. There was no response. "Ben," I called. "Benji, you in there?" I tried the knob, but it was locked. I shouldn't have been worried — Benjamin was a solid kid — but still with his being booted from the Navy and then our fight yesterday, I was more than a little concerned. I banged harder, and then frantically. "Benji, open up!"

The doorknob turned and he poked his head out. He still wore the same clothes he had on the day before along with a five o'clock shadow. He looked confused as he pulled the earbuds out and let them dangle from his hands. "What's up?"

"Did you hear me? I was screaming."

He held up his iPod. "Sorry. Music."

We just stood there looking at each other. Finally I said, "I'm going to go see if I can buy Larry lunch. Why don't you come with me?"

"Where's Mom?"

"On a job interview."

He furrowed his brow. "Job interview?"

"She wants to play the piano at Tambourine's."

"Hey, that's what she was doing when you two met." Kyra had told him the story a hundred times. Probably ninety-nine more than he had wanted to hear it.

"That's right."

"Makes sense."

"What makes sense?"

"When stuff starts falling apart, people want to go back to safety. Kind of like me with Braddy's Wharf."

It did make sense. My mind was on Benji more than Kyra, though. No wonder he wanted to be a fisherman. "I'm sorry I put your dream down."

He waved his hand in dismissal. "Don't be. You were right. It's impractical. I mean, I'm a man now; it's time to put away childish dreams and face reality."

I should have been pleased with his response, but the flat way he said it and the dull look in his eyes made me uncomfortable. "Ben, you okay?"

"Better than okay."

"Yeah?" I asked, unsure.

"I think I'm going to apply for college."

My smile threatened to split my face. "Virginia Tech is a great school — Hokies, baby. Of course I wouldn't be unhappy with Chapel Hill. Go Heels!"

He sniffed and looked back into his room

as if he had something pressing to get back to. "I'll apply to both."

"Are you leaning toward a BA? You know I'd continue straight on for your MBA. We'll try for scholarships of course, but don't worry, we'll get a loan, whatever we have to do."

"Yeah, Dad, sounds great." He started to close the door.

For someone who'd just made a decision to change his life for the better, he sure didn't look happy. I put my foot in the door to keep him from closing it. "You okay, Benji?"

"I just need time to let old dreams die, you know?"

I laid my hand on his rough cheek. "Yeah, I do, Son. Every man does."

He scratched his neck. "Growing up is the pits."

"Not all the time," I said. "Just most of it."

He gave me a half smile.

"So, what about you and me taking Larry to lunch?"

He cleared his throat. "I really don't feel like it."

"It'll be good for you," I said.

He hung his head. "Sure, Dad, whatever you think."

He opened the door, and I saw his room was in even rougher shape than he was with plates and glasses scattered about the floor, his bed unmade, and the clothes he brought home still hanging half in, half out his sea-bag.

"You might want to take a shower," I said. "And shave. We have time."

"Aye-aye," he said with a two-finger salute, and closed the door.

Thirty-One

A long time ago, when I was feeling guilty about leaving my first job for greener pastures, Alfred took me aside for a man-to-man talk. He set a pot of water in front of me and told me to make a fist and immerse it. Feeling foolish, I reluctantly obeyed.

"The hole you'll leave when you take your hand out is the hole you'll leave at that job of yours when you go," he'd said.

I hated to admit it, but it was as true today as it was back then. Thompson's was running just fine without me.

Benji panned the showroom. "Wow, this place looks different than the last time I was here."

I glanced around to see if I could spot Larry. "You were a lot shorter then."

It was noisier than usual. Car horns were being tested out on opposite ends of the lot outside, while in here it was hard to hear over all the talking, overhead announcements, and car doors slamming. It was busier than it had been in a long time because of a two-day sale I'd forgotten all about. There would be some major money made today. I couldn't help but feel jealous that I wouldn't be in on any of the commissions.

Thompson, who had been talking to the receptionist, turned and waved at us.

Benji slipped up his hand in response. "Who's that?"

"My boss."

He studied him. "Oh yeah. He's gotten old."

"Happens to the best of us," I said.

As Thompson approached, he reeked of the cologne he used to attempt to hide the cigarette stench. It only made him smell, of course, like cologne *and* cigarette smoke. "How's my best employee?" he asked.

"I'm good," I said. "Just ready to be back."

"I was talking about this fine young man." He chuckled and fake-punched Benji's arm.

Benji gave me a weary side glance.

"So, when you coming to work for me, boy? If you're anything like the workhorse your father is, you'll be running this joint in no time."

"He'll have to take a rain check on that." I wrapped an arm around Benji's shoulder.

"My son here's going to be heading off to college in the fall."

Thompson grinned, revealing a piece of what looked like some kind of meat caught between his bottom front teeth. "Is that right? What are you going to study?"

When Benji didn't answer, I said, "He's going for his MBA." I figured if that wasn't right, he would have corrected me. I was thrilled when he didn't.

"A go-getter, I like that." Thompson turned to me and patted my shoulder. "You enjoy the rest of your R & R, Yoshida, and get back here quick as you can. We're a mess without you."

I looked around the showroom floor with customers running their fingers down polished paint, salesmen standing by to close the deal, and the finance department running numbers. Even though it was an obvious lie, I thanked him just the same.

Jacobson walked by. "Hey, man, can't stay away?" He carried a cup of coffee that was most likely meant for the tall Barbie type eyeing one of our most expensive models.

"You seen Larry?" I asked him.

He pointed to Thompson's office.

Jealousy nipped at me, but I forced it away. Just because Larry was hanging out there didn't necessarily mean anything, and

I was here to make peace regardless. I stuck my head in Ruby's door. She turned her nose up at me as usual.

"Hey, Ruby. Is Larry Wallace in there?"

She folded her hands and set them on whatever form she'd been reading. Glancing over her shoulder at Thompson's closed door, she said coolly, "He is."

"Can you tell him I'm here to see him?"

Larry must have heard me because the door swung open. On his chin, smooth skin replaced the goatee he'd worn as long as I knew him, and he had donned a three-piece suit that actually fit him. He looked sharp for a change, though I couldn't say so without risking him calling me gay.

"Hey, bro, I thought you were still on vacation," he said, looking like nothing had ever happened between us.

I hadn't realized how tense my muscles had been until they relaxed. "I thought if we were cool, we'd buy you lunch."

"We're always cool." He looked over my shoulder. "Who's we?"

I smiled. "My son and I."

His face lit up. "Benji? Where?"

I pointed toward the showroom.

"Sweet, I'm starving. Let me just run it by Thompson."

Ruby, who was now tapping away on her

computer, looked up. "I'll tell him you've gone. He couldn't care less when you take your lunch. Believe me, he'll be happy for the break."

When Larry frowned at her, she added, "Nothing personal."

"You know," I said, "one of us is going to be your boss pretty soon. I'd think it would behoove you to at least try to pretend you can stand us."

She smiled smugly. "I'm retiring the day he does."

"Glad to hear it," I said. "Nothing personal."

Her cheeks mottled as her nose rose higher in the air. She typed twice as fast.

Larry turned to me. "So, where we going?"

"Let's leave it up to my eating-machine of a son."

When we returned to Benji, I found him talking to Danielle. My blood turned to ice.

Danielle's eyes glinted with humor as she looked at me. "Wow, Eric, you didn't tell me your son was such a fox."

My skin crawled as her hand touched down on his arm. As usual, she was dressed to draw attention to her body in a thigh-length skirt and plunging neckline. When her attention was fixed on me, I couldn't help but notice my son checking out her legs. She turned in time to notice it too. A knowing smile slithered across her lips.

She fingered her low-lying necklace, successfully drawing Benji's eyes upward. "Well, Benjamin, it's so nice to finally meet you after hearing so many wonderful things. Your father really needs to update the picture of you he has on his desk, though. You're definitely not that little boy anymore. What are you, twenty now?"

His eyes were fixed on her fingers still toying with her necklace. "I'm nineteen, and you can call me Benji."

It occurred to me then that she was much closer in age to my son than to me. I wondered if they would have hit it off if she had met him before she and I hooked up. It weirded me out to think she might have been my daughter-in-law if things had gone a different way.

"Benji," she repeated softly, her gaze still glued to him.

I decided it was time to end this little party. "Yeah, well, we need to get going. Catch you later, Dani."

I put a hand on Benji's back and ushered him forward. Larry followed us. When we stepped out of the dealership, sunlight left me blind for a second as my eyes adjusted.

Shielding them, I pointed to the general area where I'd parked. "We're over there."

"How about if I drive?" Larry said.

I was about to argue that my SUV was closer but stopped myself. "That'd be great. Thanks."

He gave me a double take.

"Hey, I can change," I said.

As we drove along the main strip, he looked at Benji in the rearview mirror. "Where we headed to, sailor?"

I thought Benji would jump on him like he had me when I referred to him as a squid, but he just said, "General Tso's chicken would be good."

Larry did his famous man-grunt. "A fine military choice. Great Wall Buffet it is!"

Once checked into the restaurant, the three of us stood side by side in front of the Plexiglas-protected buffet. The air smelled of sesame oil, ginger, and soy sauce. Larry piled his plate high with just about everything they had to offer, with the exception of anything resembling a vegetable. I mostly stuck to my old standbys — beef with broccoli and lo mein. Benji's plate remained empty except for two lonely nuggets of General Tso's. When he saw me looking disapprovingly at his plate, he plopped a heap of chow mein onto it. Unless something had changed in the Navy, Benji hated chow mein.

We sat in a booth, Benji and I on one side, Larry on the other. I was pleased when Benji offered to say grace.

Larry wasted no time shoveling food into his mouth. We all ate silently for a few minutes, except for Benji, who just pushed noodles around with the cheap, throwaway chopsticks that he hadn't even bothered to split apart.

Larry took a drink of his Coke. "Hey, Ben, you not liking my restaurant choice?"

He shook his head. "I've just got a lot on my mind."

"Your dad told me." Larry speared two shrimp with his fork. "So what's the next step?"

Benji didn't look up. "I just wait for them to make it official and then get to work on plan B."

"Ant bites? Man, that must have been one heck of a reaction."

"I swelled up like a water balloon."

"That's scary," Larry said. "I wouldn't think on a ship you'd run into too many fire ants, though."

"That's what I said, but they told me we didn't know what I'd be running into in the line of duty. I wouldn't be out to sea a hundred percent of the time."

"You'd think they'd just let you carry around one of those shot pen things like I do for bee stings."

Benji turned over a miniature corncob with his chopstick. "You'd think."

The waiter came by and filled our water glasses even though none of us had taken more than a sip. We each mumbled a thanks.

"So, what's plan B?" Larry said with his mouth full.

"I guess I'll go to college."

"You sound thrilled."

"It's not what I planned, you know?"

"You ever hear that saying that we make plans and God laughs?" Larry twirled lo mein onto his fork.

Benji finally took a bite, probably so he wouldn't have to talk.

"What will you major in?" Larry asked.

Benji looked at me to answer for him.

"He's thinking about getting his MBA."

"Why?" Leave it to Larry.

"Why what?" Benji asked.

"Why business?"

"Because he's a whiz at it," I said.

He locked eyes with Benji. "Ben? Why business?"

Benji took a sip of his Sprite. "It's as good a field as any. At least I'll have the potential to support a family someday."

"Wow," Larry said.

"Wow, what?" I asked.

Overhead, Asian instrumental music cut in suddenly when a second group of patrons entered the restaurant.

"Wow, that's so not what your son wants," Larry said, looking serious.

My fork clanked against the plate as I dropped it. "How can you say that? You don't know what he wants."

"MBA — wasn't that *your* dream, Eric?"

Why was he picking another fight? "No, it wasn't my dream, Larry. It's something I wanted him to do before he decided on the Navy, but —"

"Guys, please," Benji said. "MBA is fine. It's not like I have a better plan."

"Oh, come on," Larry said. "There's got to be something that fires you up."

If Larry wanted to be a parent, he should have his own kids. What did he know about making sure his family's future was secured? He needed to step off, and I was about ready to tell him so.

"I like the ocean," Benji mumbled.

Larry shoved another bite in his mouth, chewed a couple of times, and swallowed. "Okay. Great. Oceanographer. What about that?"

"What's that?"

I was suddenly a third wheel completely out of the conversation.

"It's a . . . Well, I don't know but I'm pretty sure it has to do with the ocean."

"Huh," Benji said, considering it.

"Or a marine biologist. They study the sea creatures, I think."

"I don't want to study them," Benji said. "I kind of just want to catch and eat them."

I pasted on a smile. "There's no jobs out there for seafood eaters, Ben." I ripped my teeth into a bit of spring roll. I could kill Larry for trying to get Benji on this rabbit trail when he'd finally decided on school.

"Maybe not," Larry said. "All I'm saying is you need to find your passion. Life's too short to spend most of your waking hours in a job you're miserable in."

"Dad does," Benji said.

"I do not."

Benji finally broke apart his chopsticks and held the two, now separate, sticks the way I'd taught him long ago. "Yeah, you do. You've said it yourself. You only do it for the money."

I felt heat rising up my neck. "I love cars."

"Yeah, just not selling them," Benji mumbled.

Larry furrowed his brow. "You don't like

what you do?"

"I wouldn't say that." I glanced at my watch, hoping it was time to go. We still had a little time unfortunately. "It just doesn't inspire me."

Larry gave me a funny look. "Really?"

How the conversation suddenly turned into an attack on my job preference, I didn't know, but I was suddenly feeling under attack for the one thing I was actually doing right in my life. "Be honest, Lar. Does it inspire you?"

"Yeah," he said. "I guess it does."

Yeah right, I thought, but I didn't say it. I was sick of fighting, and if he wanted to pretend to be inspired by pushing metal, let him.

The way I figured it, inspiration was for artists and dreamers, and apparently Larry. Perspiration would have to do for regular people like Benji and me.

THIRTY-TWO

Somehow Benji and I had beaten Kyra home. When she finally came in, instead of greeting me, she went straight to the kitchen and returned carrying a dust rag and bottle of furniture polish. Looking over the top of my newspaper, I watched her place books back on the shelf she'd just dusted.

I took it she didn't get the job.

Her voice was barely a whisper. "You'll be happy to know they rehired their old pianist."

"Why would that make me happy?" It was true that I didn't want her working in those kinds of places. It was like seeing a Monet hanging in a fast-food restaurant. But I certainly wasn't happy that she was upset.

She slid off her suit jacket and looked around the house as she laid it on the back of the dining room chair. "Where's Benji?"

"Upstairs." I folded the paper in half and set it on the end table beside my chair.

"Why were you gone so long?"

I braced myself for her to tell me that once again she was painting the town with Marcello. I'd had quite enough of that man.

"I was out with Cello." She stopped dusting long enough to study my reaction. "I was helping him buy a new car."

"Is that right?" She had managed to hit two of my hot buttons with one stone, and she knew it. "Why didn't you tell me your boyfriend needed a car? That is, after all, what I do. It's what pays for your little outings and European vacations."

Her eyes turned into slits. "I took him to your dealership, *darling*, but you weren't working today, remember?"

"If he's buying a car, that means he's staying in the States?"

"That's right," she said smugly.

I immediately thought of Danielle. Blood rushed to my face so fast I thought I'd pass out. I just prayed they hadn't talked. The only thing I could do was play it cool until I knew for sure.

"Who sold you the car?"

"Stan Jacobson."

"Did he give you a fair price?"

"Better than fair. He cut him a deal and Marcello insisted he split the commission with you."

"How thoughtful of him." So, Mr. International thought he could buy me off? I thought of my wife showing up at my place of business with a handsome Italian in tow, instead of me, and how that must have looked to the guys. It hurt my pride and ticked me off at the same time, but I knew it would have been hypocritical to say so.

When she crossed her arms, I knew I was in trouble. "Guess who took his check?"

I was still picturing the two of them touching and laughing right out in the open where everyone could see them when I remembered that Danielle was now F&I.

Kyra's face distorted in anger. "That's right. Your girlfriend, Dani. You know what that tramp had the audacity to ask me?" She stared at me expectantly as if she really expected me to guess. *"If I knew."*

I could barely hear her over the pulse pounding against my eardrums.

"If I knew," she repeated as she rubbed her rag hard enough against the wood to take off the finish.

Feeling light-headed, I covered my face.

"I told her very calmly that yes, I did." She turned around. "You should have seen the look on her face. She didn't expect me to say that, I can tell you that. She thought she was going to shock me, I guess."

I sat there waiting helplessly for the guillotine to drop.

"I told her I'd forgiven you, and we were doing better than ever." She let out a mirthless laugh. "Her jaw hit the floor."

I dared to peek at her. "Really, that's what you said?"

Her eyes shot laser beams of death at me. "I lied, Eric. Just like you did."

She threw her rag down and began pacing the floor, her ankles wobbling every so often in the heels she seldom wore. "How old is she? Is she even Benji's age?" She shook her head. "It all makes sense now. Why your jacket smelled like watermelon the day you brought me home from the hospital. You'd probably come straight from her bed! How could you? How could you carry on these past weeks as if that hadn't happened? How could you act like everything was fine between us, when you'd already destroyed our marriage?"

Knowing anything I said could and would be used against me, I chose to remain silent.

I caught a glimpse of movement from the corner of my eye and turned to find Benji standing in the kitchen doorway. He'd heard every word.

Kyra turned to see what I was looking at. "Benji, your dad and I need privacy."

Benji walked over and picked up each of our hands, just like he used to do when he was little and found us arguing. "Mom, I know what he did was awful, but trust me, so does he."

She gave him a hurt look as she slid her hand from his. "Your father cheated on me, Benjamin. I'm entitled to be mad."

Benji stepped back, looking unsure.

"Kyra, please," I said. "This isn't his fault. You're embarrassing him."

She looked on the verge of tears. "*I'm* embarrassing him? You're the one who did this. You're the one who's embarrassed our family. You know how stupid I felt to find out you cheated on me with that girl?"

Kyra covered her face and began to sob. I motioned with a nod for Benji to go to his room.

I watched my wife for a moment and then took a chance and pulled her to my chest. I held her as she cried into my neck.

After a few minutes, she pulled back and wiped the tears and mascara from under her eyes. She looked up at me and touched the tears I hadn't even realized I'd cried, with the saddest expression. When she laid her hand on my cheek, I thought she was going to say something to comfort me, utter

314

forgiveness or an apology of her own. Instead she whispered, "Please leave."

THIRTY-THREE

I looked over my shoulder at Larry, who had just walked through the door carrying a grocery bag.

"What a circus," he said.

"When isn't work a circus?" I asked. "Hey, thanks for letting me move back in."

"Mi casa es su casa." He walked the bag to the kitchen and I followed.

I watched him put away a bunch of diet food — protein shakes, rice cakes, diet soda, and even carrot sticks and a bag of apples. "What ya got there?" I asked.

"Just decided it's time to make a few changes."

I raised my eyebrows. "Wow. I never thought I'd live to see the day Larry Wallace went on a diet."

With his hands buried in a place I doubted they'd ever been before — the fruit and vegetable drawer of his refrigerator — he turned and gave me a harsh look. "Not a diet. I'm just trying to eat a little better. We're not going back to work and announcing I'm on a diet, understand?"

"But you are."

He stood and closed the fridge door. "You want to get a hotel room?"

"Fine, you're not on a diet. So, how'd the two-day sale treat you? You make some serious bills?"

He grabbed a diet soda and set it on the cocktail table, before kicking off his dress shoes into the pile by the door. He performed his version of the moonwalk, then made a V for victory on each hand, raising them high above his head. For the finale, he hung his head with thc Vs still raised to the ceiling. Sweat stains marked his armpits.

I hit the mute button on the remote, and the canned sitcom laughter was gone. "That good, huh?" Flickering light from the television made the room glow, dim, and glow again.

Larry made guns with his hands and blew on the make-believe barrels of both. "I was on fire, man. Hat trick, baby. Three cars — out — the — door." He curled his lip up Elvis-style. "Thank you. Thank you very much."

"Well, you sure had a better day than I did."

He loosened the knot of his tie and slid it over his head. "I made enough to buy that ultimate home gym thing I've been wanting. You know what Thompson said today?" He smiled. "That I'm irreplaceable."

"You are," I said, "and not just at work. You think you're really going to use that gym? It would make an awfully expensive coat rack."

He patted his gut. "You ever know me to say I'm going to start eating better and working out?"

I shook my head. "Can't say I have."

"That's because until now I had no desire to. You know I only started eating like this when Tina cheated on me. I think I've been trying to kill myself with food ever since. Stuff happened at work today that made me realize that it's time to move on and stop letting what she did rule my life. I might actually have something to offer a good woman someday, and when that day comes, I want her to want me for my body as well as my mind."

"Wow," I said. "Sounds like someone's been watching Oprah."

"You're a funny man."

"My wife doesn't think so," I said. "Did you see Kyra come in with her boyfriend, Marcello?"

Larry plopped on the couch beside me. It made a *whoosh* sound like he'd knocked the air out of it. "I saw a lot of stuff today, but not that. I was doing a test drive with a couple bent on seeing the entire city. They put so many miles on the car, if they hadn't bought it, I would have been ticked. I heard when I got back that Kyra was in there with some old Italian helping him buy a car."

"Old?"

"Stan told me he was like a million years old or something." He picked up his diet soda and popped the can. "Thompson said he was glad the dude was paying cash because he probably didn't have four years left in him to make the loan."

"Marcello's old?" I asked again. All the times I pictured him, not once was it with age spots.

"Yeah, old and rich apparently. I mean I guess that was him. Jacobson said he was a happy, old Italian man. She can't know more than one Marcello, can she?" He kicked his feet onto the table. "Listen, I'm sorry about Kyra. But at least everything's out in the open now. That's got to feel good."

"Not particularly," I said, still trying to wrap my mind around Marcello being ninety. I owed Kyra yet another apology.

He nodded toward the TV. "Watching anything good?"

I shook my head. "A hundred and fifty channels and nothing on."

He took a swig from his can and grimaced. "So, how mad is she?"

"She wants a divorce." I crumpled my empty, full-calorie soda can and tossed it across the living room, actually hitting the kitchen garbage for a change.

I unmuted the TV and stared at the screen, not really seeing or hearing it. My mind was again on Kyra and what she might be doing at this very moment. Probably thumbing through the yellow pages for a lawyer.

Larry unfastened his top two buttons and stood. "Let me get out of this monkey suit so I can fill you in on the Barnum and Bailey show we had at work today." He went into his bedroom and closed the door.

After a few minutes his door opened, and he reemerged wearing purple pajama bottoms and a matching T-shirt.

I looked over my shoulder at him and laughed. "You look like Barney."

"Wanna know what you look like?" Not waiting for a response, he went into the kitchen.

The refrigerator door opened and shut.

He walked out holding two rice cakes and collapsed on the couch next to me. He held one out.

"I'll pass on the Styrofoam, thanks."

He bit into one and scrunched his face. "This is going to take some getting used to." He sneered at his diet soda before taking a swig. At least this time his grimace was less dramatic. Maybe he'd get used to the taste. I hoped so. The man was a heart attack waiting to happen.

"So, fill me in. What happened at work?"

"Where to begin? How about if I start with the six o'clock news and save the Jerry Springer episode for last?"

"I'm all ears."

"Thompson officially announced his retirement."

I silenced the TV again and whipped around to face Larry. "You're kidding."

He took another drink. "Nope."

I hadn't expected Thompson to retire for at least a few more months. What was even more surprising was that he chose to announce it while I was off. It didn't look good for me that I was the last to know when I should have been the first.

"Wow."

"I'm just warming up," Larry said. "You ready for the real kicker?"

I was still trying to choke down the first pill; I wasn't sure I was ready to swallow another one. "I don't know. Am I?"

"Danielle and Santana got caught fooling around in the parking lot during hours."

"Get out!" A myriad of emotions hit me, ranging from jealousy to elation, all of which left me feeling soiled.

"Yuppers. Ruby caught them making out in that new white bimmer we just got on the lot." He smiled and shook his head. "That biddy dragged Santana out by his ear all the way to Thompson's office. I told you she used to be a nun."

Danielle and Santana — I just couldn't picture it. "Are you messing with me?"

He took another swig of his drink and chased it with a second bite of rice cake. "Nope."

"So, were they both fired?" It seemed everything that possibly could happen at Thompson's had happened all in one day. Thompson announcing his retirement, Benji meeting Danielle, then her and Kyra's confrontation, and now this. Larry wasn't kidding — it really was a circus . . . and all on sale day.

Larry shook his head. "Wait, I haven't even gotten to the best part. Thompson was still trying to figure out what to do with them when Santana's wife flies into the office and snatches Danielle by the hair."

"No way," I said, riveted with morbid fascination. This was more melodrama than a soap opera. "Man, Santana's wife isn't exactly petite. How'd she find out?"

"That's the weirdest part. Danielle told her herself."

I sat there speechless, trying to make sense of it.

"Yeah," Larry continued. "From what I could piece together, when she and her little lover were brought into the office, to save his job, he claimed she threw herself at him and he was trying to fend off her advances. You know Danielle ain't going to take that lying down, even though that does seem to be her preferred position these days."

He took a sip from his can, like he needed a breather. I couldn't wait to hear the end of it. I hadn't been this riveted since *Fatal Attraction*. "Finish the story," I said.

"So, to get even, Dani calls Mrs. Santana and rats him out, but instead of crying and divorcing him, like Danielle figured she'd do, the woman goes postal on Dani and drags his butt home. Literally, I might add."

"Was Danielle hurt?"

"She just lost a wad of hair, which may or may not have had a little flesh attached to the end of it . . . and her job, of course."

"Man, I missed all the excitement."

"Be glad you weren't there. You could have been implicated."

"That would have made your life easier."

"How do you figure?"

"Good-bye, competition."

"I don't want the job that bad."

I ran a hand through my hair. "Man, I can't believe Danielle and Santana are gone."

"I know, right?"

"That could have just as easily have been me."

Larry set the half-eaten rice cake down on the table and rubbed the back of his neck.

"What if —?"

"Reality check — your what-if has already happened. You're living with me, and she's going to divorce you."

"What can I say? I'm a pathetic excuse for a man." I knew what I was saying was true. It didn't matter what Kyra had done to push me away, I'd made a promise before God for better or for worse, and I broke it. In the end, I was no different than my father after all.

Sliding his legs off the cocktail table, he knocked the mangled box of tissues onto the floor and got a weird look on his face.

"Shoot, what time is it?"

I looked at my watch. "Nine. Why, you got a date or something?"

"Yeah, and so do you."

"Reality check — I'm married."

"Not that kind of date, doofus. I want to show you something I think will cheer you up."

I doubted there was anything that could do that, but figured with him taking me back in on such short notice, I owed it to him to go to Alaska if that's what he wanted.

THIRTY-FOUR

Twenty minutes later, I was dressed in jeans and a hoody standing next to Larry at a bus stop, wondering what we were doing here. "Why are we riding the bus when we have two perfectly good vehicles?"

The night air was cooler than usual, and we were in a part of town I tried not to go through if I didn't have to. A bleached blonde in a waitress uniform sat on the bench beside where we stood, clutching her purse as if we might be waiting to do a grab and run. The air reeked of urine and fried onions.

As it grew nearer to the projected time for the bus's arrival, more people showed up, all working class, all weary looking, all going home after a long day's work as far as I could tell.

An elderly man with a long white tuft of beard showed up last, pulled a battered guitar out of the case he'd been carrying, set out a paper cup, and started to play "Bad, Bad Leroy Brown." Before he could even get to "Badder than old King Kong," the city bus screeched to a stop in front of us, bringing with it a heavy dose of exhaust. Larry threw a dollar in the guitarist's cup, and the man gave him a gummy smile.

I leaned into his shoulder to whisper, "You shouldn't encourage those people."

"Of course I should. The man's making a living."

Some living. I followed Larry onto the bus and thanked him for paying for the both of us. With the exception of public school transportation, I had never ridden a bus and had no clue how much I was supposed to give them anyway. I didn't see a credit card slot, and I seldom carried cash these days.

We took a seat at the very back of the bus, which was a bench seat that forced me to sit next to the musician with the missing teeth. He smelled like garlic. When he smiled at me, I held my breath and smiled back.

"You like my song?" he asked.

I hesitated. "Sure."

"No, you didn't. I can see the lie in your eyes."

I turned to Larry. "Why are we here?"

He smiled. "Hold your horses. You'll see."

The bus rolled away from the stop, filled to about half its capacity. I could feel my brain vibrating in my skull as the bus jostled me about. Between that and the exhaust and garlic smell, I was starting to get a little motion sick. I was about ready to pull the cord for the next stop just so I could get some fresh air, when a young man stood up and started giving a speech. After a minute I realized it wasn't a speech at all but a sermon.

I looked at Larry, who grinned back at me. Judging by the look on his face this kid was what we'd come to see, but I didn't see what point there was in taking the city-turned-church bus when we could have stayed home and watched a TV evangelist if he wanted to be preached to.

The kid held the overhead bar with one hand and a small wooden cross with the other. "God's light came into the world, but people loved the darkness more than the light, for their actions were evil."

Some scrawny twentysomething sitting next to an even scrawnier twentysomething yelled, "Sit down, Jesus freak."

The preacher kid looked over at us and smiled. Larry smiled back, then stood up with all his three hundred plus pounds and said, "I want to hear what he has to say."

The scrawny duo crossed their arms but said no more.

The kid continued, bolder than ever. "The Lord says He will give eternal life to those who keep on doing good, seeking after the glory and honor and immortality that He offers. But He will pour out His anger and wrath on those who live for themselves, who refuse to obey the truth and instead live lives of wickedness. There will be trouble and calamity for everyone who keeps on doing what is evil."

Larry whispered, "Recognize your protégé?"

I studied the kid as he preached. "My what?" I looked a little closer. He had more hair on his face now and less on top, but I was pretty sure it was him. "Angelo?"

Larry just smiled. "Listen to him. You won't believe it's the same kid."

So, there we sat, shaking from the poor condition of the road and poorer condition of the bus's shocks and listened to Angelo give a sermon that would have made Billy Graham proud. I noticed the young woman dressed in the waitress uniform listening intently.

He finished by holding up the cross one more time. "Who can tell me what this is?

"The cross," Larry said. "The symbol of Christ."

"Crucifixion," the toothless musician called out.

"Forgiveness," I said.

The bus pulled to a stop and let out the twentysomethings and a middle-aged woman. Angelo and everyone else remained silent until the doors whooshed shut again and the bus began to move.

"What I see when I look at this is a crossroad," Angelo said. "I see a place where anyone can turn and take a different path." He looked at me and smiled. "Like I did. You know what else I see?"

"What?" the musician asked.

"When I look at the cross, I see a *t* for truth. God is truth. Satan is the father of all lies. The Bible says you will know the truth and the truth will set you free. It also says whoever the Son sets free is free indeed. Who here wants to be set free?"

He said a little more after that, but I didn't hear another word. I zoned, looking out the window, thinking about what a surprise Angelo turned out to be and all the stuff he'd said. I began to think about what the cross meant to him and what, if anything, it really meant to me.

When the bus had made its full rounds

and had dropped us back off where we started, Angelo didn't move. I imagined he was preparing himself to speak to the next group of passengers.

"You did good, Angelo," I said as we passed him.

I put my hand out to shake but he hugged me instead. "I'm going to be an urban missionary," he said.

I smiled. "Looks like you already are."

Larry and I walked back to where we parked. The streetlights made buzzing sounds above us, and the highway roared with traffic just behind the bend.

"Wow," I said. "I didn't see that coming."

"God's amazing." He looked over at me. "You just never know what a person has in them. His parents are mad because he quit community college. Can you imagine that? You've got a preacher for a son and you're mad because he won't become a paralegal."

"No." I thought of Benji. "I can't. I'm surprised that bus driver didn't make him stop."

"He's an elder in our church. He's the one that encouraged Angelo to do it. I don't think he likes the job much anyway."

I laughed. "Well, that's one way to get fired. Hey, thanks for taking me to hear him."

"No problem." He slid into the front seat of his Jimmy. "Couldn't have my best friend believing he can't do anything right."

I felt myself choke up. "Thanks," I whispered. "I needed that."

He gave my shoulder a quick squeeze. "We all do sometimes."

Thirty-Five

As I lay on Larry's couch, light from the nearly full moon streamed through the part in the curtains and across my face. I should have gotten up and pulled the shade, but I was warm in my blanket, and walking all the way across the room seemed like a ridiculously far distance at one in the morning.

Racing thoughts, along with the blaring music from the tricked-out Jeep parked outside the rental house beside us, had kept me tossing and turning for the last hour. I would have liked to yell for the punks to shut up, but again, that would have taken effort, especially if they decided to yell back.

I flipped to face the wall, but still couldn't get comfortable. I missed my bed. More than that, I missed lying next to Kyra in it. I wondered how long it would take for someone to take my place there.

Men were like vultures when they sensed

vulnerability in a woman. As I stared at a scuff on the wall, I hoped she wouldn't fall prey to the bombardment of seduction attempts she was sure to have to endure in the coming months, when word got out about our divorce.

The thought of another man in my bed, touching my wife, made me insane with jealousy. The fact that the punishment fit the crime only managed to make me feel worse.

I reminded myself of her strong moral character and that whatever she did from now on was really no business of mine. According to her, we were no longer an *us.* We were a used to be, a should have been, and if I hadn't been such an idiot, a would have been.

Laying there on my lumpy pillow, listening to AC/DC shake the neighborhood, my mind ran amok. I thought of just how much like my father I turned out to be. Just like him, if I died tomorrow, what I had done to Kyra and our family would be the legacy I'd leave behind. If he'd lived, he would have had all his life to make amends. I considered, for the first time, that he might actually have tried. I hated it for him, and me, that he'd never had the chance. I hated that my forgiveness for him had come only now, four decades after he'd died.

I also thought of Angelo and how brave he was to preach on the metro like that.

Who would have dreamed that a shy kid with a chip on his shoulder had that in him? I mulled over the Scriptures he'd quoted about truth and being set free. Freedom was exactly what I needed — from my sin, from my guilt, and from the web of lies I had spun around myself and my marriage. I thought about what my own preacher had said years earlier — that if we confess our sins, God is faithful and just to forgive them. I'd never given that promise much thought, but as I lay there covered in the filth of my guilt, I found myself clinging to it.

There was nothing left to do but take God up on His generous offer, and so I confessed it all. With each sin that I admitted came a release from guilt, until I felt nothing but the freedom I'd been promised.

It couldn't have been more than a few minutes, since the same song was playing on the car radio outside when I finished, but it felt like hours as I admitted to every sin I could remember ever committing. I'm sure I left out a lot of them, but still I felt like I'd thrown off a boulder.

He is faithful and just to forgive us. . . .

Lord, I'm holding You to that.

I truly believed that I had His pardon at that moment. Down to my marrow, I felt it. Now I just needed Kyra's. How stupid I'd been to think I could throw a few shallow gestures at her and expect her to absolve me from what I'd done. She wasn't stupid. She could see as well as anyone through the superficiality of a person.

I thought of the waitress clinging to Angelo's every word and wondered if she had been carrying a burden as heavy as mine and if she was able to throw hers off like I did. I hoped so.

This, in turn, led me to think of the toothless musician and how happy he looked strumming that guitar of his, which then led me to think of Kyra and her desire to be a lounge pianist, and Benji's to be a fisherman. When had I gotten it in my head that money equaled happiness? It certainly hadn't worked out that way for me.

How different might our lives have turned out if we had stayed in Braddy's Wharf? Somewhere along the way, my family had sacrificed not only the home they loved, but their dreams for mine. No wonder Kyra stopped wanting to make love to me. How attractive is a person who belittles your aspirations every chance they get?

Too bad the epiphany hadn't come to me before I'd dragged my family to Rolling Springs and into Danielle's bed. Looking back, moving here was really the first nail in the coffin, and while sleeping with Danielle might turn out to be the last, there were plenty of others along the way: too many nights working late and put-downs, cancelled vacations, hours spent watching TV while pretending to listen — the list could go on forever.

It seemed my whole life played out in my mind as I lay there staring at the wall, but the thought that revisited the most was Alfred's advice to apologize. I knew Kyra deserved at least that much. Not one of my halfhearted attempts at half-truths, but an apology for what I had really done.

I knew if I had to look her in the eye while doing it, there was a good chance I'd chicken out, so I decided to put it in writing. She might never forgive me, but maybe coming clean would eventually help me forgive myself.

Since I couldn't seem to fall asleep anyway, I figured now was as good a time as any. Tomorrow was my last day of vacation and then I'd likely be caught up in the whirlwind of either being promoted or else teaching Larry everything I knew so he could be. I would deliver the letter tomorrow and let the chips fall where they may.

I rolled out of bed and pulled out a legal pad and pen from my briefcase. Sitting at Larry's desk, I put the pen to paper and prayed that he was right — that the truth would somehow set me free.

~~Dear Kyra,~~
My dearest Kyra,
It seems like yesterday I was watching you play the piano at Sophia's. Even then I knew you were too good for that place. Too good for me.

You were, and are, the most beautiful, talented, and wonderful woman in the world. What I did was bad, honey. So, so bad. I don't just mean with Danielle; I mean telling you that my idea of a life well spent was more important than yours. You should be able to play at restaurants if it makes you happy. I'm sorry I tried to make you feel bad about wanting that. What you enjoy is what you enjoy, and you shouldn't have to justify it to me or anyone else.

You could have made me feel bad about wanting to sell cars for a living, but you didn't. Instead you let me uproot you from a place you loved, a job

338

you loved, and friends you loved, so I could follow my dreams. (I realize now just how small they were in the grand scheme of things.)

Kyra, my love, my soul mate, my best friend, we've gotten so far offtrack, but I believe your accident was God's way of giving us a second chance. It's up to us what we do with it.

Words are inadequate to describe just how in love with you I am . . . and how very sorry. If you somehow find the grace to forgive me, there will be no more lies, no more omissions of truth, and no woman on the face of this earth that will tempt me away from you again. You promised in Milan that you would never leave me no matter what. I know it wasn't fair of me to ask that of you, but fair or not, I'm begging you to find it in your heart to keep that promise.

Darling, I am the thief on the cross beside Jesus, the woman at the well, and the man who loves you more than his own life.

Even if you can't forgive me, I'm going to spend the rest of my life trying to make this up to you.

Love always,
The man who used to be your samurai

I read and reread the letter. Maybe it wasn't great, but at least every word was the truth for a change.

The next day, I slid on a pair of dress pants and light sweater, shaved, combed my hair, brushed my teeth, and even polished my shoes. I had never been so nervous in my life. I checked myself in the mirror, rebrushed my teeth and hair, and checked myself again.

I tilted my head back and pinched a drop of Visine into each eye. Looking at myself I realized I still looked every bit as worn out as I felt.

"You need a miracle," I said to my reflection, and so he prayed for one.

Letter in hand, I pulled up outside my house to find Kyra, dressed to kill in a black skirt and silk blouse, getting into her car. She didn't even throw me a glance as she shut the door.

I looked up at the rain clouds strewn across a gray sky, and a raindrop hit my windshield, followed by another. I smiled and rolled down my window.

"The drought's over," I called to her.

The look on her face reminded me that ours wasn't.

I inched my vehicle forward so that my

window met hers. "Where are you headed?"

She pulled the rearview down and dabbed at the lipstick at the corner of her mouth. "I have another job interview."

"Piano?"

"Yes, I am a pianist, Eric. At least I was until I married you."

She pushed the mirror back into place. "What do you want?"

I started to open my door.

"Don't get out. I'm in a hurry."

"Kyra, please," I said.

She turned the ignition. "Please what? Please forget that you want to make out with someone half your age under the northern lights? Isn't that what you promised her in that e-mail?"

I picked up the envelope from the passenger seat but then set it down again. I couldn't give it to her right before an interview. Instead, I said, "Good luck, sweetheart. I hope you get it."

I watched her car turn the corner, then pulled into the driveway of my soon-to-be ex-home. Rain soaked me as I hurried up the walkway. When I stepped into the house and closed the door, I was drenched. Benji was lying on the couch staring at a black TV screen. "Is it raining?" he asked looking at me.

"Can't you hear it?"

Unless he had more than one pair of sweatpants stained with ketchup on the right thigh, he was wearing the same pants as when I'd last seen him. I held up the letter I'd written to Kyra. "Can you please make sure your mother gets this?" I laid it on the table by the door.

"Mom tell you she's auditioning at Sal's?"

I sat beside him. "Yeah."

"You know how much that stupid job will pay, and that's if she even gets it?"

I shrugged.

"Straight tips. Guess she'll be living on alimony."

"How are you?" I asked.

He laid his head on the armrest. "Good, I guess. I started filling out college applications."

"Do you actually want to go to college?"

He opened his mouth to say something but closed it again.

"Go ahead," I said. "Tell me the truth. This is your life, Ben, not mine."

"I can't think of anything I'd rather do less."

My heart sank, but I did my best to hide it. "That's okay. College isn't for everyone. You still thinking you might want to make a living from the ocean?"

He looked at me a long time, then said, "I was thinking that I could maybe get a job as a sales associate and work my way up like you did."

"No," I said so gruffly that I think it shocked the both of us.

He sat up. "Why not? You make good money."

"Money isn't everything."

"Since when?" He kicked his bare feet against the base of the couch and looked over at the envelope I'd laid down. "Is that divorce papers?"

"If your mother wants a divorce, she'll have to be the one to do it. It's just a letter."

"She's so mad at you."

"I know."

"She probably is going to divorce you, you know." There was vulnerability in his tone and I hated it for him. Hated it for all of us.

"I hope not."

"Me, too." He scratched at the ketchup stain. "Mom says we're going to sell the house."

Hearing it made me sad, but it didn't surprise me. "She did?"

"Yeah. She said she hates it here. She wants to go back home."

"To Braddy's Wharf?"

He gave me a sad look. "She's just talking. She wouldn't leave us here."

"She'd leave me," I said.

"If she were serious about moving, she wouldn't be applying for jobs here."

"I hope you're right."

"So, will you get me a job at Thompson's?"

I hated the thought of my son spending his adult years the way I had, but I reminded myself that they were his to do with what he wanted. "Is that what you really want?"

He shrugged. "Will you?"

"Sure, but Benji, money really isn't everything, which is good because you won't be making a whole lot of it in the beginning."

"That's okay," he said. "As much as I like money and love the ocean, working at Thompson's would give me a chance to spend time with you."

"I'd like that," I said. "We've never gotten to do much of that, have we?"

He shook his head.

"Ben, I'm sorry I didn't spend more time with you when you were growing up. I want you to know that I regret that."

He looked at me for a long time. "Me, too," he finally said.

THIRTY-SIX

My first day back to work I felt completely disoriented, but then I hadn't been off more than two days in a row for years. I suppose it made matters worse that two of our regular employees were now gone, and Thompson kept me from getting anything significant done by calling me into his office every five minutes. It might have given me confidence if he hadn't been doing the same thing with Larry.

I had no idea what he was talking to Larry about, but in my case, it was mostly just a lot of questions about operations. At first I assumed he was doing sort of a stream of pop quizzes just to make sure I knew my stuff before he made up his mind, but then I caught him taking notes, which made me wonder if he was trying to extract as much practical information as he could just in case I decided to quit.

The funny thing was, for the first time

since I had started working for Thompson, I didn't feel like the world would end if I didn't get the promotion. If I did, great; but if I didn't, well, that would just mean that Larry had. I actually found myself wanting it for him as much as I ever had for myself.

Despite feeling a little disoriented at being away so long, dealing with the tension over who Thompson would pick to succeed him, and the avalanche of paperwork that had built up on my desk in my absence, being at work felt more comfortable than it had in a long time.

It was a relief to not have to deal with Danielle anymore. Santana, on the other hand, I kind of missed. He was the only other guy on the lot with a sense of humor that mirrored Larry's and mine.

The sales associate Thompson had hired to take Danielle's place when she was promoted tried to fit in, but his jokes were corny, and most of the time he walked around looking like his head might explode at any given moment. Maybe once he learned the job a little more he'd loosen up and his jokes would get better, though I doubted it. I knew the wound-too-tight type when I saw it.

At the end of the day, Thompson took Larry and me aside and said he'd announce his final decision tomorrow, but no matter what happened, he wanted us to know that he thought we were both excellent employees and hoped there would be no hard feelings. It was all starting to feel a little drawn out and melodramatic, but that was Thompson for you.

I was on my way out, preparing to crash hard, when Benji called my cell phone to say that Kyra wanted me to stop by on my way home. I assumed she'd read my letter and was ready to lay me out once and for all. Gathering my resolve, I headed up the walkway and knocked on the door before I could lose my nerve. No matter how ugly it got tonight, I told myself that after this, for better or worse, we could all finally move on.

Kyra answered in sweatpants and a T-shirt. Instead of hello or a string of expletives like I expected, I was met with "Steve's dead."

I stepped inside. "Who?"

"Our fish. I think he starved to death. Did you feed him when I was in Milan?"

"Yes, of course." I remembered sprinkling flakes into his bowl at least once, but I was at Larry's more than here. Why wasn't *she* feeding him? I closed the door behind me.

"When was the last time you fed him?" she demanded.

"I don't know," I said. "Recently."

She wore her hair in a ponytail, which swung as she turned to walk further inside the house. "You've got to flush him. I can't do it."

"Hey, Dad," Benji said from the couch. He was still wearing those same stained sweatpants.

"Son, you think you might want to shower sometime this month?"

Kyra scowled at me. "Leave him alone. This isn't his fault."

"I didn't say it was." Smelling smoke, I looked around but didn't see anything out of the ordinary. "Is something burning?"

Kyra grunted and hurried to the kitchen. "That's just great. It's ruined!"

"What's ruined?" Benji asked.

"Really, Son," I said, "at least change your clothes once in a while."

"I'm officially no longer a sailor as of today," he said.

"Oh no." My heart sank. Here I was giving him a hard time about something so shallow when he just received a blow like that. I guess I'd have to work harder than I thought to keep the 180 I'd just done from becoming a 360. "I'm sorry, Ben."

He stared at the ground. "It's fine. It's not like I didn't know it was coming."

Kyra stepped out of the kitchen with an oven mitt on her right hand and a smear of black on her left cheek. "Thanks for ruining my brûlée. This was supposed to be for Marnie's dinner tomorrow. Now what am I supposed to bring?"

"Yes," I said, watching wisps of gray float across the room, "I'm sure it was all my fault."

She turned and marched into the kitchen. "Are you going to flush Steve or what?"

"How long has he been dead?" I called to her.

"Since about ten this morning," Benji said flipping to the Food Network. "Dad, check this out. They're making stuffed rainbow trout. You can't catch a tastier fish."

"Just flush him!" Kyra yelled from the kitchen. "He's starting to stink."

"There's no way he's starting to stink that fast," I yelled back. I turned to Benji. "Yeah, rainbow trout are the bomb. Where's Steve?"

He pointed to the fishbowl that was now just half full and sitting on the entry table. A hard-water stain formed a ring around the top of the bowl, where his water would normally be filled to.

"Why didn't you do it?" I asked him.

"She wouldn't let me. She said since you

were the one who killed him, you should do it."

"*I* killed him?"

He shrugged. "She's not exactly being rational. I think she just wanted a reason to call you."

"Did she read my letter?"

He gave me an apologetic grimace. "Yeah, she tore it into a million pieces, then set it on fire and shoved the ashes down the garbage disposal. Did you know that Brenda Harrington has breast cancer?"

"What?"

"I don't hear the toilet flushing," Kyra screamed.

"How did you find that out?" I asked him.

He picked up one of his mother's *Southern Living* magazines from the end table and thumbed through it faster than he could even look at the pictures. "I told you I go over there."

"Eric!" Kyra yelled.

"Ben, go flush the hall bathroom so we can finish talking."

Always the obedient child, he did as I asked and walked back to the living room. "Bram's devastated. He shaved his own head so she wouldn't feel bad when she starts losing her hair to chemo."

"That's terrible," I said, feeling guilty for

all the things I'd said about them over the years. I had no idea.

"He says they caught it early, so she should be able to beat it."

I pulled the curtain back and looked out at their house. A For Sale sign stood in the front yard.

"Are they in financial trouble?" I asked.

"I don't think so," he said. "I think they just want to be near her parents in Wyoming."

"But isn't his whole family here?"

"Yeah, but she's the one who's sick."

"What about his job? He just got promoted."

Benji frowned. "Are you serious, Dad? That's his wife."

Kyra walked out of the kitchen carrying a baking dish with what looked like a glob of charcoal pudding stuck to it. She glared at the fishbowl, then me. "Why is he still here?"

Benji's gaze bounced between his mother and me.

"I asked Benji to flush the toilet so you'd be quiet long enough for him to finish telling me about Brenda Harrington's cancer."

"Typical," she said. "My husband, the liar."

"How is that a lie?" I asked.

"How isn't it?"

"Kyra, please don't do this."

"Or what? You'll fall in love with another woman?"

"I'll be upstairs," Benji said, looking miserable.

I waited for him to go, then reached for Kyra's hand. "I never loved her. I love you."

She yanked away from me. "You don't have an affair on someone you love."

"It wasn't an affair," I said. "I only slept with her once, and I'll spend the rest of my life regretting it."

Her face distorted in rage as she threw the dish. The brûlée hit the wall right before the dish shattered against the floor. "No, you didn't just sleep with her once. You slept with her a thousand times and will sleep with her a thousand more. And every time I close my eyes, you'll sleep with her again. As long as I live I'll never get that image of you and her together out of my head."

I laid my hand across my eyes. "You wouldn't let me touch you."

"I didn't even know you anymore! You were so wrapped up in your stupid job, I felt like I was married to a stranger. You stopped talking to me, you stopped thinking about me, and for all I could tell, you stopped caring about me." She paused and looked like she was trying to regain her composure. "And besides, I knew what you really wanted."

I looked at her. "What did I really want?"

"The stupid routine is getting old."

"What did I want?" I repeated. At this point I honestly had no idea what she meant. I wasn't sure *I'd* even known what I really wanted.

"That Latin bimbo."

My mind reeled trying to figure out what in the world she was talking about. I drew a blank.

"I was standing on the landing when you kept rewinding and playing that thriller with Chantico Lopez."

I felt like I'd entered the twilight zone. "Who?"

"The woman with the long dark hair, brown eyes, and the big —" she cupped her hands in front of her chest. "You think I want you touching my body while you're fantasizing about her?"

The only thing I could figure was that the concussion had planted false memories. "Honey, you're confused —"

"Don't even try it," she hissed. "Don't you dare try to confuse me. I watched you rewind, pause, and replay the clip where she took her shirt off, over and over and over. How do you think that made me feel?"

I was about to tell her again that she was mistaken, when the lightbulb finally came on. "The beige lamp?"

She bent over, picked up two of the largest pieces of broken dish, and used them to scoop up the brûlée. "I don't remember the name of the stupid movie. I just remember your obsession with her breasts."

"No, not the title," I said. "The movie was *Just Another Murder in Mexico*. I'm talking about the beige lamp I was looking at. That's what I was rewinding and replaying the movie for, not some stupid woman."

She stared me down.

Heat flooded my cheeks as I realized what had happened. "I couldn't pick the actress out in a lineup, but there's a beige lamp in that scene. It had a maroon flower on it one second and then the flower was gone. They must have spliced the scene, and the lamp got turned so the design wasn't showing or something. It was a blooper. *That's* what I was looking at."

"Yeah right," she said weakly.

I just stared at her, digesting the magnitude of what she was saying. All those nights I spent racking my brain to figure out what I could have done or said to turn her off.

Without warning, her balled-up fist hit me dead in the chest. She threw another weak punch, followed by another. "Get out," she screamed, pounding my chest, harder and harder, screaming that she hated me.

I grabbed her wrists. "Stop it. I didn't lust after some actress on TV. Our issues started far before then and you know it. You can't blame your years of frigidity on one misunderstanding. You wanted nothing to do with me long before that movie even came out, so don't even try it. Put blame where blame belongs, Kyra. Admit that you stopped being attracted to me. And it wasn't because of some stupid actress."

She let out a wail like a grieving mother. "How could you sleep with that girl?" Pulling free, she punched me again, but this time I grabbed her and pulled her against me.

As she struggled to get away, I held on like my life depended on it. "What happened to us?" I asked.

She tore away from me and thrust her arm out toward the fish floating upside down in his bowl. "That's what."

THIRTY-SEVEN

Today was the day I'd been working toward for the last six years. I would find out in the next fifteen minutes whether it would be me or Larry running the dealership from now on. All those twelve-hour, six-day work weeks, dragging myself in even when I felt like death and missed family functions — not to mention all of Thompson's bull I had to endure — it all came down to this moment.

But it was my wife, not the job, that took precedence in my thoughts as I sat at my desk, listening to phones ringing, incentive announcements blaring from overhead speakers, and the rest of the usual midday commotion.

Last night was all I could think of as I stared through the wall of windows at the showroom floor. I watched Larry slink out of our boss's office looking like he'd had his million-dollar lottery ticket stolen, which could only mean one thing — the job was mine. I should have been happy; I'd sacrificed so much for this. But instead, I just felt terrible for my friend, and in a way, worse for myself. The thought of spending the rest of my life here in this dealership, without Kyra to go home to, felt a little too much like a one-way ticket to purgatory.

Sitting alone at my desk, watching my coworkers scurry around like ants, I forced my thoughts back to rehearsing what I would say when Thompson finally offered me the job — promises to fill his big shoes to the best of my abilities, suggesting Larry be given my old job, if he hadn't already thought to offer it to him, and of course, I'd have to lavish the appreciation on him as thick as honey for choosing me.

As I tapped my pen against the desk blotter, my thoughts once again turned back to Kyra and our unraveling marriage. I doubted that we'd have any trouble selling the house and considered what I might do with my half of the money. With the raise I'd be getting, I could easily afford payments on a new condo. That meant that the proceeds of the house on Macabee could go into a special account set aside for the specific purpose of wooing back my bride. No matter what a long shot it was, I had to at least try.

Maybe I could begin by surprising her with a trip to a place she'd always dreamed of visiting, like Hawaii, Europe, or better yet, Israel. She'd always wanted to be baptized in the Jordan. We could do it together maybe. It could be symbolic of not just the change in me, but the change in us.

My mind reeled. If I was going to be the supportive husband I had made my mind up to be, I'd need to be at as many of her gigs as possible — the guy at the front table, clapping the loudest, whistling obnoxiously. I just didn't see how I'd be able to make that happen now, but I'd have to find a way. That was all there was to it.

When I glanced up at the wall clock, I noticed a young man dressed in a suit a lot like one of mine, standing by the front desk talking to the receptionist. It had been so long since I'd seen him cleaned up, I almost didn't recognize my own son. I hurried over to meet him.

Larry must have noticed him right when I had, because we both called his name at the same time.

"Wow, nice reception," Benji said smiling between us. The suit he wore *was* mine. I couldn't believe just how well it fit him.

"Looking good, Ben," Larry said. "You

come to wish your old man luck?"

Benji gave me a questioning look. "Luck for what?"

"Today's the day," I said, feeling self-conscious with Larry's eyes on me. "What are you doing here?"

"I decided to go ahead and set up an interview."

"You did?" Larry and I asked at the same time.

Larry grinned at me and gave my arm a jovial punch. "You owe me a beer."

I rubbed my arm. "What are you, twelve?"

"Do twelve-year-olds drink beer?" he asked.

A woman with a preteen in tow walked up to us. "Can one of y' all help me?"

I pointed to the closest salesman. "Phil, over there, will be happy to."

She thanked us and dragged her son over to him.

"Hey, you should've let me have her," Benji said with a wink in his tone. "I'm ready to make some moola." Not only was he wearing my suit, he smelled like my cologne.

"You really want to sell cars?" Larry asked him.

Benji buried his hands in his front pockets. "I've got to make a living somehow."

"It's not like this is the only way." Larry gave me the same *do something* look Kyra liked to use.

There was something about seeing my son dressed like every other sales guy on the lot and standing against the backdrop of the busy showroom floor that made me realize the magnitude of this crossroad in his life.

I thought of how different my life might have turned out if I had never come to work here. If I'd given my family what I'd given this place. I also thought of Angelo and what his life might be like if he gave up being what he was called to do — to sit in a lawyer's office all day with his nose stuck in a book.

"He's right, Ben," I said. "You don't want this. Selling cars isn't really your thing. The ocean is."

He scrunched his face at me. "But you said —"

I set my hand on his shoulder and gave it a squeeze. "You can't listen to me. Your father's an idiot. For you, working here would be like a prison sentence; trust me. How about for now we keep your options open, okay? I'm sure we can find something you enjoy that you can also make a living at."

He frowned. "What gives?"

"I just want you to be happy; that's all."

His frown turned up into a half smile. "Really?"

"Believe it or not, it's what I've always wanted. I just didn't realize until recently that the path there might not always be paved with money."

"So, you're not going to ride me about college anymore?"

"I didn't ride you. I just encouraged."

He picked up pretend reins and made a giddyap clicking sound.

Larry nodded at me. "I like this kid."

"Of course you do," I said. "He's just like you." I glanced at my watch. "Listen, Ben, I'll stop by the house tonight on my way to Larry's, and we'll talk about this some more if you want. Maybe set up a game plan for figuring out what you were put on this earth to do."

Dimples formed on Benji's cheeks. I couldn't remember the last time I'd seen them sink so deep. "Thanks, Dad. That's really cool."

I shrugged like it was no big deal, but inside I felt like a hero. "Better go cancel your appointment."

The bounce in his step as he walked into Ruby's office to tell her he'd changed his mind was worth more to me than the commission on a thousand cars.

Larry turned to me as we watched Benji walk out the front door. "Good call, man."

"Thanks," I said, giving my watch another glance.

"You better go in." He nodded to Thompson's office. "Destiny's waiting."

THIRTY-EIGHT

When I stepped into Thompson's office, it reeked of that cheap cologne of his and cigars. One smoldered in the ashtray, already half smoked, as if he'd started the party without me. I couldn't blame him I guess. If there was ever a reason to celebrate, retirement would be it.

He lifted open the fancy wood box sitting on the edge of his desk, revealing a row of fat, brown cigars. Two were missing, which made me wonder if he'd already given one to Larry as a consolation gift. "You know, Yoshida, I've done a lot of nail-biting these past few weeks. Choosing who will run the business that'll be funding your retirement isn't for the faint of heart."

I took the cigar from him and slid it under my nose. Rich and woody, it smelled like victory. As I rolled it back and forth in my fingers, I felt for the crunching of the tobacco inside, but it was smoother than I was used to, with just a tinge of oil to the casing. The band circling it even managed to look expensive with its fancy gold and red lettering.

He picked a fresh one from the box and inhaled it before gently setting it back down beside the others. "You'll be able to afford your own now."

He slid a lighter from his front pocket and clicked out a flame. With my stomach already churning like a cement mixer, I was afraid smoking might make me hurl. "Thanks very much, Mr. Thompson, but would you mind if I save it for later?"

He let go of the button and the flame retreated. "I think you can guess what I'm about to say." He motioned for me to have a seat, but I just stood there.

He raised his eyebrows, drawing my attention to that one unruly hair coiling up from the rest. "Yoshida, you've worked hard these past years. I want you to know that I appreciate it, even if I didn't always remember to say so. You've been the first one here and the last to leave. Sure, you've slacked off lately with your personal problems, but I've decided to overlook that," he pointed the lighter at me, "with the understanding that you'll get your nose back to the grindstone."

His beady eyes narrowed. "You will, won't

you, son?"

As he stood staring at me, my life flashed before my eyes. I saw Kyra's father walking her down the aisle to entrust her to me, and the smile that met me when I pulled back the lace veil. I saw the beads of sweat pouring down her forehead as she struggled to push our son into the world and the tears she shed when we buried each of her parents.

I also saw the future I'd dreamed for us that would never be now. We might still retire to the ocean like we planned, just not together. Benji and our grandchildren would always feel pulled, splitting their time between us . . . and I'd always feel like half of me was missing.

Thompson slapped his hands together an inch from my face. "Snap out of it, Eric. This is the day you've been waiting for. I'm offering you up a six-figure salary and an office with a view. This kind of opportunity doesn't come around often for a man without a bunch of letters behind his name." He slapped me hard on the shoulder. "You've done it, son. You've made it."

Trying to clear my head, I looked up at the dropped ceiling and noticed that the aluminum suspension brackets holding the tiles in place formed a string of crosses — a line of tiny crossroads.

"Wow," I said, finally looking at Thompson. "I'm honored. I'm just not sure what to say."

He picked his cigar out of the ashtray and chewed the tip. "What do you mean you don't know what to say? Doggone it, boy. This is the part where you accept."

I glanced up at the ceiling again.

"Yoshida, stop playing coy with me. Just tell me what you want."

I thought about the Harringtons and what Bram was giving up for his wife. I thought about Larry's advice, and my mother's, and finally I thought about me. So what did I want? It was time to be honest, not just with Kyra and everyone else, but with myself.

He tapped his hairy knuckles against the desk. "So?"

Part of me wanted to say yes, to step onto the showroom floor and announce to everyone that I was worthy after all, but Thompson had been right when he said that getting what you wanted in life required sacrifice. And what I really wanted was Kyra. She probably would never forgive me, but if there was even the remotest chance, I had to try.

I opened up the box and set my cigar back down beside the others. "I appreciate the offer, Mr. Thompson, but Larry's your man."

He scratched his cheek. "If I didn't know better, I'd think hell was freezing over. First Larry turns down the job because he wants you to have it, then you turn it down?"

I felt like I'd been slapped. "Wait, what?"

He had this stammering look on his face as if he'd just realized he might have said too much. "All I'm saying is this is a good —"

"You offered Larry the job first?"

He rubbed his mottled neck. "Don't look so surprised. He's a heck of a salesman, shows up every day on time, everyone respects him, and he doesn't molest the help. You used to be my right-hand man, Eric, but lately, you've been somewhere else. Women, they'll ruin a good man if you let them. And you've been letting them."

I walked out of Thompson's office feeling scared about how I'd make a living now. I hoped the old adage would prove true for once, and that the grass really might be greener on the other side of the fence.

Now, I just needed to figure out where that fence was.

When I stepped into the hallway, I found Larry leaning against the wall pretending to talk on his cell phone and trying his best to look like he wasn't dying to find out what the outcome was. He acted like he was hanging up, then looked at me.

"It's all yours," I said. "I just quit."

"I know," he said with a smirk. "Thompson called me before you even made it through the door and begged me to reconsider."

"He told me what you did for me," I said. "You're unbelievable."

He shrugged. "It was no different than what you did for me."

"Not for you," I said, trying out my new vow of honesty. "For me." I looked past those black-rimmed glasses of his into his gray eyes. The eyes of the man who was like a brother to me. I put my hand out for him to shake, but he grabbed me into a bear hug.

"Since you don't want it, mind if I take it?" he said, letting me go.

"You better."

He grinned. "Good, because I already have."

I turned to find the showroom staff and a few customers watching us with curiosity. I took Larry's arm and raised it in the air like the winning prizefighter. "Ladies and gentlemen, I give you Larry Wallace, your new boss."

Everyone looked a little embarrassed and

unsure, until I started clapping. As everyone joined in, I whispered to him, "I'll clean out my desk when the place is empty if that's okay."

"Of course," he said. "See you tonight?"

"Not if I can help it," I said.

Thirty-Nine

The week we listed our house, we ended up with a bidding war that resulted in an offer fifteen thousand above asking price. That was the beauty of living in a neighborhood so many coveted. I was sad to leave but excited to begin the rest of my life.

Kyra had sold just about everything we owned, and what she hadn't was boxed and waiting for the movers to take to her sister's house. Marnie, who was over helping her finish packing, came down the walkway to where I stood on the sidewalk and gave me a hug. "I'm sorry how things have worked out."

"It's not over until it's over," I said.

She pulled back. "No offense, Eric, but it's over."

"Do me a favor?"

She sighed and gave me a weary look. "What?"

"Keep her at your house as long as you

can. If she wants to buy a place, try to talk her out of it."

She shook her head. "I'm not going to do that. She needs to move on, just like you do."

"Please?" I said. Her expression dripped with pity. "You take care of my nephew or I'll have Marcello send over some of his mafia friends to take care of you."

"By the time they get their walkers loaded on the plane, I'll be long gone," I said.

A smile tugged at her lips. "Be careful on the road — 85 percent of accidents happen during moves."

I had to laugh at that. "You know, I've always wanted to know where you get your statistics."

She looked taken aback by the question, then recovered with, "Ancient Chinese secret."

"More like ancient Chinese nonsense."

She twisted her mouth, but the humor glinting in her eyes told me I hadn't really offended her.

She leaned over to hug Benji. "You sure you want to go back to Braddy's Wharf? I have plenty of room at my house."

The look on his face must have given her the answer she was looking for, because she grinned and nodded. "You two take care of each other."

"You take care of my wife," I said, taking her hand.

She gave my fingers a squeeze. "I'll take care of my sister."

Benji watched her disappear inside the house, then turned to me looking as sad as the day we'd first moved here. "Guess I better go in and say good-bye to Mom."

"You know," I said, "you don't have to come with me right now. You can come when everything's done."

"And do what in the meantime? Count silverware for Aunt Marnie?"

I nodded toward the house, trying my best not to let the choked-up feeling in my throat turn into tears. "Go on and kiss your mother for me."

"Don't worry, Dad; this is a really great idea. If I know chicks, she's going to love it."

I opened the car door. "*A,* don't refer to your mother as a chick, and *B,* you don't know chicks. No man really does. And *C,* get your butt up there and kiss your mother so we can get this party started."

I slid into my vehicle as I watched him jog up the walkway. It struck me that if I accomplished nothing else good with the rest of my life, at least I'd done one thing right.

After a few minutes, he ran back to the car and got in. As we backed out the driveway, Kyra called to me from the porch. Hope made my heart quicken.

I rolled the window down the rest of the way. "Sweetheart, did you need something?"

Benji elbowed me. "Go up there and talk to her."

Feeling more self-conscious than the first time I'd approached her at Sophia's all those years ago, I meandered to where she stood on the porch.

Even dressed in sweatpants without a stitch of makeup on her face, she looked beautiful. She wrapped her arms around herself. "I just wanted to wish you luck."

It was then that I saw her. Really saw her in a way that I hadn't since I'd first fallen in love. I saw the freckles on the bridge of her nose, the lines around her eyes and mouth that hadn't been there when we met, and the strands of silver that had started weaving their way through her red hair. "I wish you'd come with us," I said.

She rubbed absently at her arms. "If wishes were dollars, we'd all be rich."

I reached out to touch her, but she flinched and I withdrew.

"Tell Benji to call me when you get there and let me know he's safe," she said.

You used to want to know that I'd made it somewhere safe, too, I thought. "Will do," I said. "Call me if you need help getting situated. It's only a few hours away. I could be here in —"

She glanced at the open door behind her. "You take care, Eric."

"You, too," I said.

And just like that, my marriage was over.

FORTY

Soft music played from the newly refurbished speakers as Benji and I sanded opposite ends of the bar in a steady rhythm. My arm began to ache, so I stopped to rub the muscles around my shoulder.

Benji's now-longish black hair was speckled with sawdust, which made it look almost gray. He blew a strand from his face. "You okay, old man?"

I threw my sandpaper down on the ground like I intended to fight. "Those are big words coming from a little boy. Come here and I'll show you who's an old man."

He wiggled his fingers at me. "Ooh, I'm shaking." He glanced down at the front of his jeans. "Uh-oh, I better go home and change. I think I just peed a little."

On a whim, I charged after him. Instead of shrieking like he used to do when he was a child, he widened his stance and raised his fists out in front of him like a boxer. I pretended to throw a right hook to his side, but when it came time for impact, I tickled him instead.

He tried hard not to laugh but finally gave in. I was about to tell him he laughed like a girl when I heard a familiar little snort. Both Benji and I turned toward the door at the same time to see Kyra standing there in a white sweater and faded jeans, holding a fishbowl. She wore her hair shorter now, angled and trendy. She looked good, but then she always had. Her face seemed narrower than it was last time I'd seen her, and I imagined with the weight I'd lost since our separation, mine probably did too. Turned out that impending divorce was the best appetite suppressant known to man.

"Kyra," I said, surprised. "You weren't supposed to come yet. We're not ready." I brushed dust from my face and tucked my shirt in. "I wanted everything to be staged."

She smiled shyly. "You know me. As soon as I got your message, I had to see it for myself." Holding out the fishbowl, she said, "Here, I brought you a housewarming gift."

When I took it from her hands, our fingers brushed. I felt like crying when I saw that her left ring finger was bare. "Oh, cool, a beta fish. Thanks."

She gave me one of her Mona Lisa smiles.

"Let's see if you can keep this one alive."

When I set him on the bar, the water swayed back and forth, carrying him with it. "If he dies, I promise you it's not going to be from neglect this time." I watched the small blue fish swim through the tiny rock bridge underpass. "What should we name him?"

"I was thinking maybe Benji Jr." She winked at our son.

Laughing, I said, "I think that name already belongs to a certain crab."

Benji walked over to the bowl and peered in. "He looks more like an Eric Jr anyway."

I gave the back of his head a playful tap.

Kyra eyed the place, looking more awestruck than I even hoped. "Did you really buy it?"

"Lock, stock, and barrel. What do you think?"

She looked down at the plank floors Benji and I had spent a week refinishing, then over at a life-size mermaid statue standing guard over the bar we were just about ready to stain. "Love the mermaid. Gosh, this place looks way better than it ever did when it was Sonny's."

"You really think so?" I beamed at the approval in her eyes.

"It's amazing." She walked over to Benji

and hugged him. "So, I gather you've known about this the whole time?"

"He's worked beside me every step of the way," I said, feeling another surge of pride. "Turns out our son has talents we never knew about."

"Looks like you both do." Her gaze slid across the freshly painted walls and stopped at the piano. A look of recognition passed over her. "That looks just like my old . . ." She walked over to it and sat down on the bench.

I held my breath. I'd spent at least an hour every night for the past few months working to refurbish it. Her fingers traced the key cover and slowly she opened it. She looked up at me as her hand flew to her chest. "It *is* mine. Where did you . . . ?"

I walked over and sat beside her, trying not to be obvious as I inhaled her vanilla-almond scent. "It's not like we got rid of it. It was always in storage." I realized then why she'd acted so bitter about me replacing it with the baby grand. "You didn't know that, did you?"

She shook her head, looking like she might cry. "I guess I just assumed . . ."

I didn't bother saying what we were both probably thinking.

Bending over, she touched the scrolled

legs. "It looks like new. When did you have it redone?"

"He did it himself," Benji said.

With the sleeve of my shirt, I dusted off the keys. "Except the tuning. I had to hire someone for that."

When she wiped at the corner of her eyes, I knew I had done all right.

"Play something, Mom."

She looked up at Benji, then set her fingertips down. The old piano didn't have the satiny sound the baby grand did, but watching Kyra play with her eyes closed, completely engrossed in the music, made it sound like a song from heaven.

Suddenly, as if ripped back into reality, she stopped playing and turned to me. "I never knew you wanted to own a restaurant."

"I don't," I said.

She gave me a questioning look and then Benji.

Benji bounced around like he used to do on Christmas morning. "Dad, show her the sign."

A curious smile worked its way across Kyra's mouth. "What sign?"

"Well," I said, standing, "I was going to wait until your birthday to show you, but I guess the jig's up."

"The jig?"

I took her by the hand and led her outside. The sun was preparing to set, and the horizon had never looked more lovely with its blending hues of orange, pink, and purple. Waves roared in the distance, and as I stood there beside my wife, wishing she was still wearing my ring, I had to fight an overwhelming urge to kiss her.

Benji stood on the other side of his mother looking up at the tarp covering the sign. "Can I do it?"

"You want a drum roll?" I asked.

"Sure," he said.

I looked at Kyra. "You're the musician."

She moved her wrists up and down in quick succession, accompanying it with the appropriate sound. Benji waited for her to hit the pretend crash cymbal, then yanked the end of the tarp revealing a blue shingle hanging from thin metal chains. The white cursive letters read *Kyra's by the Sea.*

Her eyes turned into saucers as her mouth dropped to the sand. "I don't understand."

My stomach was tied in knots as I choked out, "Happy birthday, honey."

She looked troubled. "You named your restaurant after me?"

It dawned on me then that she might have outgrown this dream. "No, I named *your* restaurant after you. But if you don't want it," I said, "we can sell, or —"

"I'll take it," Benji said.

Kyra made a face at him. "Back off, Benjamin. It's my birthday, not yours."

"So you like it?" he asked.

She stared up at it and finally, reluctantly, turned to me and gave me a hug. It wasn't the reaction I dreamed of all these months, but it was more than I hoped for.

"I'm going to need someone to help me manage it," she said.

"Guess I'm free for the next twenty years," I said.

Her skin flushed. "I'm not talking about getting back together."

"Of course not."

"Just a business partnership."

"That's all," I agreed. "You're going to need somewhere to stay, aren't you?"

"We have an extra bedroom," Benji offered — a little too eagerly, I thought. I wanted to tell him to go easy so he didn't scare her off.

She gave me a stern look. "Just until I get my own place." Turning back to the sign, she smiled. "So, when do we open?"

"It's up to you," I said. "It's Kyra's by the Sea, not Eric's."

Looking at her profile, my heart melted.

"Can I show her the rest?" Benji asked.

"There's more?" she asked.

I took her hand and walked her over the hill. I pointed to the docked troller in the distance. "That's Benji's."

She furrowed her brow. "The pier?"

"No, the boat. Dad bought it for me," Benji said. "We're in the fishing business now too."

"We are?" she asked, not realizing what she'd just implied.

"We're renting it out for now. We've got a deal with a local guy: in addition to rent, he has to supply all the seafood we need for the restaurant."

"Wow," she said. "I feel like I went to sleep and woke up in Wonderland."

I slipped my fingers into hers. "What are you thinking?" I asked.

"Just that I'm happy." She looked down at our hands together and back up at me. "This doesn't mean we're back together."

"I know," I said, though neither of us let go.

FORTY-ONE

Days turned into weeks as the three of us worked to put the finishing touches on Kyra's by the Sea. By day, you would never know we were anything but a happy little family, working side by side to accomplish a common dream.

By night, we mostly did our own thing. Her on her side of the rental house, me on mine. Gradually, she joined Benji and me in front of the TV. At first she sat on the opposite end of the couch, then closer and closer, until one night, it hit me that she was lying beside me watching the evening news, with her hand in mine and my ring back on her finger. I was afraid to say anything about it for fear I would ruin the miracle I'd been given.

The day before our grand opening, Benji walked through the restaurant door holding a bag. Kyra finished the song she had been practicing and walked over to him. "Did you get it?"

He pulled a small lamp out of a shopping bag and handed it to her. "Is this okay?"

She held it up like it was some kind of trophy. "It's perfect."

I watched her walk over and set it on the small table beside her piano. "Hey, baby, if you need more lighting I could turn up the spotlight," I offered.

She grimaced. "Please don't. I'm already going to need sunglasses to play."

"So, why the lamp?"

Her fingertips trailed down the small column base. "I just don't want to ever forget."

"Forget what?"

She gave me a look that told me I ought to know. "Do you really have to ask?"

I started to say no, I didn't have to ask, but I was working hard to break myself of that habit. Instead of pretending to know what I didn't, I said, "I have no idea."

She frowned. "What color is this, my love?"

"Tan."

"Try again."

Then it hit me and I smiled. "The beige lamp."

"You're as smart as you are good-looking."

"We'll pretend that's a compliment," I said.

She wrapped her arms around me. "Let's not pretend anything anymore, okay?"

I kissed her forehead. "Deal."

She went back to stringing white lights on the artificial trees we were using to brighten dark corners, while Benji disappeared into the kitchen to double-check that our newly hired chef had everything he needed for the following day.

I was behind the bar polishing glasses when the red of a woman's dress caught my eye. She was tall, curvy, and pretty enough to be a swimsuit model. My eyes flew to Kyra, who glanced up at her, then went back to winding the string of lights.

"Can I help you?" I asked, stepping out from behind the bar.

She flipped her long dark hair over her shoulder. "The place looks great."

"Thanks," I said. "What can I do for you?"

Her eyes moved slowly down me, then back up. "Word on the street is that you're looking for a waitress." A flirty smile lifted her glossy lips as her painted fingernails traced the base of her neck, just above her cleavage. I refused to let my eyes wander. Instead, I looked at Kyra, who was now watching us intently. I smiled at my wife, thinking how much more beautiful she was than this, or any other, woman and turned back to the brunette. "I'm sorry, but the word on the street is wrong. I have all I need."

EPILOGUE

I turned to Kyra to answer the question she had just asked me and found myself, once again, not really seeing her. Sometimes, it was like I was looking through the glasses perched on my nose, vaguely knowing they were there, but not being fully conscious of them. And so, like I did every day for the last twenty years, I forced myself to not just look at her, but actually see her.

Her hair was no longer red, but silver, reminding me more of moonlight than the sunshine it used to be. Although her sweet face was now fractured by fine lines, her skin was still the same lovely porcelain it had always been, and her blue eyes shone every bit as bright as they did on our honeymoon . . . and I thought of that too. Of how she'd made love to me the first time and how I couldn't imagine anything ever comparing. But I had been wrong.

Somehow, even after decades of marriage

and familiarity, there were moments we shared, even today, that made that first time pale in comparison. I lived for those moments, and every one in between.

As it turned out, Benji wasn't a commercial fisherman after all, though he seldom spent a day off not trying to put a hook through a gill-breather. To the surprise of all of us, though, he was an incredible cook.

Looking more content than we'd ever seen him, he worked alongside Jim Kelly, who had been the head chef at Sonny's and was now ours, learning all there was to learn. Jim wasn't exactly young anymore, but what he lacked in stamina, he made up for in knowledge. He and Benji made a great team and kept our customers and the critics happy.

It was good to have the chance to watch my son as he discovered his place in the world and even better to have a part in it. Besides helping run our kitchen, he handled the bookkeeping and business end of things. He was surprised to find out what I had known all along: not only was he a natural at business, he actually enjoyed it.

I, on the other hand, did not, so I decided to give fishing a try.

While Benji built his life running the most

successful restaurant in Braddy's Wharf, my wife and I dabbled in what we loved — she playing the piano for our patrons and me struggling to earn my captain's license.

Kyra had said it would take a lifetime for her to get over what I'd done, but it didn't. In the end, she forgave me far sooner than I forgave myself.

Looking back on my life, it's strange to think just how far I'd fallen and how far I had to claw my way back up. When I'd first become a Christian, I read what Adam and Eve had done in the Garden of Eden, and it really ticked me off. Now, I knew that I was no different than they were. I guess none of us are.

I would give anything to go back and undo my infidelity, but true to His word, God had used even that for my good. If Kyra and I hadn't weathered our drought, I don't think we would have really appreciated the rains when they finally came. Like Alfred said, without the desert, an oasis is just another watering hole.

Dry as Rain is a story of infidelity and one couple's decision to forgive and heal together.

There are clear, biblical reasons to divorce, and infidelity is the clearest of all. While we are admonished to forgive, that doesn't always equate to staying together. Realistically, I doubt that most husbands or wives who have done what Eric did repent so quickly or love so deeply.

If you have found yourself in a similar situation and were not willing or able to make your marriage work after such a betrayal, please know that this novel is not standing in judgment of that decision. I, as the author, certainly am not.

If you are struggling with the unfaithfulness of a spouse, know that God sees your struggle. He hears your cries.

While I haven't myself been in exactly this situation, I do know what it's like to feel abandoned and worthless in other ways. I've been in the dark tunnel where tears fall freely but hope does not, and where all I could do was cling to the promise that God would never leave me.

There is light at the end of that tunnel, and it is so worth the forgiveness and time that will get you there. Boy, is it.

Thanks for reading.

Gina Holmes

DISCUSSION QUESTIONS

1. Just when Eric has taken what could have been the final step away from his marriage, he gets a phone call telling him that his wife has been in an accident. How does that help keep him from doing any further damage to his marriage?
2. Have you ever been in a situation where a seemingly random event made you stop and think twice about something you were doing or were about to do? How do you explain such happenings?
3. Eric decides to let Kyra remain in ignorance about the state of their marriage, and specifically about what he has done wrong. Do you think that was the right decision? Why or why not? What would you have done in his position?
4. Did you like Eric at the beginning of the book? Why or why not? In what ways could you relate to him? How did your

opinion of him change as the story went on?

5. Eric and Kyra both try to boil down the problems in their marriage to one or two specific things the other spouse did — or failed to do. How have you been guilty of that same approach in some of your relationships? What are some practical ways we can try to step back and see the bigger picture when we are tempted to oversimplify things?

6. Eric is disdainful of his friend Larry's Christian faith. Did you feel Larry was obnoxious or off base in the things he said? Why or why not? In what ways was Larry a true friend to Eric?

7. Some of Eric's issues stem from the loss of his father at an early age. What losses have you experienced that have affected you in profound ways? What are some ways you can work on forgiving (if necessary) and otherwise letting go of these things?

8. In some ways, Eric has never felt worthy of Kyra's love. How does that feeling contribute to some of his poor choices? How can we avoid making the same mistakes?

9. Everyone close to Eric advises him to tell Kyra the truth. But he resists that advice

for a long time. Why is it so hard for him to be honest with her? What is he afraid of?

10. Can you think of a time in your own life when you were afraid to be honest with someone? How did that situation eventually work out?

ABOUT THE AUTHOR

Gina Holmes is the author of the bestselling and award-winning debut novel *Crossing Oceans*. In 1998, Gina began her career penning articles and short stories. In 2005 she founded the influential literary blog Novel Journey. She holds degrees in science and nursing and currently resides with her husband and children in southern Virginia. To learn more about her, visit www.gina holmes.com or www.noveljourney.blogspot .com.

The employees of Thorndike Press hope you have enjoyed this Large Print book. All our Thorndike, Wheeler, and Kennebec Large Print titles are designed for easy reading, and all our books are made to last. Other Thorndike Press Large Print books are available at your library, through selected bookstores, or directly from us.

For information about titles, please call:
(800) 223-1244

or visit our Web site at:
http://gale.cengage.com/thorndike

To share your comments, please write:
Publisher
Thorndike Press
10 Water St., Suite 310
Waterville, ME 04901